**Unable to stop herself,
Kate glanced over her shoulder,
but the drifting fog only heightened her
sense of isolation. Did anyone actually
live here in the west of Ireland?**

A car's yellow hazard lights drew close, fog curling around the lamps like ghostly ballerinas. Out on the footpath, Kate saw two figures. A moment passed, and the smaller of the two broke away and began to run. The tall one followed in swift pursuit, both moving, wraithlike, in and out of the fog. When it cleared again, she saw only the larger figure, motionless, before it, too, disappeared, leaving the footpath as empty as if Kate had imagined the whole thing.

Teeth chattering, she started her car. The tall one had done away with the little one, she decided. He was probably out there somewhere looking for his next victim.

Really panicked now, she let out the clutch. The car shuddered to a halt. Cursing manual transmissions, Kate started the engine again and let it idle. Her hands on the wheel were shaking. *Get a grip. There's no one out there. This is Ireland, not Santa Monica.*

Then she looked up to see a man at her window.

Dear Reader,

The Man on the Cliff is set in one of my favorite places in
the world, western Ireland. I love the wildness of the
Connemara coast, the absolute hush of silence that falls
over the countryside and the warmth and hospitality of the
people. And, as the Irish say, the *craic* (Gaelic for a good
time) in the pubs is first-rate. I made extensive notes for
this book during a vacation in Ireland where we stayed in
a converted coast guard cottage in Clifden, County Galway.
We also washed down our fair share of Guinness as we
listened to the music. I am, incidentally, a huge fan of Irish
music and particularly enjoy a ballad singer by the name of
Christy Moore, whose lyrics I think are poetry.

Kate Neeson, the heroine of this book, is a California writer
who arrives in Ireland to do an investigative piece on a
young folk singer who fell to her death from the Connemara
cliffs. Kate is cynical and a little world-weary. She doesn't
trust men. When she finds herself falling in love with a
man no one trusts, she's definitely disconcerted. From
signposts that point in the wrong direction and hovering
mists that make her doubt her eyes, to the secrets and
hidden agendas of the villagers, Ireland seems oddly
unreal and slightly off-kilter. Before long she's doing
things she wouldn't dream of doing back in Santa Monica.
Personally, I think Kate just fell under Ireland's spell. As I
have myself.

I hope you enjoy the book.

Janice Macdonald

P.S. I enjoy hearing from readers. Please e-mail me through
my Web site, www.janicemacdonald.com.

The Man on the Cliff
Janice Macdonald

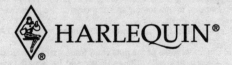

HARLEQUIN®

TORONTO • NEW YORK • LONDON
AMSTERDAM • PARIS • SYDNEY • HAMBURG
STOCKHOLM • ATHENS • TOKYO • MILAN • MADRID
PRAGUE • WARSAW • BUDAPEST • AUCKLAND

ISBN 0-373-71077-1

THE MAN ON THE CLIFF

Visit us at www.eHarlequin.com

Printed in U.S.A.

The Man on the Cliff

CHAPTER ONE

IF THERE WAS ANY correlation between bad luck with men and a poor sense of direction, Kate Neeson thought it might explain a whole lot about her life.

She was lost. Again. She turned off the ignition and peered gloomily through the window of the rented Peugeot at the unfamiliar Irish countryside. Isolated cottages, stunted windswept trees and stone walls. Endless stone walls. Around the twists and turns of the road, she'd caught glimpses of pale ocean merging into pale sky. Before the road started climbing again, she'd heard the low roar of waves breaking. On the coast, obviously, but in Ireland that wasn't much help.

With a sigh, she reached for the map and spread it out over the passenger seat. Cragg's Head, the village where she'd arranged to meet a local reporter, was barely more than a dot on Connemara's ragged coast. She'd set up the meeting before she left the States, but had forgotten to ask him for directions. Jet-lagged and cold, she rubbed her eyes. On the map, the area looked like a piece of china, picked up and hurled to the ground in a tantrum.

Moruadh had fallen from Connemara's steep cliffs nearly a year ago. Kate tucked her hands under her arms, chilled by the damp air seeping into the car. Moruadh, the young Irish folksinger whose songs of love, doomed, lost and unrequited, rang uncomfortably true to life. Or at least to her own life. Moruadh was why Kate was in Ireland, but she didn't want to think about Moruadh right now. Specifically, she didn't want to think about Moruadh's death. Tomorrow would be time enough for that. Tomorrow—after a decent night's sleep—she wouldn't be plagued by a spooked feeling that had her glancing over her shoulder and checking door locks.

Tomorrow, she would wear down the widower's resistance. If Niall Maguire had something to hide, she would ferret it out. Reluctant interview subjects didn't discourage her.

Unable to stop herself, Kate again glanced over her shoulder, but a drifting fog only heightened the sense of isolation. Did anyone actually live in the west of Ireland? With her palm, she wiped away condensation from the windshield and tried to decide whether to plough on, in the unlikely hope she was headed in the right direction, or turn back to the last village.

Through the swirling air, she saw two figures out on a narrow footpath. She rolled down the passenger window to ask for directions, then changed her mind. Irish advice on such matters, she'd discovered, was picturesque, convoluted and usually wrong.

A car's yellow hazard lights drew close, fog curling around the lamps like ghostly ballerinas. Out on the footpath, the two figures merged briefly. A moment passed and then the smaller of the two broke away and began to run. The tall one followed in swift pursuit, and both moved wraithlike in and out of the fog. When it cleared again, she saw only a tall, dark silhouette, motionless before it, too, disappeared, leaving the footpath as empty as if she'd imagined the whole thing.

Teeth chattering, she started the car. The tall one had done away with the small one, she decided. He was out there now looking for his next victim. A deranged woman hater. She could feel his eyes boring into her head. Probably deciding whether to drag her out of the car or just roll the car with her in it over the cliffs.

Panicked enough to convince herself that the scenario might not be that far-fetched, she let out the clutch. The car shuddered to a halt. Cursing manual transmissions, she started the engine up again and let it idle for a moment. Her hands on the wheel were shaking. *Get a grip. There's no one out there. This is Ireland not Santa Monica.*

And then she looked up to see a man at the window.

She screamed.

His face, like an apparition in the swirling fog, was narrow with dark eyebrows and light gray eyes. For a moment he stood motionless at the open passenger window, evidently immobilized by her scream. Then, hands up at his chest, palms out, he slowly backed away from the window.

"God, I'm sorry," he said. "I didn't mean to scare you."

Kate stared at him. Even as the adrenaline rush of fear slowly faded, the scream still rang in her ears. She took some deep breaths. He was probably about her age, mid-thirties, tall and slender. He wore a rough woolen jersey, unraveling slightly at the neck, and an open sheepskin jacket, dark with moisture. A couple of cameras were slung around his neck, a leather gadget bag over one shoulder. A smile flickered tentatively across his face.

"Are you all right?

"I'm fine." Given her panicky state a few minutes earlier, the presence of this complete stranger was oddly reassuring. "It's kind of deserted out there, I don't see a soul for a couple of hours. Then I see two people in the fog. One of them disappears and then the other, and suddenly you're at my window." She managed a shaky laugh. "Another minute and I'd have had my can of Mace out."

"Would you now?" The faint smile appeared again. "But what if I'd been wanting to help you? Which I was."

"I'm naturally suspicious," she said, distracted momentarily by his eyes. Pale as the fog and fringed with dark lashes, they seemed focused on something beyond her shoulder. In a split second, though, she realized they were actually watching her. It was disconcerting. Like looking through a one-way mirror and finding someone looking back at you.

Moments passed. She stared through the open passenger window at him. He gazed into the car at her.

"Did *you* see anyone out there on the edge of the cliffs a few minutes ago?" she asked, thinking again of the disappearing figures.

"I didn't. But I was supposed to meet a girl up here at six…" His glance took in the mist-shrouded landscape, then he looked at Kate again. "I was beginning to think I'd been stood up, but maybe it was her you saw. A few minutes ago, you say?"

She glanced at the dashboard clock, then up at him and felt vaguely envious of the girl who'd stood him up. "About that, I guess."

"Did she have long fair hair?" he asked.

"I don't even know if it was a girl. I just saw two people. One was smaller, I assumed it was female. She—if it was a she—wasn't alone, though."

"Right." He studied her face for a moment. "Well, I'll take a look around then. Maybe she's just late."

Kate eyed the cameras slung around his neck. The breast pocket of his jacket bulged with what she guessed was film and, in a lower pocket, she could see the corner of a green-and-white carton. "You're shooting a new Waldo book? Find Waldo in the fog?"

He gave her a blank look.

"Waldo? Little blue-and-red-striped figure? You have to find him in a page of... Never mind. I was just curious about what kind of pictures you could take under these conditions." The thought flashed through her brain that she wanted to prolong this encounter.

"It isn't ideal," he said, "but there are certain settings and film speeds that compensate." He leaned into the window a little. "Listen, I'm sorry I frightened you just now."

"You didn't *frighten* me." She met his eyes. "You startled me."

"Ah."

"There's a difference."

"Right, of course. I didn't mean to suggest..." He shifted his bag to the other shoulder. "Can I do anything? Your car's running all right, is it? You're not out of petrol?"

"No." Kate took another look at the clock. It was five minutes to six. "Am I headed the right way for Cragg's Head?"

"You're almost there," he said with a smile. "But I'll draw you a little map in case. It can be a bit tricky."

She watched as he reached into his inside pocket and pulled out a notepad. Something metallic fluttered to the ground.

She craned her head to see better and caught a glimpse of a thin gold chain. As he reached to pick it up, she saw a gold letter she couldn't make out. Briefly their eyes met, then he shoved the locket in his pocket and finished drawing the map.

"All right, here's what you do," he said. "It's five minutes at the very most. Follow the road to Bally-conneely. You can't miss it."

A REASSURANCE THAT probably fell into the realm of Irish mythology, she decided thirty minutes later as green fields and more stone walls gave way to a village and a jumble of signposts, not one of which pointed to Cragg's Head. She braked to let a couple with a stroller cross the street, her eye momentarily caught by a shop window's picturesque clutter of paraffin stoves, candles and Wellington boots.

At the next village, she slowed the car, rolled down the windows and called out to an elderly woman in a raincoat and elastic stockings.

"Hi." She smiled. "I'm trying to get to Cragg's Head, and the last guy I asked told me to follow the road for Ballyconneely. He said I couldn't miss it, but I guess I did."

"Cragg's Head is it?" The woman peered through the driver's window. "Sure, well it's easy enough, but there's been a bit of signpost twisting going on, so things aren't always what they seem, if you know what I mean." She shifted a bulging string bag to the other hand. "Give me a minute to think."

Kate waited.

"Right then." The woman's eyes briefly registered the cake crumbs and candy wrappers on the passenger seat, then she looked back at Kate. "Here's what you do. D'you see that church over there?"

Kate craned her neck to look in the direction the woman was pointing. At the bottom of a hilly street that wound and bumped down to the water, she saw a small stone building with a Celtic cross. "Sure."

"Pay no attention to it. You'll be going in the opposite direction."

"Ah." Kate bit her lip.

"Go right and you'll pass a… Oh, wait now, you can't go that way anymore." The woman thought for a moment. "Righto then, here's an easy way, you can't miss it…"

The directions would be wrong. Kate knew that, even as she steered the Peugeot up the hill the woman had indicated. "You can't miss" was like "Trust me." You always did and you never should.

LONG AFTER HE'D packed his camera gear back into the Land Rover, Niall Maguire found himself thinking about the woman in the car. What, he wondered, was an American woman, apparently traveling alone, doing in western Ireland in February? Despite Annie Ryan's efforts at the tourist office, Cragg's Head wasn't exactly a sought-after destination.

Back in the mid-1800s, the town had been a commercial center, but more recently it was trying to reinvent itself as a tourist destination. A few bed-and-breakfasts had sprouted up, and from May to August there were quite a few tourists milling about. By autumn, though, accents in the village were strictly local.

To his mind, the summer tourists missed a lot. Sure, the weather was warmer in July and the flowers were out, but it was an easy, uncomplicated prettiness. Niall far preferred winter's dark melodrama. The white foam of the Atlantic during a winter storm. Stars distant and bright in the wind-scoured sky. The swift fall of darkness.

Thoughts drifting from one thing to another, he drove slowly along the length of Cragg's Head Walk. Earlier in the day, he'd done a photo shoot near Roundstone. A collection for one of those big, glossy books Americans put on their coffee tables. Ireland's relics. Ruined keeps and towers, roofless cottages and abbeys. Everything moss smothered and ivy strangled.

In the gusting wind, he'd climbed a small drumlin to take pictures of the disused graveyard where, as children, he, Moruadh and Hughie Fitzpatrick had played hide-and-seek among the gravestones. One hot summer day, Moruadh had lain very still on one of the marble slabs, telling them to pretend she was dead.

Today, he'd used nearly a roll of film on an old woman, her body bent into the wind, her clothes the colors of the earth and bogs. But his thoughts had returned to that summer day and a girl in a red cotton dress. Finally, his concentration shot, he'd packed up and moved to another spot.

As he turned into the Market Square, an image of the American flashed across his brain. With her red hair and green eyes, she could be Irish, but her accent and demeanor gave her away. In Dublin, he could spot Americans a mile off. A certain self-confidence about them. I've a right to be here, they seemed to say. Still, he'd noted the way fear had pinched her nose, giving lie to her bravado. Her bitten nails said something, too.

Slowly, he drove along the harbor, past the courthouse and jail. Moments later, he pulled up outside the Pot o' Gold, the bed-and-breakfast run by Annie Ryan—when she wasn't working at the tourist office. Once it had been a convent run by the Mercy Nuns and then, much later, an orphanage. By the time he was born, the place was long disused and abandoned, but that had never stopped his old man from threatening to pack him off there with just the clothes on his back.

All done up now with lace curtains and amber lights in the windows, but Niall could still recall the cold, hollow fear that had gripped him as he'd stared up at the blank windows. Watching for the boy-eating rats that he'd been told lived inside.

Slowly, it had dawned on him that his wailing and begging and tearful promises to behave himself had quite entertained the old man and that a sure way to prolong the ordeal was to let on that he was scared. He'd learned to hide his fear by pretending to himself that it wasn't really him standing there. That it was all happening to someone else, and he was just a bystander.

A twitch of the curtains broke his reverie, and he got out of the car and walked up the pathway. Given the speed with which Annie Ryan answered his knock, she'd evidently been at the window. Her hand went to her throat, and her eyes registered his mud-splattered boots. A lamp behind her cast an amber glow.

"What can I do for you, Mr. Maguire?"

"I was looking for Elizabeth Jenkins. I have it right, do I? This is where she's living?"

"It is," Annie said. "For now at least. She's visiting from England. The daughter of a friend of mine."

Niall heard the sound of the television from inside the house. Behind Annie, he could see the polished wooden floors in the hallway and off to one side the floral chintz of a chair cover. He had never eaten a meal at the Pot o' Gold, but Annie's cooking was legendary and as he stood there, he caught a whiff of a roast or stew that made him suddenly ravenous and more than a little lonely. "Elizabeth was to meet me tonight at Cragg's Head Leap," he said.

Annie's eyes narrowed.

"She's a student in the photography class I teach at the college," he explained.

"Ah." Her expression cleared momentarily. "Well, that's the first I've heard of it."

"We were going to take some pictures—" He stopped, unable to remember if he'd said that already. Uncomfortable suddenly, he turned to leave. "Anyway, I'll not keep you. I thought I'd just drop by and see if you might know where she is."

Annie cupped her chin in one hand and gave him a long look as though she had something to ask him but didn't quite know how to put it.

"Do you do that often, then?" Her eyes didn't leave his face. "Meet students after class?"

He felt an unaccustomed surge of anger. Her tone was polite, but the inference was unavoidable. He took a deep breath, shoved his hands into the pockets of his jacket.

"No, I don't, Mrs. Ryan. Hardly ever. Most students don't show the promise and enthusiasm Elizabeth does. I don't do it because it takes time out of my own schedule that I could use to do other things, but I try to encourage students when they obviously have the talent."

"Elizabeth's a very young and impressionable girl," Annie said as though she was justifying her question. "It wouldn't take much to turn her head." Her face had colored slightly, though, and her glance shifted beyond his shoulder. "It's awful foggy out, isn't it? Could you have seen much?"

"Sure, it's a bit patchy," he said, wanting to end the conversation. "Drifts in and out, but it allows for some interesting effects. If you wouldn't mind, I'll give you my card. Perhaps you'd have Elizabeth ring me when she gets home."

She took the card from him and dropped it into the pocket of her skirt. "Right then. If there's nothing more you need then, Mr. Maguire, I've supper getting cold."

He was already on the road back up to Sligo when he remembered something Sharon, his business partner, had said that morning about a meeting at the bank. For a moment he hesitated, then, with a sigh of resignation, he turned around and headed back for Cragg's Head to make peace with Sharon. The conversation with Annie Ryan played on in his head as he drove. It had been no more hostile than other encounters he'd had since Moruadh's death, but he was usually able to ignore them all. Tonight he couldn't, and he wasn't sure why.

THROUGH THE MISTED GLASS of the Gardai car, Kate could see a uniformed man slumped down in the driver's seat, his head thrown back. Sound asleep from the look of it. It was the same car she'd seen half an hour earlier. Somehow she'd managed to drive in a circle. Maybe as a penalty for past transgressions she'd been sentenced to spend the rest of her life driving along the cliffs of western Ireland.

She rapped on the window.

The man stirred, opened his eyes and muttered something unintelligible. Then he fixed her with a bleary-eyed stare. Early twenties, she guessed, with a mop of dark hair and a ruddy complexion. His blue uniform shirt was open at the neck and pulled out of his trousers. She couldn't make out the letters on the brass name badge.

"Hi." She smiled and caught a strong whiff of alcohol. "I'm trying to get to Dooley's Bar in Cragg's Head and somehow—"

"Straight ahead," he said. "Five minutes down the road."

"I think that's what I did, but—"

"It's the only way," he said. "Go in any other direction and you'll fall into the water."

"*Okaay.*" Kate slowly nodded. "Well, thanks." As she started to leave, a thought struck her and she turned back. "Listen, one other thing. I may have seen something out on the cliffs." She glanced at her watch. "About an hour ago, I guess. It could have been a fight...the fog made it kind of difficult to tell, but you might want to check it out."

The man stared at her for a moment, then seemed suddenly aware of the state of his clothes. One hand moved to his midsection. His eyes became fractionally more alert.

"Right then," he sat up. "I'll see that it gets written up. Good evening now."

Kate glanced over her shoulder as she walked back to her car. "Five minutes, you said?"

"That's right," the Garda said. "Five minutes at the most."

CHAPTER TWO

HALF AN HOUR LATER, with apologies to Hugh Fitzpatrick for being late, Kate squeezed into one of the narrow wooden booths at the back of Dooley's main lounge. "Obviously, I should have allowed more time for getting lost," she said, peering at the reporter through a blue haze of cigarette smoke.

"Ah, don't worry about it," Fitzpatrick said with a grin. "Sure, it's no crime to waste a little time now and then." He glanced over at the bar where half a dozen men in cloth caps and heavy jackets sat nursing pints, then lifted his empty tankard in the direction of the bartender. "And this is as good a place as any to do it."

Kate studied him for a moment. Mid-thirties. Hawkish nose, sallow complexion. His hair dark, lank and a shade too long. Old tweed jacket, jeans and a black turtleneck. Struggling-writer type, she'd dated a few of them. They were always bad news. Lost in the world that existed between their ears. She watched him light a new cigarette from the one he'd been smoking. Judging from the empty glasses on the table and the speed with which he'd consumed the last pint, she figured he'd had some firsthand experience wasting time in bars.

In the window behind him, she caught a glimpse of her own reflection and moved her chair slightly to avoid the image. She didn't need confirmation that the damp air had frizzed her long red hair, or that fatigue had created circles under her eyes and made her skin paler than usual, which caused her freckles to stand out.

A headache had been gathering strength for the past hour. Kate wanted to ask Fitzpatrick to extinguish his cigarette, something she would have done without hesitation back in Santa Monica. Since they were on his home turf and she needed his assistance, she decided to tolerate the discomfort.

She could hear the click of billiard cues, raucous laughter and American rock music coming from the next room. The smells of beer and fried fish hung heavily in the air, potent if not particularly appetizing reminders that she'd eaten nothing all day but cake and chocolate.

"Are you still serving food?" she asked the rotund and balding bartender when he brought Fitzpatrick's drink to the table.

"We are." He wiped a cloth over the table. "Fish and chips. Sausages and chips. Egg and chips."

"Anything that's not fried?"

"Not fried?" He scratched his ear. "Let's see. Raw fish, raw sausage and raw potatoes."

She grinned. "I'll just have some chips then."

"She means crisps," Fitzpatrick told the bartender. "I speak a bit of American. What flavor?"

Kate shrugged, stumped.

"We've only prawn," the bartender said.

"Prawn then. And a Diet Coke, please." Over at the bar, one of the cloth caps muttered something in the ear of the man next to him, and they both looked over their shoulders at her. She smiled sweetly, maintaining eye contact until they turned away.

When she returned her glance to Fitzpatrick, he grinned at her.

"You're a novelty," he said. "Cragg's Head isn't exactly a mecca for American tourists at this time of year."

The surreptitious glances had been going on ever since she'd arrived. If she'd walked in stark naked, she could hardly have provoked more interest. The sensation was strange and one she didn't particularly enjoy. Back in Santa Monica, the tweed jacket and beige wool pants she'd picked up at Nordstrom's annual sale had seemed to strike exactly the right note of country chic. Here in Dooley's they apparently screamed American tourist.

"Why is it you're interested in Moruadh?" Fitzpatrick asked.

He pronounced the name the way Moruadh had taught her to do. *Mora*. "It's Gaelic," she'd explained. "Some sort of sea creature." And then she'd laughed. "Let's hope it's a mermaid and not a whale." No last name. "Moruadh is plenty," she'd said.

Kate considered Fitzpatrick's question. "I knew her. Kind of." The bartender bought over the chips and the Coke in a glass with no ice. She tore open the bag. "About three years ago, I interviewed her for a magazine article. She called me several times after that and we became…" She hesitated. Friends would be a stretch, they'd never actually met and their lifestyles couldn't have been more different. Moruadh sang to packed crowds all over Europe. Kate wrote about sheep-herding contests in Bakersfield. Moruadh

spent long weekends in ancient and picturesque stone
cottages in Provence. Kate spent weekends shuttling
her ancient Toyota Tercel between the Laundromat
and the supermarket. Moruadh had enjoyed success
and recognition Kate herself never dreamed of. Still
there had been this connection. Which was why the
news of the singer's death had come as such a shock.

"We shared dating horror stories," she told Fitzpatrick. "Moruadh's were a lot more glamorous than
mine, but we'd both come to pretty much the same
conclusion."

Fitzpatrick looked at her.

"Men are jerks." She bit into a chip. "Nothing
personal, of course. Just the combined wisdom of our
experiences."

He moved his head slightly to exhale a cloud of
smoke, turned back to face her again.

"And then I read about the accident—"

"Moruadh's death was no accident." Fitzpatrick
tapped ash off his cigarette. "She was murdered."

"You believe that, too?" Kate asked and felt her
face color. She'd suspected that herself, but at least
wanted to create a semblance of objectivity. She dug
into her bag for a notebook, looked at Fitzpatrick.
"So what's your theory?"

Fitzpatrick laughed. "My theory, huh? Well, let's
just say, my theory is that murder is cheaper than
divorce, which incidentally wasn't legal in Ireland at
the time of Moruadh's death. Maguire could have
gone to England or France, of course, but he must
have worried she'd go after his money." He drank
some beer. "That's more than just a journalistic theory. I know Maguire."

"But her career was going fairly well. I mean she must have been making pretty good money herself?"

"Nothing compared to Maguire's money. The three of us grew up together. His family had plenty, Moruadh was the daughter of the gardener. We had that in common, she and I, peasant stock." He lifted his glass again, wiped the back of his hand over his mouth. "My mother was a housekeeper on the Maguire estate. Moruadh enjoyed playing the two of us off against each other."

"You and Maguire?"

He nodded. "For as long as I can remember. Of course, he had an unfair advantage. More pocket money than either of us had in a year. More of everything. And nothing has changed much over the years. He's always had it all. Money, looks, women falling over themselves for him."

"Was she in love with him?"

He shrugged. "Moruadh never knew her own mind. Maguire's an aloof bastard. The more he kept his distance, the more she ran after him. He didn't pay her a lot of attention until her career started taking off. When that began to wane—a year or so before she died—so did his interest in her. Pushing her off the cliff was an expedient way to end things."

Kate kept her expression neutral. She fished in the bag for a chip, bit into it. "The Garda ruled it an accident. I read the investigation report. The cliffs were unstable. She lost her footing—"

"Ach." He made a gesture of contempt. "*Investigation.* It was a farce. The old superintendent had been in the Maguire family's pockets forever and he was a bit of an idiot anyway so he was easily taken in by Maguire."

"Yeah, but pushing her off the cliffs seems a bit...well, extreme, don't you think?"

He shrugged. "That's Maguire. Have you met him yet?"

"Not yet."

"You'll get along famously." He gave a wry smile. "Niall Maguire always gets along famously with beautiful women."

"You're not exactly Maguire's biggest fan, huh?" she asked, deciding to ignore the compliment.

"You could say that." He inhaled, narrowed his eyes against the expelled smoke. "Sure, it's hard to feel a lot of warmth for someone who gets away with cold-blooded murder." He tapped ash off the cigarette. "To be honest, though, I've never liked him much. No doubt it goes back to the stale cakes and bags of his old clothes my mother used to bring home from the big house. I've had an aversion to castoffs ever since."

Kate watched him for a moment. Face twisted with emotion, he stared off across the room in the direction of the bartender who was drying pint glasses with a white cloth. She understood only too well how resentment and envy hardened into hate.

At fourteen, gawky and freckled with a mouthful of braces, she'd overheard an aunt say how unfair it was that, while Ned had heartbreaker written all over him, his little sister, Katie had none of the looks in the family. Months later, her father had to grab Kate's arms to stop her clawing Ned's face after they'd had a minor spat. She felt a stab of sympathy for Fitzpatrick.

"Sorry." He shook his head, smiling slightly as

though embarrassed. "You're not here to listen to me vent my spleen about Maguire."

"Hey." She shrugged. "We all have our hang-ups."

"I have these letters from Moruadh," he said as though she hadn't spoken. "Letters she wrote from Paris. I'll show them to you. She complains bitterly about Maguire, saying how much happier her life would be if he would leave her alone. Sure, we'd both have been a lot happier." He gave a harsh laugh. "But for Maguire, she'd still be alive and we'd be married."

Kate looked at him. He'd answered a question that had been floating around in her brain since they'd started talking. There was something about the way he said Moruadh's name, the look on his face as he spoke about her. But Moruadh had once confessed that she was only attracted to good-looking men and, while there was a certain appealing quality about him, Hugh Fitzpatrick was far from handsome.

"That surprises you, doesn't it?" He was watching her face. "I can see that it does. Thinking that I couldn't possibly be her type, weren't you? A beautiful girl like Moruadh could have anyone. Why Hugh Fitzpatrick, who doesn't have two pennies to rub together? That's what you're thinking."

"I don't like being told what I'm thinking," Kate said. *Especially when it happens to be right.* "And you're absolutely wrong." She felt her face color. "If I looked surprised, it's because I don't remember her mentioning your name."

Fitzpatrick seemed unconvinced. His face had darkened. Kate felt a tension that hadn't been there moments before.

"I've always thought that there are two types of women," he said after a moment. "Those who can't see beyond pretty faces like Maguire's and those who can."

"Listen, Hugh," she said, feeling rebuked, "in my fantasies I'm a tall, well-endowed blonde named Ingrid. Men flock to me." She paused to let that sink in. "My reality is a long, long way removed from that. So don't think I'm unaware of what it's like to be judged on appearance."

His broad smile, and the way his eyes lingered on her face told her that he'd read into her remark something she hadn't intended. They were two drab birds in a gaudy flock, the look said, sensitive and undervalued. Let's appreciate each other, it said. Kate yawned. The bar had almost emptied out. There were other things she wanted to ask him, but they could wait for another day.

Fitzpatrick was only one source, so it was too early for gloating, but she felt encouraged by what she'd learned so far. Clearly her theory about how Moruadh died wasn't as off base as her editor at *Modern World* believed. Establishing her credibility with Tom was important if she ever wanted to move from the financially precarious world of freelance assignments to the more stable and lucrative staff job he'd hinted might be coming up. Still, he'd teased her for her stubborn refusal to accept the accidental death verdict. "Kate the Intrepid," he'd laughed. "Relentless in her crusade to prove that beneath every male chest lurks a murderous and dowardly black heart. News flash, kid. Accidents happen."

Kate drained her glass. *Yeah, and husbands get away with murder.* In the end, she'd worn Tom down and he'd given her the assignment. The trip had maxed out her credit card, but if she left Ireland knowing the truth about Moruadh's death, it was worth the expense. And if she wrote a good article, Tom might even offer her a full-time position.

"You're here for how long?" Hugh asked.

"Ten days."

"There's a lot to see. Galway is interesting. Would you like to go out one evening? We could have something to eat, talk a bit more. Hear some music."

"Thanks." Not wanting to step on his feelings again, or to mislead him, she hesitated. "But I really need to focus on the article." She feigned a yawn. "And if I don't get to the place where I'm staying, I'm going to fall asleep. My body clock is still on California time."

Disappointment flickered in his eyes. "Are you interested in looking at the letters Moruadh sent to me?"

"Sure. I've got interviews scheduled for the next few days, but I could come by your office."

"Right." He appeared to be about to say something else, then he leaned across the table. "Maguire's guilty, Kate." His voice was low, impassioned. "He murdered Moruadh. He thinks he's free and clear, that he got away with it, but he's wrong. If it had happened today, under the watch of the new superintendent, he would be behind bars, but we can still make that happen. The two of us—"

"Hold on a second." Startled by his sudden intensity, Kate leaned back in her chair, widening the distance between them. His eyes, dark and deep set, seemed to bore into her as though by sheer concentration he could make her believe. "You're getting ahead of yourself. I still have a lot of people to talk to before I reach any conclusions.''

''What can I tell you to convince you?''

''What you've told me already has been helpful, but I'm going to need more than that.'' Across the room, the remaining patrons were getting in their last curious looks at her before they toddled off into the night. ''For starters, I want to talk to Maguire himself.''

''Sure, and Maguire will turn on his charm, and you'll believe whatever he chooses to tell you.''

She met his eyes for a moment. ''Obviously you don't know me.''

KATE REMAINED at the table after Fitzpatrick left, making a few quick notes while the information was still fresh in her mind. Engrossed in her thoughts, she didn't notice the bartender until he reached for the empty glasses.

''Anything else for you?'' he asked.

''No.'' With a yawn, she gathered up her notebook and purse. ''Well, actually, you could tell me how to get to the Pot o' Gold. It's the B&B I'm staying in.''

''I know it well,'' he said. ''My wife runs the place. Just around the corner, you can't miss it.''

Kate thanked him and dropped a handful of coins on the table. As she started toward the door, he called out to her.

''Listen, love, are you married?''

Kate stared at him. God, he had to be sixty. Was he trying to pick her up?

''Oh, not for me.'' He laughed, obviously seeing the shock on her face. ''My wife.''

''Your wife?''

"My wife. Look, do yourself a favor. When you get to the house and she asks you, tell her you are, otherwise she'll have you engaged to a pig farmer faster than you can say Lisdoonvarna."

"Lisdoonwhat?"

"Exactly. Married with two kiddies, tell her. Better yet, say you've a bun in the oven."

Kate smiled and stepped out into the night. After the warm smokiness of the pub, the air hit her like a cold blast. She darted down the narrow alley behind Dooley's to the muddy patch of grass where she'd parked. Vapor streaming from her mouth, she put the purse on the roof of the car while she unlocked the door. Inside, she buckled her seat belt then remembered the purse and got out to retrieve it. The car's sudden movement sent the purse sliding from the roof and into a puddle of water. Naturally, she'd neglected to fasten it.

A tube of lipstick glinted up at her from the murky water; the apple that she'd saved from the flight bobbed and sank. As she bent down to retrieve her floating passport and airline ticket, the day seemed to cave in on her and she felt herself on the edge of hysteria—not knowing whether to laugh or cry.

She picked everything up and got back in the car again. As she started the ignition, a combination of fatigue and jet lag and—why not admit it?—loneliness left her suddenly so desolate and empty that her chest hurt. *Married.* No, she wasn't married. If falling in love with the right guy was a college course, she would have flunked half a dozen times. A Love 101 dropout, auditing courses on Intro to Celibacy and Elements of Spinsterhood.

For a moment she just sat there with the windshield

fogging, the car shuddering beneath her. Here she was in a rental car in some dark alley in a remote village thousands of miles from home and no one was waiting back in Santa Monica for her to call and say she'd arrived safely. No one was counting the days until she was home again. No one gave a damn and that was the truth of it. Sure, she could do her conjuring tricks. Divert the eye. Look over here, look over there. See how busy and full my life is. When she faced it right on, though, there was nothing. No center. Nothing but black emptiness.

"Get over it." She put the car in gear, adjusted the rearview mirror and peered into it for a minute. "Quit feeling sorry for yourself," she told the face with the under-eye circles that stared back at her, "or you'll blow the assignment. Tom will replace you with some twenty-something and you'll end up jobless, homeless, wandering around Santa Monica with all your stuff packed in a shopping cart and sleeping on benches on Ocean Boulevard. Is that what you want?"

It wasn't and by the time she parked outside the Pot o' Gold some fifteen minutes later, she'd pulled herself out of the funk. Imagine the worst and whatever happens probably won't be quite as bad. One of the tools in her coping kit. That and the breezy, confident mask that only slipped when she was too tired to maintain it. By the time she rang the bell, it was firmly back in place.

The woman who answered the door wore a red wool dress that hugged her slim figure and set off her black hair and blue eyes. Recalling the sixtyish bartender at Dooley's who looked a good ten years older, Kate wondered if she'd misunderstood what he'd said about his wife running the place. If she'd got it right, the two seemed an unlikely pair.

"Kate Neeson." She stuck out her hand. "I'm really sorry I'm late."

"It's all right, darlin'. Patrick called to say you were on your way." Smiling, the woman shook Kate's hand. "Annie Ryan. Sure, I did get a bit worried, it's the way I am. My houseguest isn't home yet and I'm running to the window every five minutes." She peered at Kate's face. "You're all right, are you? Your eyes are a bit red."

"I'm fine," she said, but Annie looked so doubtful, Kate felt the need to offer more reassurance. "It's allergies." She improvised. "Probably the damp air."

Annie patted her arm, as if to say she wasn't convinced but she'd go along with it, and ushered her along the hallway and into a brightly lit room that smelled of wood smoke, furniture polish and flowers. Kate glanced around. Flower-patterned couches and armchairs grouped cozily around the flickering fire. The glow of amber lamps on the teacups set out on a low table by the hearth.

"This is really nice." She smiled at Annie, her spirits revived. "It's so warm and inviting. I was… well, ever since I arrived, I've been getting lost and everything's kind of strange, but I think it's all going to work out." She stopped, embarrassed. Why was she blabbering like this to a complete stranger? It wasn't even like her. But Annie, who was bustling around the room, poking at the fire, seemed to find nothing amiss.

"Make yourself at home now. I'll have someone bring in your suitcases." She helped Kate off with her coat, disappeared with it, and returned moments later. "While you're here, you're part of the family. Now, will you have a cup of tea and a bit of supper? I've a lamb stew in the oven, but if that's not what you fancy, there's a chicken pie. By the way, love," she said as Kate started up the stairs, "there's a phone in the hall, should you want to ring your husband. You are married, aren't you?"

NIALL LOOKED across the vast stretch of Buncarroch Castle's great hall to the mantelpiece where his business partner, Sharon Garroty, stood, hands on her hips, her expression one of severely strained patience. She had on narrow black trousers and a black silk blouse, her pale blond hair pulled into a tight bun at the back of her head.

"What I really can't understand," she was saying, "is exactly how you could just forget about signing papers on a fifty-thousand-pound loan because you were too busy snapping shots with a little twit of a coed who obviously has designs on you."

"Put that way," he said, pulling off a boot, "I'm sure it must be hard to understand."

"And how would you put it then?"

"I've explained already that I forgot we were to meet at the bank. I've also apologized for forgetting. Either accept it, or don't. I won't spend the night justifying myself to you."

He removed the other boot and stood dangling it by the laces as he looked at her. If he'd told her that anger enhanced her beauty, she'd no doubt throttle him, but it was true. The faint pink of anger that tinged her creamy skin was as flattering as the most artfully applied cosmetic. Often his assignments involved photographing beautiful women, but few of them had her classic sort of beauty. Clearly, though, it wasn't the moment to mention it.

He averted his eyes from Sharon and from the eagle on the chimney wall immediately above her head. It had been there for as long as he could remember, but the sight of it, wings outstretched in frozen flight, had always depressed him and they'd talked of taking it down. Or he had. Sharon thought it should stay. They'd talked of turning the castle into a small and exclusive hotel, and Sharon had argued that the eagle—along with the various hunting trophies and stuffed animal heads that adorned the walls—were what tourists would expect to see.

He had dropped the subject. Although he didn't like the thought that the trophies might suggest his endorsement of blood sports, he disliked a fight even more. Whatever gene the Irish had for volatility had bypassed him completely. Tonight unfortunately, the likelihood of avoiding confrontation was as remote as a month without rain.

Bits of mud had flaked off his boots, and Niall scooped them up and threw them into the grate. While he was the castle's owner, Sharon made no secret of the fact that she rather fancied herself as lady of the manor, graciously opening her stately home to wealthy tourists. Where he fit into that picture, he wasn't quite sure. He was hardly the lordly type. More the groundskeeper, he reflected, his thoughts drifting to the *cromlech* that dotted the grounds and an idea he'd had for a series of pictures of Celtic stones.

"Who is this Elizabeth girl?" Sharon demanded. "Is she the one who's always ringing the studio?"

He ignored the question, carried his boots across

the great hall, down a stone-flagged corridor and into
the kitchen. Behind him he heard the tap of Sharon's
heels. He opened the pantry door and did an inventory
of the nearly empty shelves. Two tins of mulliga-
tawny soup, some pilchards and a bit of moldy
cheese. He thought of the savory smells in Annie
Ryan's house and wondered whether the American
woman might be staying there.

Again he regretted not making sure she'd found her
way safely. Tomorrow, perhaps, he'd ring Annie
Ryan just to check whether the American was there.
He peeled waxed paper from the Stilton. After tonight's inquiry about Elizabeth, a call would almost
certainly convince Annie that he had an obsession
with stray women. Sharon's voice again interrupted
his thoughts.

"You didn't answer me. The girl you were supposed to meet? She's the one who's always ringing
you, isn't she?"

"She is." In the bread bin, he found half a loaf of
brown bread. It had gone stale, but he didn't care.
Aware of Sharon behind him, he hacked off a piece,
sandwiched it around the cheese. After he'd finished
eating, he brushed the crumbs into the sink, put the
bread back in the bin and went to the back door.
Through the windowpane, he looked out into the dark
night and after a moment heard a flurry of movement
outside, followed by a frantic scratching at the wood-
work.

"Rufus." He pulled the door open, and a large gray
dog burst into the kitchen on a blast of cold air.
"You've awful-smelling breath, d'you know that?"
He scratched the dog's wiry head. "And you're a bit
of a scruff bag, too. If you ever hope to interest that

little Pekingese down the road, you'll have to do something about yourself.''

"Oh, I see." Sharon spoke at his shoulder. "You're just going to ignore me, is that it? Sure, the bloody dog gets more attention than I do. Maybe I should get down on all fours and bark at you. Would that do it?''

Over the dog's head, he met Sharon's ice-blue stare.

"It's a character flaw, you have," she said. "You know that, don't you? Your head's always up in the bloody clouds. You're not grounded in reality.''

He pushed the dog down. The charge wasn't exactly new. Three years ago when they'd first become partners in the small art gallery, she'd teased him about mentally disappearing. For a while, it had been a joke between them. Sharon would knock on his head, inquire if anyone was home. Gradually, the teasing started to get a bit of an edge. It wasn't until they'd started sleeping together that she'd taken to calling it a character flaw.

On the dresser, there was an unopened bottle of whiskey that he'd bought to take up to Sligo. The converted lighthouse he'd bought a few years back was his favorite place in the world, remote and beautiful—with a constant crash of the ocean all around. He could do with a little of that solitude right now, he thought, with a glance at Sharon. He poured a little whiskey into a couple of glasses and handed one to her. She downed it in one gulp, carried her empty glass to the sink, then returned to where he stood.

"She's a bit young, isn't she, Niall? Have you thought of what people will think?" She put one hand up as though to ward off an outburst. "All right, you

say she's just a student in your class and it's all perfectly innocent. Maybe that's true, but people talk.''
She gave him a meaningful look. ''As you well know.
I didn't say it to the bank manager, of course, but can
you imagine if I'd told him you weren't there because
it was more important to be with this…this little
tart?'' A faint flush of pink stained her face. ''Can
you?''

''I can.''

''But you don't care, do you? It really doesn't matter to you what people think. You lock yourself away
in your own little world, and nothing else exists.'' She
stopped, left the room and returned a few moments
later with a large white envelope. ''Maybe this will
bring you back to earth. It came today.'' She handed
it to him. ''From that boyfriend of Moruadh's in
Paris. It was addressed to you, so I opened it, but the
letters inside were for her.''

He took them from her. Half a dozen gray envelopes.

He riffled through them. All had been opened. Letters from him sent during the year before Moruadh
died, forwarded by one of the many men who had
drifted through her life at that time. He looked up and
met Sharon's eyes.

''Did you open these?''

''They were already open.''

He looked up at her. ''Did you read them?''

''One of them, I glanced at. It said something about
her needing to get help and—''

''I know what it said, Sharon. I wrote it.'' He got
up and walked across the kitchen to the window and
stared out at the dark night.

''I don't make a habit of reading your personal

mail," Sharon said. "You know that. You had that exhibit in Paris last month, and I thought that this was something to do with that. A business matter. We're supposed to be partners, aren't we?"

He didn't answer.

"Whatever you think you understand from what you read," he said a moment later, "you understand nothing at all."

"But Niall—"

"You understand nothing," he repeated. "Moruadh was a talented young musician, greatly loved and admired by everyone who knew her." He said the words as though by rote. "She was also a beautiful woman who had a lot of admirers. Her death was a tragic accident and an incredible loss to us all."

Sharon stared at him as though transfixed.

"Is that clear?"

Various emotions played across her face. For a moment, she seemed about to speak, but then she shrugged and took his glass to the sink.

"There's another matter I wanted to talk to you about." He sat down at the table, watched as she pulled out a chair. "Look, I think we both know this isn't working, Sharon. Us, I mean. We spend half our time together arguing over one thing or another. There's just—" he shrugged "—nothing there anymore."

"Oh, really?" She got up from the table, crossed the room. Regarded him, arms crossed, her back against the wall. "Nothing there, you say? And do you know why that is? Niall? Do you have the faintest bloody idea why there's *nothing* there?"

He waited for her to tell him.

"No, of course you don't, because you're as oblivious to what's happening with us as you are to everything else going on around you. Well, I'll tell you. You've lost touch with yourself, Niall. You can't connect.''

He bent to pick out a burr from the dog's coat. "You're right, Sharon. I can't. Don't. Won't. I've never been much on giving guided tours of my psyche. Go and find someone who *emotes*. There's a drama teacher at the college who'll sob at the drop of a hat. I'll find out if he's available.''

"Sure, make a joke of it. It's the easy way, isn't it? Well, fine. It's over, finished. I'll survive. And you'll meet someone new and it'll be fine at first, just as it was with us. She'll fall in love with your looks and the way you have about you, so bloody interested with all your questions and rapt attention, but you're like a collector. You take what you need, but you give nothing back.''

"Well, that's my problem, isn't it?''

"Yes it is, Niall. And frankly, I'm glad to be done with it. You've got something locked away up there and you'll sacrifice anything before you let it out.''

AN HOUR OR SO AFTER Sharon left, Niall sat at his desk in the study, going through the rest of the mail. Press notices from his show in Paris, an invitation to a gallery opening in Dublin. Another letter from the American writer who wanted to interview him about Moruadh. For a moment, he held the blue envelope in his hand, its color triggering a memory of a spring day five years ago. Wisps of clouds, a lark high in the sky. A windy hillside...

Moruadh had found a gentian, the first of the year. A bright blue flower that she'd held out for him to see. There was a bit of doggerel that went along with finding the first one. They'd both learned it as children, and he had recited it in Irish, one of the few scraps of Irish he knew.

"May we be here at this time next," he'd said.

"I won't be," Moruadh replied. "I'm going to die."

Her eyes as blue as the flower in her hand looked right into his and he felt a chill across his back.

"What is it? Are you ill? Is there something wrong?"

"There is not." She smiled, one of the lightning-quick smiles that lit her face like sunshine. "Nothing at all."

"Then why would you say something like that?"

"Because it just came to me."

"You're standing in a field on a sunny day and it just comes to you that you're going to die?" He started to become angry with her. "Sure, it makes perfect sense."

"No, it makes no sense. It just came to me."

At a loss for words, he shook his head at her.

"Ah, Niall." With a laugh, she tossed the flower aside. "Don't try to understand. Some things aren't meant to be understood."

By the same time the next year, she'd claimed not to remember that day with the gentians. Niall looked at the blue envelope again, and without bothering to open it, threw it into the wastepaper basket at his feet.

CHAPTER THREE

STILL GROGGY, Kate stood in the doorway of Annie's sitting room. Instead of the quick nap she'd meant to take, she'd slept through dinner. When Annie tapped at the door to say she'd made sandwiches and tea, it was nearly eleven.

Kate's glance shifted from the bartender, dozing now by a blazing fire, to Annie, who sat at a little desk talking on the phone. A girl with cropped orange hair and thickly mascaraed eyes sat on the couch next to a dark-haired boy who was whispering in her ear. Arms folded across her chest, the girl dangled a shoe from her toe, studying her foot as she listened.

Apparently sensing Kate in the doorway, the boy looked up and his eyes widened slightly. It took Kate a moment to recognize him as the Garda she'd seen earlier, changed now into jeans and a red sweater. He half stood and smiled at her.

"Didn't I meet you on the cliffs earlier this evening?" she asked.

His face went blank.

"About six-thirty?" She waited for him to recognize her. "I told you about seeing a fight, or something."

He shook his head. "Must have been someone who looked like me."

"Rory was out on the Galway Road investigating

an accident.'' The girl draped her arm around his neck, eyeing Kate as though she might constitute competition. ''Weren't you, love?''

''I was.'' He winked at Kate. ''But sure, all the Gardai look alike, don't they? Tall, dark, handsome and irresistible to women.'' He nudged his thigh against the girl's. ''Right, Caitlin?''

Kate shrugged. Maybe she was wrong. She'd been tired, her brain still on California time and the light hadn't been good. She started to speak, but Rory had turned his attention back to the girl, his mouth at her ear. Awkward and more than a little confused, Kate was about to go back upstairs, when Annie got off the phone.

''Did you have a little snooze then?'' Annie put her arm around Kate's shoulder, drawing her into the sitting room. ''This is my daughter, Caitlin.'' She laughed. ''Kate and Caitlin, funny that. And this is Rory McBride, soon to be my son-in-law.''

''June fourteenth.'' Caitlin gazed adoringly at Rory, who had one arm around her shoulder, the other draped along the back of the couch. ''And we're going on honeymoon. Majorca,'' she added with a little giggle.

''And this Sleeping Beauty over here—'' Annie tweaked the bartender's cheek ''—is my husband, Patrick, who you've already met.''

''Whaa?'' The bartender stirred and opened his eyes.

''Nothing, Pat. Go back to sleep. Kate, you make yourself comfortable, now.'' Annie flapped her hand at Rory. ''Move over and give Katie some room on the couch.''

''No, stay where you are.'' Kate dropped down on

a hassock by the fire and looked over at Annie. "Did your houseguest come home yet?"

"She did not." Annie poured tea into flowered cups and handed one to Kate. "But that was my brother Michael on the phone. He's the sergeant in charge at the station. 'Don't worry about Elizabeth,' he tells me. 'Teenagers are like that.'"

"He's right, Annie," Rory said. "Elizabeth's been on and on about wanting to go to Galway. It's natural enough. The whole reason she's here with us is to see a bit of the country. She's not seeing much of it stuck in Cragg's Head."

"It's true, Mam," Caitlin said. "All I hear from her is how boring it is in Cragg's Head." She eyed Kate for a moment. "It's very quiet, especially in the winter. If you're looking for excitement, you'll not find it here."

"Kate's not here for excitement," Annie said. "She's writing about Moruadh Maguire. Big American magazine, right, Katie?" She laughed. "Just think of it, a celebrity right in my sitting room."

Kate grinned, thinking about her maxed-out credit cards and depleted checking account. "Hardly."

As Annie went on to tell Caitlin about a mutual friend she'd seen that day, Kate looked around the cozy room. Overstuffed armchairs, flowered curtains drawn across the dark night outside. A feeling of well-tended comfort. The kind of room in which you'd curl up with a good book. Her eyes moved from Annie, presiding over a small table set with a china teapot and plates of sliced cake and sandwiches, to Caitlin pouring milk and tea into teacups, and then to Rory who was staring into the fire. Kate watched him for a moment. At first glance, he appeared at ease, but his fingers rapped a continuous tattoo on the back of the couch. He reminded her of an engine idling—motion barely contained, ready to bolt in an instant. When Caitlin offered him a teacup, he jumped as though he'd just realized she was there. His head, Kate was almost certain, was not in this room.

"Come on, Kate." Annie broke into her reverie. "Tea? A bit of treacle bread. It's nice. I made it just this afternoon." She held out the plate. "A bit over-done, I suppose. Took my eye off the stove for a minute and the next thing I knew I was smelling smoke."

"How did you hear about Moruadh then?" Caitlin sipped her tea and looked at Kate. "Was she popular in America?"

"She wasn't really well-known, but I wrote about her three years ago and we talked on the phone a few times." Kate glanced down at the slice of cake Annie had just put on her plate. "Even though I'd never met her, I felt as though I knew her somehow."

"Moruadh could make you feel that way," Annie said.

"She could." Patrick spooned jam onto a piece of bread. "And she had a way of making you think there was no one in the world she'd rather be talking to than you yourself." He laughed. "Even a tubby old baldy like me."

Caitlin smiled at her father. "Da had a little crush on her."

"Tell me a man under ninety who didn't," Annie said. "She was a pretty girl. I don't think Hughie Fitzpatrick ever got over her marrying Maguire."

Kate thought of the reporter she'd met in Dooley's, the bitterness in his voice as he'd spoken about Maguire. Time had obviously done little to lessen his hatred for the man.

"Hughie and Moruadh were sweethearts, until she started making a name for herself," Annie said. "The next thing I hear, she's married to Maguire, and they're living in Paris."

"A cool one, that Maguire," Patrick said. "I suppose his money won her over in the end." He looked over at the couple on the couch. "How would you describe Niall Maguire, Rory?"

"Ah, he's just…" Rory's forehead creased in a frown. "Sure, I don't know how to put it. He can look right at you and it's as though you're not even there. And you'll never see him having a laugh down at the pub or out kicking a football. He's just never been one of the lads."

"But he's lovely looking, though," Caitlin said with a little smile. "Those eyelashes of his. No matter how much mascara I used, I couldn't get mine to look that long. You've not met him yet, Kate?"

"No. I'm going to try and see him tomorrow." She'd left her notebook upstairs, but made a mental note to jot down the comments she'd heard as soon as she got back to her room. At this rate, and given her own suspicions about Maguire's guilt, it was going to be hard to maintain even a semblance of objectivity.

"He's very polite." Caitlin examined her nails. "Makes you feel as though what you're saying is really important to him."

"*Very polite.*" Rory traced circles in the air near his temple. "Go and varnish your nails or something, Caitlin."

"What's the matter with that?" Caitlin asked, wide-eyed. "I'm just saying he has nice manners."

"Sure, Caitlin," Rory said quietly, his head bowed, "if he's got nice manners, he couldn't possibly have pushed Moruadh down the cliffs, could he? Not without saying 'pardon me' as he shoved her over."

"Rory." Caitlin slapped his arm. "That's terrible, no one knows that for sure."

"I'm no fan of Maguire, mind you, but in my opinion, Moruadh fell," Patrick said. "She was a great one for the outdoors. Out there every day she was, in all weather, going for her walks. For years, people have been clamoring at the council to put a fence up. 'Tis a tragedy that it took this to make it happen."

"He's right." Caitlin looked at Kate. "People should stop all this gossip about Mr. Maguire. It isn't nice. Wait till you meet him, Kate. You'll fall in love with him, I'm telling you."

"Oh, but Kate's married," Annie said, smiling. "Aren't you, Kate?"

Kate and the bartender exchanged glances. Time for her to bow out, she decided.

"No." She grinned. "I like to play the field. Love 'em and leave 'em, that's my motto." She stood and put her teacup on the tray. "I'm going to say goodnight. I'm about to fall asleep on my feet."

BUT AS TIRED as she'd felt downstairs, when she got to her room Kate was suddenly wide-awake. Fully dressed, she stretched out on the bed, her eyes fixed on the repeating pattern of the wallpaper. Tiny sprigs of white flowers against a yellow background. Her thoughts drifted back to Moruadh. At home, she would listen to Moruadh's clear high voice as she drove. Haunting and ephemeral, the music weaving its spell as it conjured visions of mists and hills, yearning and heartache. Of sadness too unbearable to endure.

"And tell the world," Moruadh sang. "That I died for love."

After Kate's article came out, Moruadh had called her a few times from Ireland and Paris. Usually in the early hours of the morning. For the most part, Moruadh talked while Kate listened. Inevitably, the topic turned to men and relationships and love. Moruadh fell in and out of love with a succession of men. Nothing lasted, and she would talk about the howling-in-the-wilderness bouts of loneliness that gripped her in the early hours. "Ah God, I could die of it," Moruadh said once. "I've crawled into the beds of men who meant nothing at all, just to have someone's arms around me."

Her last call had been short and perfunctory. She was marrying a man by the name of Niall Maguire, she'd told Kate. No time to talk, but she would call again soon.

But she never had. Kate had read about Moruadh's death in the obituary section of the *Times*. A small reference just a couple of paragraphs summing up Moruadh's career. While walking along the cliffs near her home in Cragg's Head, the article said, Moruadh Maguire had fallen some three hundred feet to her death. Ruling it an accident, the Gardai had blamed wind and rain and the unstable cliffs. Kate had thought about love and loneliness and had been unable to get Moruadh off her mind.

Restless now, she got up to examine the framed prints that hung on the walls. Sylphs and sprites in a field of bluebells. A gnome on a toadstool. More sprites and bluebells. Everything felt oddly unreal and slightly off-kilter, as though she'd been dropped into the middle of another world that bore a superficial resemblance to her own but functioned in a way she didn't entirely understand. Unanswered questions. Confused directions and screwed-up road signs. The shadowy figure up on the cliffs. The young Garda in the car. The way the gray-eyed man had suddenly appeared out of the fog.

The sensation was similar to the way she felt after she'd taken her car to be washed at one of those full-service places. She'd get back in and find that everything—radio, seats, mirrors—had been slightly changed. Not enough that she couldn't drive, but sufficient to send her neuroses into overdrive. Kind of the way she felt right now. Just a little thrown off. She yawned again and moved back to the bed. On the other hand, maybe she'd just overdosed on Celtic intrigue.

Through the closed door, she could hear the soft murmur of conversation from the sitting room below. Like a video, images of the evening ran through her head. The play of firelight on the faces around the room. The clink of flowered china teacups and saucers, the crackle of flames. Patrick dozing in his chair. The smells of baking and fresh flowers.

Annie bustling around. Smiling, urging food on everyone. Annie had a natural warmth—an openness that instantly turned strangers into friends. A quality Kate envied but couldn't master herself. Probably because it required a certain willingness to let yourself be vulnerable. Her own defense mechanisms were too finely honed to allow that. Compared to Annie, she felt world-weary and a little jaded.

A fleeting childhood memory drifted across her consciousness. A night spent at a friend's house. A girl with lots of brothers and sisters. The house was full of warmth and light and people laughing and talking. It had seemed perfect, like a page from a storybook. When she grew up, Kate had vowed, she would have a house just like it. Full of happy children. A smiling husband.

More memories, dim and fragmentary. Herself at ten, wakened from sleep by raised voices coming from downstairs. Her father's voice, cold, dispassionate. No, he wouldn't be back. He had fallen in love. A student in one of his classes. Her mother's sobs.

A memory of walking home from school after her parents divorced. Looking through brightly lit windows of other houses. The little rituals she had developed that, if followed exactly, would make everything all right again. *If* she touched every mailbox on her street as she passed, her mother wouldn't be crying when she walked in. *If* she skipped for four blocks, she would smell cookies baking when she opened the front door. *If* she held her breath for two minutes, her mother would be sober.

She got up, dug out a robe and toilet bag from her suitcase and walked down the hall to the bathroom. It was after her mother committed suicide that she'd pretty much stopped believing in magic. Or love.

TO CALL BUNCARROCH CASTLE gloomy, she decided the next morning, would be like calling Trump Tower upscale. She stood in the damp air, craning her neck to look up.

Niall Maguire's ancestral home stood at the crest of a small hill, surrounded on three sides by the ocean. Massive and vaguely misshapen, it sprouted various architectural embellishments that she guessed had been added over the years. Battlements, gargoyles, wartlike turrets. One wing, jutting awkwardly like a broken limb, seemed in imminent danger of crashing into the ocean.

Niall Maguire was not home. Or at least he wasn't answering the doorbell. She rang it again, glanced around the graveled circular driveway. No cars, but she wasn't sure what that meant. Did castles have garages? Again she rang the doorbell and waited. After a few moments she walked back across the gravel, climbed onto Annie's elderly Raleigh and pedaled down the hill again.

She would try later, she decided as she rode through a waste of rock-and-boulder-smattered heather into the village. Although Maguire had ignored her letters, which suggested he didn't want to talk to her, he might be less inclined to turn her down if they actually met face-to-face. On the other hand, if he was as aloof and detached as Patrick and Rory had described him, maybe not.

She thought of what Hugh Fitzpatrick had told her about Maguire's attractiveness to women. Objectivity was becoming difficult. Her tendency was always to root for the underdog, and Niall Maguire with his castle and money and fawning women appeared to be anything but.

As she passed Sullivan's Butcher Shop, a man in a navy, striped apron sweeping the pavement looked up and waved.

"Fine day," he called.

"Terrific," Kate called back and caught her reflection in a shop window. Warm, if not particularly fetching, in her dark green parka and old black cords. An errant strand of hair had escaped from the black woolen cap she'd jammed on and it flew out behind her like a long red ribbon.

Earlier, at Annie's insistence, she'd eaten an enormous breakfast of Irish bacon, eggs, tomatoes and soda bread slathered with butter. More calories than she ate at home in an entire week, but it was amazing what food and a decent night's sleep did for the disposition. Last night Ireland had seemed strange and a little disconcerting. Today, in the glow of early-morning sunshine, all was well. A ride to burn off some of the calories and then a couple of interviews she'd scheduled. After that, she would try Niall Maguire again.

She pedaled through the village. Only a few of the brightly painted shops along the high street were open this early, but the area was already busy. Horns tooted, car doors slammed. From Claddagh Music came the trill of a flute, as pure and clear as birdsong. From Joyce's Bakery, the aroma of warm bread rose to mingle with the peat smoke and the salty tang of the harbor.

It all seemed quite idyllic. Far removed from the police sirens and gang shootings and other staples of her daily life in Santa Monica. She rode past the small harbor where men in heavy jerseys and oilskin trousers were dragging a small boat onto the shingles. Then past the Connacht Superette and Kelly's Garage.

A mile or so out of the village, the road narrowed and acrid farm smells filled the air. A light breeze moved the clouds overhead. Except for the faint sigh of the wind and the hum of her tires on the road, the silence all around her was absolute. It hovered in the air like a presence—a peaceful hush that made the whole countryside appear to be sleeping.

Back home in Santa Monica, Kate worked to the constant chatter of the all-news radio that played in her office. When she drove, it was to the accompaniment of the assorted tapes she carried in her car. When you live with noise around you, she'd heard a radio shrink say, it drowns out the knowledge that you're alone.

Deep in thought, she heard a whoosh of air and a sharp squeal of brakes. The dark green Land Rover seemed to materialize from nowhere. She swerved wildly, slammed on the brakes and toppled over into a patch of grass. For a moment she just sat there, stunned, her nose filled with the smell of burned rubber. The car's driver, a tall, dark-haired man, made his way over to where she sat.

"Are you all right?" He reached to help her up.

"I'm fine." Ignoring his hand, Kate pulled herself to her feet and brushed grass from her pants. "No thanks to you. God, you could have killed me." She glared up at him, but he towered over her by at least a foot, which meant that she had to crane her neck and squint into the sun to see his face, something that further incensed her. "Perhaps it never occurred to you that not everyone might be zipping along in a fancy car?"

"It's usually only a problem," he said, watching her, "when people ride on the wrong side of the road. Which you were."

She felt her face flame. *Tap-dance your way out of this one.* Rooted to the spot, unwilling to break eye contact and concede the point, she stood there until she saw he was fighting to keep a straight face. And then she recognized him.

"The man on the cliff," she said.

"The Mace bandit," he said.

"*Mace bandit.*" She shook her head at him. He wore an open black leather jacket over a black sweater. The somber color accentuated his fair skin and dark hair, set off the fine-boned features and clear gray eyes. His hair was clean, slightly curly and just a shade too long. The shadow on his jaw suggested he'd neglected to shave that morning. He also had a truly sensational smile, which he was turning on her now.

"I'm not sure about you," she finally said. "Last night you nearly scared me to death. Today you knock me off my bike."

"I'm bad news all around," he said. "Or so I've been told."

"I bet you have." She tried not to smile back at him. He looked wildly attractive, a kind of unstudied sexiness that perked up her hormones and pheromones and God knows what other mones. Something about the way he was looking at her told her the attraction was mutual.

"How can I make amends?" He gestured at her bike. "What about this then? I'll see what the damage is."

"There's no damage." Even if there were, she'd rather walk the damn thing back to Annie's than drive up in his car, looking like a fool because she'd forgotten which side of the road to ride on. She smiled. "It's fine."

"You've not looked."

"Trust me. I know these things."

Moments passed. A breeze rustled the grasses, tousled his hair. A car went by. Her knee started to throb, and her hands smarted where she'd landed on them. She shoved them in the pocket of her parka.

"You're all right, really? No broken bones."

"I'm all right, really," she said, imitating him. "No broken bones." Given his looks, the lyrical accent was overkill. This guy was too cute by half.

"Where are you headed?"

"Cragg's Head."

"That's the opposite direction from where you're going."

"Well…" She glanced at him from under her lashes. "I was taking the scenic route."

"Actually, you're on the road to Dublin."

"The scenic and very circuitous route," she amended.

They looked at each other until neither one of them could keep a straight face. It occurred to her that she could stand there indefinitely trading lines back and forth with him. And he seemed in no hurry to leave, either.

"If you think you're going to get me to admit I'm lost," she finally said, "give up."

"Ah, I didn't think for a moment you were lost." He lowered his voice and leaned toward her a little. "But I'll tell you a secret. Cragg's Head is that way." He gestured with his arm. "Straight ahead. You can't miss it."

"I think I've heard that before." She bent to pick up her bike and felt him watching her. Either she could prolong the exchange, shift it up to the next gear or do the safe thing and ride off. In a split-second decision, she chose the latter. He'd told her something she already knew. He was bad news. His sort always was. That attractive got-the-world-by-a-string type. They were like strawberries. When you were allergic to them, it didn't matter how tempting they looked, heaped into pies, dolled up with shiny red glaze and whipped cream. The fact was they screwed up your system and caused endless misery.

They were something to be avoided.

"Can I at least give you a lift?"

"No, thanks." She climbed on the bike. "I can make it on my own steam. I'll try and remember to stay on the right side."

"Just remember, the right side is on the left."

"Got it." With a smile and a glance over her shoulder, Kate started off down the road, praying the wheel wouldn't fall off while he was still watching her. The final image of him burned in her brain. Sunlight and shadows dappling his head and shoulders. The quizzical smile. For a moment, she almost turned around and rode back. Maybe she'd been too flip. After all, he had seemed genuinely concerned.

She kept riding. No, better this way. Better not even knowing his name. What was the point anyway? A little more than a week and she'd be back in the States.

CHAPTER FOUR

ON HER WAY back to the Pot o' Gold, Kate passed the redbrick building that housed the tourist bureau where Annie worked part-time. Through the window, she could see Annie working at her desk. She rapped on the window and Annie motioned for her to come in.

"You couldn't have stopped by at a better moment," Annie said. "First off, if you wouldn't mind making sure Rory gets the sandwiches I made for him, I'd be grateful. He's mad for cold chicken and I had some left from last Sunday's lunch."

"Sure, no problem," Kate said. "Do you want me to take them down to the station?"

"If he doesn't drop by first." Annie held up a poster for her to see. "And now I'd like your opinion on this. Tell me what you think."

"The Cragg's Head Fleadh," Kate read aloud, mentally shoving aside thoughts of her encounter with the man on the cliff. "A festival of fiddles, flutes and concertinas. It looks great."

"Flah," Annie corrected. "Rhymes with hah," she said with a smile. "That's all right, though, you're not the first to say it wrong. I've so much to do I can hardly see straight and now, with this worry over Elizabeth, it's all I can do to keep my mind on anything."

"You still haven't heard from her?" Kate asked.

"I haven't directly, but that was a friend of hers on the phone just now. Swears she saw Elizabeth at a coffee bar this morning. Would have spoken to her, she says, but she ran off. Still, it's good to have even a wee bit of news."

"I'm sure it must be." Kate glanced again at the poster. "So you're in charge of putting this whole thing together?"

"I am. Well, we've a committee, of course, but in the time it takes for them to decide on anything, I can already have it done." She retrieved a slim blue book from under a pile of papers on her desk and handed it to Kate. "Sometimes I wonder why I bother, though. Last year, Cragg's Head wasn't even in here. This year they put a little note that said it wasn't worth a detour."

Kate riffled through the pages and smiled up at her.

"Well, we're never going to have the crowds flocking here," Annie said, returning the smile. "But it's home. I'd never leave. My sister left for America, a few years back. Boston. Pat and I went over there for a holiday and they took us to an Irish bar of all places." She shook her head. "All of them singing 'Danny Boy' and shedding tears for dear old Ireland as though they'd go back in a minute, if they could. And few of them ever would."

"You've lived in Cragg's Head for a long time?"

"My whole life." Annie gestured to the stack of wooden desks in the corner. "Until this year, this room used to be a classroom. Caitlin sat at one of those desks in this room and so did I…" She smiled. "Too many years back to remember. My father and grandfather tilled those fields out there. We've been here for as long as anyone can remember. Pat's family too.''

"It must be nice to have that sense of continuity," Kate said, recalling her own childhood. "My dad was always getting transferred. By the time I was nine, I'd been enrolled in a dozen different schools."

"Ah God." Annie gave Kate a horrified look. "What kind of a start in life is that? Your mother didn't mind it then?"

"Well, they finally got divorced, so she probably did. But she tended to go along with whatever my father wanted and he was always looking for something he never seemed to find." With her finger, she pushed scattered paper clips into a pile, lost for a moment in her thoughts. "We did okay, I guess. My brother and I. We both got decent grades. We made friends." She grinned at Annie. "Of course they never lasted long, but then we made new friends."

Annie clicked her tongue. "Sure, it would be like pulling up the daffodil bulbs every morning to see if they're growing," she said. "If you dug me up and put me somewhere else, I'd not be the same person."

"In California, where I live," Kate said, "almost everyone is from somewhere else. People talk about putting down roots and that sort of thing, but it's more like we're seeds blown on the wind. You could land anywhere and, just as easily, pull up and go somewhere else."

Annie shook her head as though the thought were too outlandish to comprehend.

"That's why you're not married," she finally said. "You've no idea who you are or where you belong. Come to think of it, that's probably Hughie Fitzpatrick's problem. Him growing up on the Maguire estate as he did. Like planting a potato in among the roses and expecting it to grow petals. Sure, who wouldn't be confused?''

SHE WASN'T JUST CONFUSED, Kate thought later that morning as she sat at a small desk in Annie's front parlor, she was besotted. For the last hour she'd been trying, unsuccessfully, to focus on the notes from an interview she'd just completed with an old school friend of Moruadh's, but her brain was refusing to cooperate. All it wanted to do was think about the gray-eyed man. The man on the cliff.

Why *had* she turned down his offer of a ride home? Maybe he would have asked her out. Dinner perhaps. A little pub with mullioned windows and a fireplace. The stories of their lives exchanged over a couple of Guinnesses.

She shook her head to clear the images. *You're in Ireland to work. Not for a fling.* She drank some coffee from a cup patterned with pink cabbage roses, picked a raisin out of a piece of soda bread, wrote three headings on her yellow pad: Accidental death. Suicide. Murder.

The school friend had said that Moruadh had occasionally suffered with bouts of depression. Spells, she'd called them. Kate recalled her mother's incapacitating depression after the divorce. Days when she never left the bed.

But there were degrees of depression. From the friend's description, Moruadh's appeared to have been of the mild blues variety. Kate got up and wandered over to the window. Beyond Annie's neatly planted front garden, she saw the dark turrets of Buncarroch Castle looming in the gray air. Something almost sinister about it. If Moruadh spent much time there, no wonder she'd had fits of depression.

Kate made more notes, drank some more coffee. Found her thoughts drifting back to the gray-eyed man. An Irish accent, but overlaid with something else. An expensive education maybe, or years abroad. She tried to re-create it. What had he said? 'Just remember, the right side is on the left.' Even now, she could feel this little tug in her stomach as she pictured him.

Restless, she got up from the table and wandered upstairs to her room. Maybe a little fling might have been fun. Since they didn't exactly live within commuting distance, she wouldn't be screening him as a husband candidate. Obviously nothing could come of it. Why not enjoy herself while she was here?

At the dresser, she stared at her reflection. Long red hair she'd worn the same way since she was about fourteen. Hanging loose down her back or tied up in a ponytail. Freckles she didn't try to cover because she hated the feel of makeup on her skin. She picked up a brush and ran it through her hair. Not that there was much point in thinking about flings, she'd probably never see him again. Although, as Annie said, Cragg's Head was a small place. She'd seen him twice already. Maybe she should take another walk.

Outside, a car door slammed, and she ran to the window. With a pang of disappointment, she saw that the car at the curb was a light green Gardai car, not a dark green Land Rover.

Get over it, she told herself as she watched Rory McBride get out. The guy doesn't even know where you're staying. She heard the front door open and close, then Rory's voice calling her name.

Thinking of the strange exchange with him the night before, she hesitated. She was alone in the house. Annie and Patrick wouldn't be home for a couple of hours, and Caitlin was at school. Paranoia, she decided. It was broad daylight and his car was parked outside in clear view. And this was Ireland, not Santa Monica.

She closed the bedroom door behind her. He stood at the foot of the stairs, backlit by the amber light streaming from the fan-shaped window above the front door. He wore a navy overcoat over his blue uniform.

"Hi." She smiled at him from the top of the stairs. "You caught me here between interviews. I was just going over my notes. What's up?"

"I saw your car outside." He pulled off his cap, shook raindrops onto the rug. "It's a lovely country, Ireland, they just need to put a roof over it."

"Well, at least the rain's let up a bit," she provided. No Irish exchange, she was learning, could start without a comment on the weather. "Maybe it will clear up tomorrow."

"Let's hope so." Holding his hat in both hands, Rory smiled hesitantly, like a suitor come to call. "I wondered…could I have a word with you? If you've a minute, that is."

"Sure." She ran down the stairs and led him into the sitting room where her notes were still spread out over the desk. "Want some coffee?" She gestured at the pot. "I can make some fresh."

"I don't. Thank you, though." He unbuttoned his coat and sat down at the table. "You might have wondered a bit about last night. My telling you I wasn't up there on the cliffs, I mean."

Kate, glad that at least one of the mysteries was cleared up, decided that no response was necessary.

"The thing is, I love Caitlin." He stuck his finger into the neck of his blue uniform shirt. "Sure, we're getting married in June, and Annie, well, she's like my own mother. But, see, yesterday I went into Galway to meet Elizabeth, the girl who's staying with Annie." Eyes downcast, he appeared to be composing his thoughts. "We'd just come back when you saw me in my car up on the cliffs but, uh, we had a few words and she left."

"And you didn't want Caitlin and Annie to know?" Kate watched his face. "That's why you said it wasn't you I saw up there?"

"Right." Faint relief flickered across his face. "Honestly, there's nothing at all between me and Elizabeth, but Caitlin...well, she's a bit green-eyed, if you know what I mean."

"Does she have reason to be?"

"She doesn't, no. I sowed my wild oats some time ago." He smiled at her, his eyes exactly the same blue as his shirt. Easy to understand why Caitlin would find him attractive, although she suspected that Caitlin's jealousy wasn't unfounded.

"So you've no idea where Elizabeth is?"

"I have not." His look suggested the question was stupid. "Would I be letting Annie worry if I knew where Elizabeth was?"

"Well, I'd hope not," she retorted and then something occurred to her. "By the way, did you check out whatever it was I told you I saw on the cliffs?"

"I did. Up and down the footpath. There were a few people about. Teenagers. Probably a couple of them larking about was what you saw."

"Probably." She folded her arms across her chest. He clearly wanted her assurance that she wouldn't blow his cover, but something about the whole thing made her uncomfortable. "I don't know your relationship with Elizabeth, but…" She put her hand up to stop his protest. "I'm not going to lie to Annie or Caitlin."

"I'm not asking you to lie. You don't have to say anything. They think I was seeing into a car crash, and that's what I want them to think. Besides, Elizabeth'll show up tonight and the whole thing will blow over."

She met his eyes for a moment. He reminded her a bit of her younger brother. Before Ned had married and settled down, he'd come to her to bail him out of various scrapes he'd gotten into. He'd go into some torturous explanation of what had happened and then look at her, anxiety all over his face, as he waited for her reaction. Just the way Rory McBride was looking at her now.

"Listen, Rory. I'm going to tell you something about myself. I can't stand liars. And I can't stand cheating men. And, trust me, I've had plenty of experience with both." Kate saw the flicker of interest in his eyes as though what she'd said had cast her in a slightly different light. "Here's the deal. I won't bring it up, but if anyone should ask me whether I saw you on the cliffs last night, I won't lie, either. Okay?"

"Right." He gave her a little smile. "Thanks, Kate."

"And I better not find out that you were cheating on Caitlin."

"I told you, I love her."

"Yeah, well…" She shrugged. "I'm not much of a believer in that sort of thing."

He grinned, relief now clear on his face. "Your work's going well, is it?"

"Not bad. I did a phone interview this morning and I've got another one later today. Niall Maguire wasn't in when I stopped at the castle. You wouldn't happen to know if he's in town?"

"He is. I saw him myself not an hour ago. You'll have the best chance of meeting him if you go directly up there." He frowned down at the table, started to speak, then stopped. A moment passed. "You'll want to be careful, Kate," he finally said. "With Maguire, that is."

"What d'you mean?"

"It's like I was saying last night, he's a bit—" He stopped as though a thought had occurred to him and shrugged. "Sure, you probably think I'm a fine one to talk, after what I've told you, but Maguire…well, he has an eye for the women. He's a fancy photographer of some sort. Does those big glossy picture books. There's always one woman or another up there visiting him."

"I'll keep that in mind." She bit back a grin. Despite her suspicions about Rory McBride, he looked so young and earnest in his blue uniform. Advising her, a woman at least ten years his senior, to be careful. "If he tries to put any moves on me, I'll sock him one."

"I'm serious, Kate." He frowned. "As a Garda, I shouldn't be saying this, but I've never doubted that Maguire had a part in his wife's death."

This was the second time Rory had mentioned his suspicions. Kate reached for the coffeepot. "This

stuff is cold. Come and talk to me while I make some
more.''

Rory followed her into the kitchen and stood with
his back to the wall, watching her as she ran water.
''Maguire's got money,'' he said after a moment.
''The rules are different for him. People will turn a
blind eye and that includes those high up in the Gardai, although you never heard me say that.''

Kate turned from the sink to look at him.

''Under the same circumstances, anyone but Maguire would have been locked up long ago,'' he said.

She measured coffee into the pot and put it on the
stove. The view from the kitchen window offered a
panorama of green fields and gray ocean and, off in
the distance, another, but equally gloomy, perspective
of Buncarroch Castle. It seemed to dominate the small
white cottages dotted all around. If she lived in one
of those cottages, she'd probably dislike Niall Maguire. She looked back at Rory.

''So what do you think his motive would have
been?''

''Well—'' he scratched the back of his head
''—myself, I think Moruadh just got to be a bit too
much for him.''

''What do you mean?''

''Anyone you speak to will tell you how everyone
liked Moruadh. Small wonder, she was a great girl. I
liked her myself.'' He stared for a moment at the
kitchen wall. ''The thing is, she had a...well, a reck-
less way about her that sometimes made you wonder
whether she was right in the head.''

''In what way?'' She sat down at the table again.
''Can you give me an example?''

''I can.'' He looked down at the floor as if in search

of a dog to pet, and glanced quickly up at her. "But you didn't hear it from me."

Kate met his eyes for a moment.

"I'm serious. If it got out that I told you this, it'd be my job. I'm only telling you because we've a bit of an understanding. You help me, I do the same for you." He watched her face. "Do you want to know?"

"Go ahead."

"A few months before she died, we got a call late one night about a bit of a disturbance at Reilly's flower shop. I was sent down to look into it and when I got there I couldn't believe my eyes. A window had been smashed, and Moruadh was inside, blood all over the place." He glanced over at the door as though scared someone might come in. "Stretched out on the floor, covered in flowers." His voice had dropped to a whisper. "Not a stitch of clothing on her."

Kate felt her breath catch.

"Still as a statue, she was." Rory reached in his shirt pocket and pulled out a pack of cigarettes. "Eyes closed. I thought at first she was dead. Christ, my heart was going like a drum. Then all of a sudden, she just opens her eyes and smiles at me as though it was the most natural thing in the world for her to be there. 'Oh, hello,' she says. 'I'm just choosing some flowers for my coffin.'"

"My God..." Kate shook her head. "That's incredible."

"It's written up in a report," Rory said, "but you'll never get anyone to show it to you. It was all hushed up quicker than a wink. That very night I was called into the superintendent's office, told that I hadn't seen a thing and if so much as a word got out, I'd find myself back in Donegal and off the force. If anyone should ask about the window, it had been broken by tinkers.''

"And it was never mentioned?"

"It never happened." He held her gaze. "The next time I saw Moruadh she was giving a recital at the library. Right as rain, she seemed. Smiling and friendly when she saw me. The funny thing is, after a bit I began to wonder myself whether I'd just dreamed the whole thing."

"But Maguire must have known about the incident, right?"

"He knew, all right. Sure, it was him she was asking for the night it happened. He was brought to the shop in the superintendent's car. No doubt he paid for the damage himself."

"And you think, what? That this sort of thing happened enough that he got tired of covering for her so he killed her?" She frowned. "It seems kind of far-fetched. I mean why wouldn't he just get psychological help for her?"

"I'm not the one you should be asking that question." Rory looked down at the pack of cigarettes in his hands. "To my mind, Maguire's odd himself. In fact, before I saw this with my own eyes, I'd have said she was the normal one and it was him who was off in the head."

Kate nodded. Cold and aloof according to almost everyone she'd spoken to. Easy enough to see how such traits wouldn't make him popular, but it didn't exactly convince her that he was capable of murder.

"No slight on the article you're writing," he said, "but I'd be surprised if you turn up anything that hasn't already been gone over. To my way of thinking, her death is a closed book. Sure, if they all want to believe it was an accident, better to just let them.'' He stood and buttoned his coat. "And about the other matter…''

"I've already forgotten it.''

"Thanks, Kate.'' He smiled at her. "And be careful when you go up to Maguire's, all right? If you're not back at Annie's by supper, I'll have a car sent up to the castle.'' He'd already taken off down the road when Kate remembered the sandwiches Annie had made for him. It took her only a minute to decide to take them down to the station. Maybe she'd run into the gray-eyed man again. A third chance encounter would be an unlikely coincidence in Santa Monica, here in Cragg's Head anything was possible.

"Rufus. Come on, boy.'' Niall whistled for the dog. After a moment it came bounding back, stick in its mouth. It panted, eyes expectant, waiting for him to throw.

"You think I've nothing more to do, don't you?'' As he ran his hands through the long hair on the dog's neck, Niall eyed the bank of purple clouds banked over the low hills, mentally composing a shot. A silver shaft of light pierced the clouds, shimmered on a ruined tower. The light was just right, but if he went back for his equipment, by the time he'd got everything set up, it would have faded.

The dog barked at him.

"Sorry. I forgot. You've got your priorities, too, haven't you?'' He flung the stick and grinned as the dog chased after it. An Irish wolfhound, rescued from a German couple who had rented one of his cottages a couple of years back, intending to make Ireland their home. After a taste of one Irish winter, they'd packed their bags and left. Rufus had become his by default.

Chin cupped in his hand, Niall studied the bruised-looking clouds again, then decided against going back for the camera. The second time that day, he thought as he started across the fields, that he'd had to forgo a bit of inspiration. The first time had been the American girl. He had a vivid mental picture of her on the grass by her fallen bike. Glaring up at him. Strands of red hair had escaped her black wool cap, and he'd fought an impulse to pull the bloody thing off her head and watch her hair tumble free.

She had green eyes. Not flecked with hazel, as he often saw, just pure green. And freckles on her forehead and throat. Seven of them over the bridge of her nose. He'd counted them. They probably multiplied in the summer. He thought of the summer he'd spent in America a few years back. California. It had been very hot, he remembered. But so beautiful you forgot about the heat until you got burned.

He walked out to the edge of the cliff, peered through the clumps of purple-red valerian. About halfway down, a rocky outcrop formed a shelf that ran for several miles and eventually down to the beach below. As a boy, he would ride his bike along the narrow ledge, thrilled at the danger of riding high above the ocean. He walked on for a mile or so, the wind tugging at his coat, his thoughts drifting.

When the talk started after Moruadh's death, he had wanted only anonymity. An escape from the hostile stares and murmurs that seemed to follow him everywhere he went. He'd considered America. New York, perhaps. Los Angeles. Any big city.

And then one day as he walked out across the fields, he had seen, as though for the first time, the vast wideness of the sky, the heather-colored landscape. He had felt the wind on his face, tasted on it the faint tang of salt from the Atlantic. And, in that moment, he had known he could never leave Ireland. He might be estranged from those around him, estranged from himself if it came to that, but here was where he belonged. Nothing would drive him away.

The dog bounded back across the grass and Niall threw the stick again. He'd stood at the car door and watched the American girl ride off, red hair streaming behind her. Stood there until she disappeared from view. Unable to remember what it was he'd been about to do before he met her. For some reason, he'd wandered back to the grassy patch where she'd fallen. Sometimes you did things without really knowing why and this was one of those times, he supposed.

As he'd bent to take a closer look at the tracks her bicycle tires had left, his hand brushed across something hard and flat beneath the grass. When he pulled the blades aside, he'd found a lichen-covered stone. Next to that stone, there'd been another, and another. A half-dozen of them in all, formed in a circle.

A *cromlech*. They were all over Ireland, circles of stones, half buried in the earth. Left there by farmers too superstitious to move them. They were also known by another name, the thought of which made him smile. Fairy rings they were called. She had fallen into a fairy ring.

Moruadh, who had claimed that rooks nesting in the turrets of the castle spoke to her, would have called it a sign.

Five minutes later, he pushed open the door to the

tourist office. Annie Ryan and Brigid Riley were eating sandwiches as they stuffed envelopes. Both of them gave him looks that suggested he was about as welcome as rain at a picnic.

"What can I do for you, Mr. Maguire?" Annie asked.

"I have those pictures you'd asked me to develop for the festival." Annie was one of the organizers of Cragg's Head's yearly music festival, and he'd offered to photograph some of the musicians for advertisements she was running in the local paper. He glanced down at the envelope in his hand. "So I thought I'd drop them off."

"Ah, good." Annie put her sandwich down and reached for the envelope. Brigid had started eating again, but she didn't take her eyes off him.

"I was also wondering about Elizabeth." He looked at Annie. "When I spoke to you last night, she hadn't come home."

"She still hasn't."

"And you've no idea where she might be?"

"None at all." Annie's gaze was steady on his face. "The Gardai are keeping an eye out for her."

He nodded. "Last weekend when she came up to my place," he said after a moment, "she said something about seeing some friends up in Donegal. Maybe—"

"I didn't know she was up at your place, Mr. Maguire," Annie interrupted. A chair creaked as Brigid shifted her weight. "Elizabeth said nothing to me about being there."

As he had the night before, Niall heard the accusatory tone in Annie's voice. "What I was suggesting, Mrs. Ryan," he said, "was that perhaps she was staying with friends up there. It might be something you'd want to look into.''

"I'll do that."

"Well, I hope you hear something soon." He ran his hand across the back of his neck, glanced down at the posters on her desk. Finally, he looked up at her. "And are you keeping busy these days, Mrs. Ryan? At the bed-and-breakfast, I mean?"

"It's a bit early in the year for the tourists. I thought there might be a few for the festival, but there's no one so far." Annie folded up the waxed paper from the sandwiches, then brushed some bread crumbs into her hand. "I've just one guest right now," she said with a glance at him. "After she leaves, there's no one until late June."

"An American is it? The guest you have staying with you. A girl with long red hair?"

"The same." Annie looked at him. She got up from the desk and took some papers over to the filing cabinet, seemed about to tell him something, then stopped.

Niall couldn't think of anything more to say so he left. As he walked away, he found himself whistling.

CHAPTER FIVE

KATE STOOD against the far wall of the Gardai station, trying not to smile as Rory attempted to settle a dispute between a couple of grizzled old farmers over some sheep one said the other had stolen.

"It wasn't like that a'tall, Sergeant," the tallest of the two was saying. "I was in me field cutting briars when I heard shouting." He gestured with his thumb to the man standing next to him. "It was him there, asking me what I'd done with his sheep. Then he starts calling me a sheep stealer. And then he hits me. Cut me lip he did and gave me two black eyes, the *eejit*."

"Away with you," the other man roared. "It's you who is the *eejit*." He looked at Rory. "I'm telling you, Sergeant, it was him that started the whole lot of it."

Rory briefly met Kate's eyes, then turned his attention back to the farmers, sending them off with a warning that the next time there was fighting he'd have them both arrested.

"Both of them older than my da," he said after they'd left, "and fighting like a couple of schoolboys. Going on for generations it has and no one remembers how it all started. I'll bet it's not something you see in America, is it?"

"Not in Santa Monica anyway." She grinned and

held up a brown paper sack. "Annie wanted to be sure you had lunch. She's worried you're not eating properly."

"Jaysus." Rory rolled his eyes. "I've put on two stone since I've known Caitlin. At this rate, they'll have to roll me down the aisle. Caitlin, too," he said with a grin. He turned to sharpen a pencil and glanced over his shoulder at Kate. "I don't suppose Elizabeth's come home, has she?"

"Not while I was there." She watched him for a moment, his expression distracted as he looked at the pencil in his hand. "You're worried about her? No idea where she might be, huh?"

"Caitlin thinks she's off in Galway, which is what I'm thinking myself." He finished sharpening the pencil and folded his arms across his chest. "There's a band she likes that was playing. Probably stayed with some of her mates after."

"Does she do this often? Take off without calling or anything?"

"All the time." Rory's eyes flickered over her face. "It's the kind of girl she is. A bit wildlike and—"

He broke off as the station door opened, and Hugh Fitzpatrick came in. Fitzpatrick didn't see her immediately, and Kate watched as he made his way over to the long wooden counter. He looked much as he had the night before in Dooley's, the same heavy black overcoat. Same edginess. A guy who existed mostly on coffee and cigarettes, she'd bet money on it. He said something to Rory that she couldn't make out, then Rory cocked his head in her direction, and both men looked over at her.

"Kate." Fitzpatrick seemed genuinely happy to see

her. "Soaking in some of the local color, are you? You've come to the right place. Rory here could keep you entertained for hours with tales of the things he encounters."

"Listen, Hugh," Rory said, visibly uncomfortable, "I've work to do, so if there's nothing you need—"

"Any word from Elizabeth?" Fitzpatrick asked. "That's really what I wanted to know."

"Nothing at all."

Fitzpatrick leaned an elbow on the desk. "From what I've been able to put together, you seem to be the last person to have seen her." He laughed and looked over at Kate. "Oh, God, that didn't sound right, did it? All I meant was—"

"Give it a rest, would you, Hughie? You were up there yourself, if it comes to that—"

"But sober." Fitzpatrick flicked ash off his cigarette. "And in full possession of my faculties."

Kate looked from Hugh to Rory. The tension between the two of them was almost palpable, and she wondered whether Hugh's slip had been intentional. She thought of Rory's admission that he'd gone into Galway to meet Elizabeth. Something didn't feel right. If Elizabeth didn't turn up in the next few hours, she wouldn't keep Rory's secret no matter what their agreement.

AFTER LEARNING that the American girl was staying at Annie's, Niall had dreamed up, then discarded half a dozen reasons to stop by and see her. Each time he hit upon a plan, the memory of Annie Ryan's suspicious voice discouraged him.

He surveyed the setting and tried to focus on the image he wanted to create. An elegantly dressed couple, clearly trying not to shiver in the cooling evening air, were posed on an upturned rowboat. A *curragh*, really, although the distinction would be lost on the models, who were both Dutch. The woman's hair was long and curly, the same color as her jet-black evening gown. Her companion had on a tuxedo. Behind them was a thatched cottage and horse and cart.

The shoot was for an American women's magazine. He'd wanted to laugh when they'd told him about the assignment. The editor had never been to Ireland, knew next to nothing about the country, but wanted something that would capture the beauty and timelessness of it all, as he put it. Niall loaded film into one of the Nikons. It had taken him the better part of two days to scout out a thatched cottage. They were hard to find these days, too expensive to keep up. Modern convenience was what people wanted. Take-out tandoori in front of the telly. He'd had to give a Traveler twenty pounds for the use of the horse and cart.

Up on the cliffs, high above where he stood, the windows of a few small cottages glinted like diamonds in the setting sun. He shot off a few exposures then zoomed in on the beach scene, focused tight on the *curragh*. He'd always been fascinated by the boats, by their craftsmanship and the folklore around them.

As a boy, he'd listened to the tales of Aran islanders rowing over to the mainland to choose a wife to bring back to the island. Eight miles each way, the feat had captured his imagination. The summer he was sixteen, he and Hugh Fitzpatrick had set out in separate boats for Inishboffin. A race against each other. It was the year he'd realized Moruadh was, if not exactly a woman, no longer the girl he always seemed to be rescuing from one childish misadventure or another.

On this day, she'd seen them off from the dock. For some reason, he still remembered the lipstick she wore. A deep, almost plum color. Remembered, too, her black hair flying, the way the thin white material of her dress had wrapped around her legs.

He had won the race, but Moruadh had kissed Hugh.

The woman on the boat called out something, and Niall forced his thoughts back to the present and to the carefully contrived scene before him. It all looked beautiful and quaint even if it wasn't entirely true. True would have been the cheap white bungalows and tourist trailers that dotted the low green hills, but true wasn't the order he'd been given. He finished the roll, started loading up his gear. We all want our illusions, he thought. We all believe what we want to believe.

Which led his thoughts back to the American girl. He bent to pick up a lens cover that had fallen in the sand. Pale, golden-brown grains stuck to the plastic case. Grains like freckles. With his finger, he slowly brushed them away. What if he were to march right up the steps of the Pot o' Gold and introduce himself?

He looked down at the grains still clinging to his fingertips. Annie Ryan would no doubt feel it necessary to warn the girl that the caller was a man who was thought by some to have murdered his wife. Of course, he could point out that no charges had ever been filed. And, of course, he could tell her that he was innocent.

And, of course, the American would believe exactly what she wanted to believe.

Ten minutes later, he sat in the car, a few yards up the road from the Pot o' Gold, close enough that he could see into the sitting room, but not so close that he'd attract unwanted attention. The lamps were on, amber glass bowls, each frilled at the edges like a baby's bonnet. Yellow light spilled out over the dark front garden.

He looked at his watch. A quarter to seven. He blew into his hands. Leaned his head back against the seat. Exhaled. Looked at his watch again. God, he felt like a Peeping Tom. Why *was* he sitting there? Why did this American girl intrigue him more than, say, the Dutch model who had certainly made no secret of her interest? He had no answer and, after a minute or so, he stopped looking for one. Some things weren't meant to be analyzed.

A car went by, trailing a comet of rock music. Inside the house, he saw a sliver of green, a flash of red hair. Pulse quickening, he reached for the horn, then drew his hand back. If he was after attention, he might as well throw a fistful of pebbles at the glass. Without looking away from the lighted sitting room, he felt for the door catch and sat there, his hand on the cold metal. He pictured his progress to the front door. Through the front gate, up the garden path. Two choices once he got there. The brass knocker, or the bell. The knocker. *Rat-a-tat-tat.* With any luck, it would be her, not Annie, who came to the door. And then he changed his mind.

KATE STOOD at the sitting-room window and watched the taillights of a car disappear around the corner, a blip in the inky blackness. In California, the night sky always seemed to glow, lit up by millions of lights. Here in Ireland, the dark was absolute, depthless.

Reflected in the window, she could see the family seated around the fireplace. Annie and Patrick in armchairs, Rory and Caitlin hand in hand on the couch just as they'd been the night before. Her eyes drawn to Rory, Kate thought of the weird tension between him and Fitzpatrick. With Elizabeth still not home, her uneasiness about keeping Rory's secret had increased another notch. Just as she'd decided to talk to him about it, a friend of Elizabeth's had called from Galway to say she was pretty sure she'd seen Elizabeth at a club the night before. Since everyone had seemed relieved by the news, Kate decided to wait a little longer before she confronted Rory.

"While you're up on your feet, Katie," Annie called out, "Draw the curtains for me, will you? Then come and sit back down, I've baked something I want you to try."

"Okay, what have you whipped up tonight that's going to make me fat?" Kate pulled a footstool up to the fire.

"*Fat,*" Annie scoffed. "Sure, a good gust of wind would blow you away." She put a slice of dark fruit-studded bread on Kate's plate. "Barm brack."

"That's a new one on me." She thought of the various bakery offerings she'd sampled so far. "Is it a traditional recipe?"

"My ma's and her mother's before that." Annie spooned sugar into her tea. "You bake different things into the batter. Rings, coins, buttons. What else, Pat?" she said with a glance at her husband.

"Pieces of wood. Peas. Get one of those and you'll never have any money." He winked at his wife.

"Must be our problem, Annie. Thimbles, too, my mother would put in there."

"Ah God, don't get a thimble," Annie said with a meaningful look at Kate. "You'll be a spinster."

"Oh, Kate'll never be a spinster." Caitlin looked up from the magazine she'd been flipping through with a free hand. "I bet you have a date every night, don't you, Kate?"

Kate grinned. "Like I told your mom, my life's a mad social whirl."

"That was me, too," Caitlin said. "Playing the field, a different one every night."

"You're nineteen, Caitlin." Annie regarded her daughter over the rim of her teacup. "A lot of field playing you had time to do."

"Ah, you'd be surprised, Mam." Smiling, Caitlin reached over and put a piece of bread on Rory's plate. "Of course, that was all before I met you, right, love?"

Kate glanced over at Rory who had hardly said a word all evening. Suddenly, he set his cup and saucer down on the table and left the room. A moment later, the front door slammed.

"He's worrying about work," Caitlin said. "That new superintendent they have is a bit of a tyrant. Takes his work very seriously," she said with a look at Kate. "Married to it, he is."

Kate nodded, but the lingering uneasiness she'd been trying to dismiss returned in full force. It was Elizabeth and not work that was preoccupying him, she was pretty certain. Maybe there was more to their relationship than he'd acknowledged. Maybe that was why Elizabeth was staying away.

"I played the field a bit myself in my day." Patrick, apparently unaware that the topic had changed, yawned and stretched. "Quite a catch I was, if I do say so myself."

Annie raised an eyebrow. "Are you forgetting, Patrick Ryan, that I've known you since you were sixteen?"

"Before I was sixteen, I meant." Patrick winked at Kate. "Quite the catch I was."

"Catch indeed," Annie scoffed. "What kind of catch I've no idea." She looked at Kate. "Sure, he'd starve to death before he'd as much as put a pot on the stove."

Patrick gave a sigh of long suffering. "Right, if you want blame, marry. If you want praise, die. I've cooked, Annie, and well you know it. Do you not remember the cake I made for Caitlin's birthday?"

"I do." Annie said. "But I'd be doing you a favor if I didn't. I was scraping burned bits from the cooker for months on end. And what about yourself, Kate?" she asked. "Do you cook?"

"Not a whole lot," she replied. "Mostly, I eat salads or stick a TV dinner in the microwave."

"Caitlin's like that," Annie said, shaking her head. "It's the way of young people these days, I suppose. Sure, I'm always trying to teach her how to bake bread, but she's not interested in the least."

"Caitlin's lucky. If you want to give *me* a lesson while I'm here," Kate said impulsively, "I'd love it."

"I'll do that." Annie eyed her for a moment. "Are you close with your mother, Katie?"

"She's dead." Uncomfortable suddenly under Annie's watchful gaze, Kate started to stack up the tea things. "We were never close," she said, mostly to fill in the silence, but also because she suspected that

Annie saw her life back in Santa Monica as less than wonderful and felt a little sorry for her. "It happened a long time ago," she said. "I'm fine. Truly. I'm happy with my life."

"Your da then…" Annie said, clearly not convinced. "Do you see him much?"

"No." Kate looked at Annie, who seemed clearly distressed "He has his own life. I have a brother, though, and a nephew." *Whom I haven't seen in two years,* she thought but didn't add. "Hey, listen, Annie, I'm fine with things this way. It saves a whole lot of money at Christmas. Plus, I can be as messy as I want."

"Ah, Katie." Annie shook her head. "It's a pity you'll not be here for the *fleadh.* There'll be a lot of nice young men coming in from Dublin. Could you not stay another week?"

Kate laughed. "Not even for a nice young man."

"Do you not have one back in America then, Kate?"

"A nice young man?" Clearly Kate's single state was of much more concern to Annie than it was to her. "I was going with someone, but he wasn't really all that nice, so we broke up."

"And what was it he did that wasn't so nice?"

"Oh…" Kate shrugged. "Basically, I found out he'd been cheating on me."

"Ah no, that won't do." Annie shook her head. "If you can't trust them, it's no good at all."

"Exactly." Kate sipped her tea. Trustworthy men—at least those she'd met—were rare. As she bit into the last piece of barm brack, she looked up to see Annie watching her.

"No ring?" Annie said.

Kate shook her head.

"Too bad. Find a ring," she said with a smile, "and you'll be married within the year."

"Yeah?" With a grin, Kate picked up her cup and saucer. "Not that I believe it for a minute, but there *was* this really cute guy I ran into today."

SHE WAS ALREADY UNDRESSED, reading on the bed, when she remembered that she'd left one of her notebooks on the table downstairs. In her robe and heavy socks, she padded silently down the carpeted stairway. Everyone had gone to bed and, except for a light in the hallway, the house was in darkness. She found her notebook, started for the stairs then spotted something white on the mat by the front door. Guessing that it was a note that someone had slipped through the letter box, she bent to pick it up. The envelope was addressed, in flowing black script, to:

"The American Girl with Long Red Hair."

Kate stared at it for a moment before she turned over the envelope and pulled out the card inside. The note read:

They say the two things the Irish do well are drinking and reciting poetry. I'll bend my elbow on occasion and, although I'd rather do it in person, I don't mind quoting poetry. So, to borrow from a fellow countryman:

We poets labour all our days
To make a little beauty be
But vanquished by a woman's gaze
And the unlabouring stars are we.

Just a reminder to stay on the right side. My apologies once again for causing you to part with the road. Perhaps one day I'll learn your name. Until then, I suppose I must remain,

      Yours, The Man on the Cliff.

"LOOK AT YOU," Annie said the next morning when Kate came down to breakfast. "Have a date, do you?"

"What?" Kate glanced down at herself. Black cords instead of the usual faded jeans. A new yellow sweater bought on impulse, instead of the UCLA sweatshirt she'd pulled on for the last couple of days. Her hair brushed until it fell smoothly down her back. *I might just run into him again.* "A date indeed," she said with a grin at Annie. "I'm in Ireland to work."

She watched as Annie set down a plate of eggs and sausage. Savory smells wafted up to greet her. Pale morning sunshine streamed through the dining-room window, shone on the flower-patterned china. Kate had a sudden impulse to break into song, to say something sappy like, "God, life is good."

She'd fallen asleep with the note under her pillow. Fallen asleep with a smile on her face. Read it again the moment her eyes opened. Thinking of it now, of the man who had sent it, she smiled down at her food. Couldn't stop smiling. *The Man on the Cliff.* Annie was standing there, watching her. Waiting for an explanation.

"That guy I told you about last night," she said, "he left a note for me. I found it last night after everyone had gone to bed."

"What did he say then?" Annie's eyes were bright with interest. "What's his name?"

"He didn't say. He just signed it, 'The Man on the Cliff.' I met him the first night I got here. I was lost."

"What does he look like? He's no doubt someone I know."

"He's tall and dark-haired and..." She shook her head. "Basically just gorgeous. And very nice, too, at least he seemed that way. Of course, they all seem that way at first."

Annie shook her head reprovingly. "*Katie*. You've just never met the right man, that's all there is to it. We'll find someone for you though."

"This guy would be a good start." She cut one of the sausages into little pieces, speared one with her fork.

A wide smile on her face, Annie pulled out a chair and sat down opposite Kate. "Ah God, I love a little romance. I mean, look at yourself. You're a different girl this morning." Her forehead creased. "I wish I knew who it was. It's not Hughie Fitzpatrick, is it?"

"The reporter?" Kate looked at her over the rim of the teacup. "Not my type, Annie. In addition to smoking like a chimney, he seems very bitter. I was hoping he could help. But he's got this thing about Maguire murdering Moruadh, and it's hard to get him to move from that."

"Well, life hasn't been easy for him." Annie buttered a slice of toast. "His mother's a right shrew who would still have him at home with her if she could and although he went off to university, he's back now writing about jumble sales and church fetes. That must get him down a bit."

"I can imagine."

"And he's had his heart broken a few too many times," Annie went on with a glance across the table.

"Starting with Moruadh. Sure, that can make you bitter, can't it?"

Kate was saved from responding when the phone rang and Annie got up to answer it. Annie's words had made her uncomfortable. Was there a similarity between herself and Hugh Fitzpatrick? Maybe they were both guilty of letting anger and bitterness taint their lives? Something she'd have to think about. Later.

"Hughie's a nice lad, though," Annie said, coming to sit down again. "You could do worse. Bit lonely, too, and both of you being writers…oh, wait. It was Liam Donohue, either him or—"

Kate laughed. "You know what? It doesn't matter who he is. I kind of like it better the way it is now. Kind of magical and mysterious."

"Suit yourself, love." Smiling, she reached over to pat Kate's hand. "We won't talk about it. You go and enjoy yourself, but I want to hear all about your day when you get back."

The phone rang, and Annie got up again. Moments later, she was back. "For you."

As she took the phone, Kate felt her heart speed up. Then she heard the American accent of her editor. Disappointment stabbed, fierce and sharp, and she struggled to focus.

"You called me yesterday, kiddo," Tom was saying. "I'm just returning your call. I didn't get a moment all day, so I thought I'd try before I went to bed. What time is it there?"

"Just after seven. I'm eating breakfast." She took a sip of tea and shook away thoughts of the man on the cliff. "You'd asked me to fill you in on what was happening. I'm finding a lot of support for the idea that the husband killed her. Apparently the reason he wasn't arrested was he's got money and influence with the guards.''

"Have you met him?''

"Not yet. He lives in some medieval castle. He wasn't in when I rode up yesterday, but I'm going to try today.'' *Unless I get waylaid by a gray-eyed man, in which case all bets are off.* Over the phone line, she could hear the all-news radio station Tom always listened to. A traffic tie-up on the southbound Golden State Freeway. "I've been talking to people. I'm just waiting to see how all the pieces fit together.''

"Sounds good. How's everything else?''

"Terrific.'' Kate smiled to herself. "Lots of great-looking scenery.''

"Well, you seem to be off to a good start. All kinds of mystery and intrigue. I like that.''

"Yeah. Well, I'll see if I can get him indicted before I leave.'' She pictured Tom at his cluttered desk. A pencil stuck in his unruly gray hair, dark eyes glimmering behind rimless frames. "Anything for a good story.''

But later, as she walked along the cliffs to Buncarroch Castle hoping to find Niall Maguire home, early sunshine gave way to clouds and her mood turned similarly gloomy. Wind whipped her hair around her face and pushed her forward like a giant hand in her back.

What if she never saw this mystery man again? The seven days she had left in Ireland were crammed with interviews and people she had to see. Anyway, maybe he'd left Cragg's Head. Maybe he was off in Dublin. *Maybe he was married.* That was it. Married with kids, which was why he hadn't signed his name.

Probably a good thing if she didn't run into him again. Which undoubtedly meant she would. God, she couldn't think about him anymore.

But as her fingers touched the note she'd slipped into her pocket, she felt her spirits lift despite herself. Obviously he wanted to see her. Maybe right now, he was driving around Cragg's Head in his green Land Rover hoping to run into her again. Maybe she should go back and get the car and look for him. Both of them looking for each other like bumper cars at the fair.

Wasn't there supposed to be something magical about Ireland? All that stuff about fairies and spirits. Maybe if she thought about it hard enough, she could *make* him appear. Conjure him up. It wouldn't be a coincidence, it would be a magic trick.

Images of his face danced through her head. He would take her hand, and they would ride off into the mist. His sole purpose, he would say as he swept her into his arms, was to give her pleasure. And, God knows, she was ready for a little pleasure. Was it Yeats who had said that if you couldn't find lasting love, transitory love wasn't a bad idea? She could go for that, a little transitory, unlasting love. Not that she ever had, but she could. And what could be more transitory and unlasting than a fling with a guy whose name she didn't know.

The more she thought about it, the more she liked the idea. An aberrant, unfamiliar version of herself seemed to have taken up residence. Tear off the bonds, it urged. Do something completely unexpected. Keep thinking along those lines, she told it, and you really will be pushing a shopping cart along Ocean Boulevard.

She shivered and pulled up the collar of her parka. Her hair billowing around her face, she looked out at the slate-colored ocean. A spot of rain hit her forehead. If Maguire wasn't home, she would walk back through the town. She picked up her pace and tried to focus on the questions she wanted to ask him.

The sudden appearance of a large, shaggy and exuberant dog effectively sent all thoughts flying. In a blur of noise and motion, the dog bounded up to greet her, and she staggered backward under its assault. Paws on her shoulders, eyes level with her own, the dog panted happily in her face. With a grin, she returned it to all four feet and bent to pat its head. A moment later, she looked up and into the gray eyes of the dog's owner.

It was him. The man on the cliff. Standing there in front of her as though she really had conjured him out of thin air. Hands in his pockets, long dark overcoat open and flapping in the wind. Kate felt the smile spread across her face. Neither of them spoke. He was smiling back at her as though they'd just pulled off the world's biggest joke.

"After you rode off yesterday," he finally said, "I couldn't get you out of my mind. I left the note because—"

"I couldn't stop thinking about you, either," she broke in, unable to hold back the words. "I slept with your note under the pillow."

"Did you?" His smiled widened. "Last night I sat in my car sat outside the Pot o' Gold, watching you through the window and wondering what I was doing there.''

''Watching me?''

''The curtains weren't drawn, and I saw your hair and a bit of your sleeve At one point, you crossed in front of the window. I tried using mental telepathy to get you to come outside.'' He shrugged as though the revelation had embarrassed him. ''My skills are a bit rusty, I suppose.''

Charmed, Kate smiled up at him, pictured him in his car thinking about her while she was just a few feet away, probably thinking about him. Suffused by a warm glow, she felt as though she'd been given a completely unexpected—but wonderful—gift.

''After I dropped the note through the letter box, though, I could have kicked myself for not asking you to meet me.''

She nodded. ''I was scared I'd go back to the States without ever seeing you again.''

''I thought about that, too.'' He glanced down at the dog who sat on its haunches, eyes expectant as though waiting for the action to begin. ''Maybe it was a bit of fatalism, not leaving a note. Maybe I was thinking that if we were meant to meet again, we would.''

''And we did.'' Kate watched her breath condense on the frigid air.

''Of course, fate might have nothing to do with it,'' he said after a moment. ''It could be that you just lost your way again. Taking the scenic road to Ballyconneely, are you?''

"Get out of here." She poked a finger at his chest. "I'm not lost. I wasn't lost yesterday, either."

"Maybe that was a bit of fate, too."

She kept smiling. Purple clouds began to form over the ocean. The wind picked up. They'd somehow moved closer as they spoke. Inches from his face, she saw the small scar above his upper lip, the beat of a pulse in his temple. She saw the tuft of dark hair at the open neck of his blue shirt. Wind whistled through the long grasses, blew streamers of red hair across his face, wrapped his long coat around her legs. She smelled the sea in the wind, felt it sting her skin in wet needlelike sprays. If she touched his hair, it would be stiff from the salty wind. His mouth would taste of it. Unconsciously, she ran her tongue over her bottom lip. She wanted to kiss him. Her breath felt trapped in her chest. If a justification ever existed for living purely in the moment, this was it. If she didn't kiss him, she would regret it forever. She looked into his eyes. He leaned closer to brush away a strand of hair that clung to the corners of her mouth. She caught his hand.

The kiss rocked her like an explosion. Fire shot through her body, made her legs tremble. Briefly, they parted and then, as though survival depended on it, they were kissing again, awareness of everything else blotted out by a sensation she'd long forgotten. The knee-buckling intensity of being in the arms of a man whose desire matched her own. The waves lashing the rocks beneath them echoed the roar of blood in her ears. Another flurry of kisses and then, arms still entwined, they stood back to look at each other, laughing with relief, happiness and wonder.

"I don't do this," she gasped. "It's not me at all."

"It's not something I make a practice of myself," he said. "Though, I have a weakness for red-haired American women."

"Really?" Absurdly, she felt jealous. "Is your weakness tested often?"

"It isn't. At least, I've never succumbed before."

She smiled. He smiled back at her. The dog, which had gone off on its own adventure, came galloping back. She patted its head. It was ridiculous how happy she felt. If this man suggested riding off into the sunset together, she had little doubt that she would willingly accompany him.

"By the way," she said. "My name's Kate. Kate Neeson."

"Niall Maguire," he said.

"WELL, YOU'VE NOT SPAT on the dirt yet," he finally said. "Or scrubbed your mouth to get rid of all the traces but from the look on your face, you'd no doubt like to pretend the last ten minutes never happened."

Arms folded across her chest, she stood a foot or so away from him. When he'd told her his name, she'd jumped back as though shot.

"I'm sorry," she said. "I'm just blown away. It's so...I'm here to write this piece about your wife and—"

"Wait. You're what?" He suddenly recalled the blue airmail letters he'd thrown away. "You're the one who wrote to me?"

"You didn't answer either of my letters. I was coming to see you today. In fact, I'm on my way up to the castle." She was looking at him as though she still couldn't believe her eyes. "God, this is so incredible. Yesterday I was convinced that you'd killed...well, I intended to keep an open mind until I'd actually met you, of course."

"Of course." He decided not to ask what her opinion was now. A movement at his feet made him look down. Rufus, who minutes earlier had greeted her so effusively, had chosen camps and now almost sat on his boots. The silence lengthened. A gull swooped low, seemed for a moment to fix him with its bright, beadlike eyes, then flew off with a raucous screech.

"Anyway." She shrugged, as though dismissing what had happened between them. "I still want to talk to you."

"Look..."

"Kate," she reminded him.

"Kate." He studied her face for a moment. Kate. It suited her perfectly. He lost his train of thought. "Look," he started again. "Obviously my identity is more of a shock to you than yours is to me, but I'd be happy to have you come back to the castle. We can talk about America or Ireland or your wildest dreams or whatever you feel like talking about, but I might as well tell you right now, I won't talk about Moruadh."

"Why?"

"Because I don't want to."

"An excellent reason," she said. "Very informative."

"Maybe it's all you need to know."

"Maybe my article could clear up all these rumors swirling around," she said. "They can't be easy to live with."

"You're assuming I've nothing to hide." He watched as Rufus, suddenly alerted by a movement in the grass, galloped off into the misty rain. After a moment, he looked back at Kate. Her eyes were fixed on something beyond his shoulder. Rain had darkened her hair and it clung to her head in heavy strands. Drops trickled down her forehead, spiked her lashes. He wanted to take her home and feed her hot whiskey. "Well," he said, "what's it to be then?"

"God, I don't know." She looked at him. "I've only got a few days in Ireland to get the information I need. I mean, this isn't a vacation for me, so if you're not willing to discuss Moruadh, what's the point of going with you?"

"What was the point of kissing me?"

Her eyes widened. The question had clearly caught her off guard.

"The truth?"

"I've always found it best."

"You were an unknown quantity. A mystery man. I thought a fling in Ireland might be fun."

He tried not to smile. "And is your thinking still along those lines?"

"No. When you were just this mystery man who I'd probably never see again, I could fantasize about you. Make you anything I wanted you to be. Now I know who you are and it's different."

"Because you believe I murdered my wife?"

She looked him straight in the eye. "Did you?"

"No. But what else would I say?"

"True." She kept looking at him, her eyes unblinking. "Still, if you talked to me a little about things, I could form my own opinion."

"Or you could just pretend you don't know who I am, and we could spend a pleasant afternoon talking about whatever else we wanted to talk about."

"Besides Moruadh?"

He nodded.

"It won't work," she said. "I *do* know who you are."

"Maybe you don't, though. Didn't we both say just now that what happened wasn't typical behavior for either of us?"

"It certainly wasn't for me."

"Or for me, but I have a theory about it. You know nothing of this, but yesterday, when you fell off your bike, you fell into a fairy ring. It's perfectly clear that this caused a spell to be cast upon both of us." He saw her trying not to smile and felt light with relief. "'Tis a frequent occurrence," he went on, broadening his accent. "Fairies will fancy a mortal to carry away into their own country and they'll leave a changeling in its place. This time, they left two."

"So I'm not me and you're not you?"

"Exactly."

"And that would justify a fling because we're both perfect strangers."

"You're a brilliant girl."

She stared at him for a moment, clearly struggling to maintain a straight face, then lost the battle. She grinned and then they were both laughing. Rufus circled, barking. Beyond them stretched the watery horizon of ocean and sky.

"I've heard some inventive come-on lines, but that takes the prize," she said.

"It's an Irish specialty." He wasn't entirely sure he'd won her over. Her eyes searched his face as though an answer to his real character might be revealed there. "What is it?"

"I'm just trying to figure out why everyone I've talked to since I've been here describes you as cold and aloof."

"It's Niall Maguire they describe that way."

"Seriously."

"I think I could give you a more reasoned answer if we were sitting somewhere warm and dry." He glanced around for Rufus, whistled, then turned back to Kate. "What do you say?"

CHAPTER SIX

GOD, THIS WASN'T FAIR. Head bowed, Kate, kicked at a clump of grass. *Not, not, not, not fair.* She looked up and into Niall Maguire's amazing eyes that right now were regarding her with just the faintest hint of amusement as he watched her ponder his invitation.

"We could toss a coin," he said. "Heads you throw caution to the wind and take your chances with the village bluebeard, tails you opt for prudence and the safety of Annie Ryan's front parlor."

"Don't patronize me." They were now locked in a stare-off, and she wasn't about to be the first to look away. "Safety isn't the issue. I was on my way to the castle to meet you when I...met you. Obviously I'd heard all the rumors, so if I wasn't concerned for my safety then, why would I be now?"

"Good point." He was clearly trying not to smile. "So why don't we continue this inside where the skies won't be emptying down on our heads?"

"Thank you, but no." Rain had seeped inside the collar of her parka and through the soles of her boots. It trickled off her hair, down her cheeks. Pouring so hard that she had to squint through the deluge to see him. "I'm researching an article and if you can't provide me with information, then I should be using my time more productively."

"I'm sure you should." He swiped the back of his

hand across his face. "But if you do happen to find
a spare moment that could be put to unproductive use,
you know where to find me. And Kate," he said as
she walked off, "I make a very good bouillabaisse if
you'd like to have dinner one unproductive evening."

BOUILLABAISSE. Back in the village again, Kate stood
under the awning of a newsagent's shop to wait out
the rain which was coming down even harder than it
had five minutes earlier. What would an Irishman
know about making bouillabaisse? *God, she'd wanted
to stay*. Even as she'd walked back down the hill from
the castle, she'd had to stop herself from turning
around and accepting his invitation. She'd been *this
close*. But how could she? She was in Ireland to write
a piece that might prove he'd murdered his wife.

A voice behind her interrupted her thoughts, and
she turned to see Hugh Fitzpatrick smiling at her.

"Kate. We meet again. After I left Dooley's Monday night, I kept thinking of all the things I wanted
to tell you. When you rang me from California, I was
ecstatic to think that someone outside of Cragg's
Head was finally going to look at how Moruadh died
and what do I do but rant on about my issues. What
can I do to make amends? Can I buy you a pint right
now?"

"No, but thank you anyway." A little startled by
the enthusiasm of his greeting, she took a step back.
"If you have a few minutes, though, I do have some
questions."

"We couldn't do it over a pint?" He read the answer on her face and grinned. "No? Right then, my
office is just over there." He pointed to a small store-
front on the opposite side of the street. The sign

painted on the window in peeling gold paint had lost a letter and read *ragg's Head Gazette.*

"Probably reminds you of the *Los Angeles Times,* doesn't it?" Fitzpatrick joked as he opened the front door.

Inside, they were greeted by a dumpy woman in a black raincoat who immediately collared Fitzpatrick. He motioned to Kate that he'd be with her momentarily, and she pulled out one of the wooden chairs that stood on either side of a large littered desk. An oil heater in one corner of the room filled the air with acrid fumes but did little to dispel the damp chill. A naked lightbulb swinging from the ceiling cast harsh shadows on the bare floor and on the yellowing newspapers stacked up around the walls.

She looked over at Fitzpatrick. Arms folded across his chest, he stood at the window, staring out at the rainy street, seemingly oblivious to the woman's ranting.

"I'm saying you need to write something about how Cragg's Head has become a honey pot for the tinkers," the woman was telling him. "Filthy scum, all of them. They'll rob you blind. Up there at Cragg's Head Leap one of them was this morning, talking to two young girls. And what would the likes of him be wanting with young girls anyway? Up to no good, that's what. Up to no good at all. You mark my words."

Fitzpatrick said nothing. Kate wondered if he was even listening. He seemed distracted. A cigarette in one hand, the other in the pocket of his tweed jacket. She felt a wave of sympathy for him. She'd spent a couple of years working for several small-town papers. Each of them had had a local citizen in a chronic state of rage over something or other and given to frequent visits to the editorial offices. The sight of them usually sent the reporters scurrying to keep appointments they'd suddenly remembered.

"They don't get their money the way the rest of us do, by working for it," the woman ranted on. "Make it off their women they do, sending them to beg in bars, babies swathed in rags. And what money they get they spend on drink. A decent woman can't even step into a bar without being accosted by one of them. Trouble just waiting to happen, I'm telling you."

After a while, Kate stopped listening and thought about Niall Maguire. The whole incident still astounded her. Last night she'd fallen asleep with *his* note under her pillow, dreaming of a gray-eyed man who'd turned out to be Niall Maguire. She'd kissed *Niall Maguire*. Going with him would have been asking for trouble. He told her he wouldn't talk about Moruadh, and the chemistry sizzling between them suggested that they wouldn't be talking much about anything.

She could imagine the conversation with Tom if she had stayed. "Yeah, I know I thought he murdered his wife, but he wouldn't talk about it and anyway we were tearing each other's clothes off, so—"

She glanced at Fitzpatrick and the woman who appeared to have run out of steam. With an abrupt good-evening to Fitzpatrick and a nod to Kate, she left. A bell jangled as the door closed behind her. After the sound of her plodding footsteps had faded away, Fitzpatrick rolled his eyes at Kate.

"Brigid Riley has her knickers all in a twist over the Travelers," he said as he walked over to the desk and sat down. "First it was them keeping chickens in the house that sent her into a right tizzy. Now she's got it into her head that they're set on ruining the virtue of Cragg's Head's female population. Jaysus." Elbows on the desk, head propped in his hands, he looked at Kate, his expression morose. "Is it nice in California?"

"Very."

"Do you surf and roller-skate and wear very small bikinis and eat avocado on everything?"

"Oh, sure," she said. "My favorite thing to do in the whole world is eat avocado while I'm surfing and wearing a very small bikini. Similarly, you probably run around saying 'top o' the morning' and chasing leprechauns, right?"

"Guilty of stereotyping as charged." He grinned and lit up a cigarette. "What do you need? Can I offer you something?" From the drawer of his desk he brought out a jar of instant coffee and a box of tea bags, held them up for her to see.

"Nothing, thanks." She pulled a notebook from her purse, looked at her notes from their previous conversation and tried to separate the Niall Maguire she'd just kissed from the Niall Maguire she'd come to Ireland to write about. "You'd said the three of you grew up together. Tell me about when you were older. When did Maguire and Moruadh began to develop a romantic interest in each other?"

He sighed. "Like I told you, Moruadh always played us off against each other. While Maguire was away at university though, Moruadh and I...well, she was my girl. We'd go to dances, take the ferry from Roonah over to Clare Island. Take off all our clothes and go skinny-dipping in the strand." He smiled.

"All the things you do when you're young and in love."

"And what happened?"

"Maguire came home one summer, and I found them together."

"So he stole her away?"

"You could put it that way, yes. But even after it happened, she still loved me. Maguire just dazzled her with all his fancy ways. It was always me she returned to, though, even after they married. Until, of course, he killed her."

OF COURSE that was just Fitzpatrick's interpretation, Kate decided as she opened the front door to the Pot o' Gold later that evening. And Fitzpatrick was obviously bitter. Still, she realized that she was reluctant to accept anything that put Niall Maguire in a bad light.

In the kitchen, she learned from Patrick that Annie had gone to Dublin to be with an elderly relative who had broken her hip. She would be back the following evening, Patrick said. In a note slipped under Kate's bedroom door, Annie wrote that she was dying to learn the name of the mystery man on the cliff.

Early the next morning, Kate wrote a message for Annie. She said nothing about the mystery man, or his real identity; nothing about kissing him. Just that she would be up at Buncarroch Castle interviewing Niall Maguire. She put the Mace in her pocket and, just for good measure, a police whistle. Kind of ridiculous, but she'd been a Girl Scout and she knew the whole thing about being prepared.

Maguire had just returned from walking his dog when Kate arrived at the castle; he seemed delighted to see her. He wore an Aran sweater and jeans and looked just as fantastic as he had yesterday. Behind him, the castle, silhouetted against the iron sky, looked just as sinister.

"I've found I do have some time for an unproductive day." Kate felt her heart beat a wild tattoo. She bent to pat the dog in an attempt to hide the color she felt flooding her face. "Will today work for you?"

He smiled. "It will. Very well. But so your time isn't entirely unproductive, what if I give you a tour of the castle? That way you won't be consumed by guilt over the time you've wasted."

"That's very considerate of you."

"Just an attempt to dispel the notion that there's a lump of ice where my heart should be."

Kate hunched her shoulders against the cold and watched him insert a large old-fashioned key into the rusted lock. The rain was back, drops tracing a familiar course down the back of her neck. Patrick had said that morning that the way to forecast rain was to look at the mountains. If you could see them, it was going to rain. If you couldn't, it was already raining.

She shivered. Buncarroch Castle was definitely not a reassuring place. Last night, Patrick had mentioned the vengeful spirits that were supposed to haunt it. In the cozy warmth of the Pot o' Gold's kitchen, the story had struck her as quite comical. Now, it was less so.

"Nothing's easy about this place," Maguire said as he finally managed to unlock the door. "The locks are old and the wood swells in the damp. One of these days I'll get around to putting new ones on, but they're low on my list of priorities." One palm flat against the wooden door, he turned to smile at her.

"A week of this and you'll no doubt be glad to get back to America."

Kate smiled back at him. The sizzle hadn't cooled one bit. The possibility of ending up in one of the bedchambers was definitely there. Which also explained why her verdict had inched still further along the spectrum from probably guilty to unjustly accused. Either that, or she just couldn't deal with the idea that she'd kissed a possible murderer. No, he wasn't a murderer. She'd know somehow. He'd be sending out murderous vibes. Plus, he had a dog. A big, goofy dog who right now was licking her fingers. That didn't go with being a cold-blooded murderer.

She absorbed the details that six days from now would be only memories. The slight tilt of his head as he turned to smile at her. The narrow planes of his face. His hand, pale against the dark wood grain of the door. Long slender fingers—an artist's hands. And then she blinked because it wasn't the wooden door she was looking at under his palm. *It was Moruadh's back.*

As clear as a picture held before her eyes, she saw Moruadh at the edge of the cliff. Tiny yellow flowers on her sundress, the way her dark glossy hair fell in smooth waves to her shoulders and there, just where the hair ended, Niall Maguire's hand.

"Kate." He peered into her face "Are you all right?"

"Huh?" She shook her head to dislodge the image. "Yeah, I'm fine. Fine."

"What is it?" Niall stood in the open doorway. "You're white as a sheet."

"I'm fine. It's just the cold." Unable to meet his eyes now, she slipped past him, through the door and into the castle's great hall. In her pocket, her fingers touched the can of Mace. Niall followed behind her.

"Have a seat." He gestured at the battered leather armchairs grouped around the fireplace, then began to move around the cavernous room. All motion, he blew into his hands, turned on lamps and sent several glances. "Will you have some tea? No. A shot of whiskey? Egg and chips? You're hungry, is that it?"

"I'm fine." The image was fading now. She smiled, touched by his obvious concern. Once, on a ski trip with a man who'd professed to love her, she'd broken her leg and he hadn't given her a fraction of the attention. But still. "Listen…" She glanced at the phone. "Could I—"

"Let someone know where you are?"

She felt her face color. "I didn't mean…"

"I understand." He seemed about to say something more, then stopped. A moment passed. "While you're phoning," he finally said, "I'll feed Rufus. Back in a minute."

The door slammed and she heard the sound of his footsteps across the gravel and then his voice as he called to the dog. She picked up the old-fashioned black receiver, started to dial, then replaced it again. Why was she hesitating? Even if the rumors about him eventually proved false, it made sense to play it safe, right? And Annie may not have found the note.

She dialed Annie's number, heard the machine click on and left a message that she was at Buncarroch Castle and would be back around four.

She hung up, blew into her hands. Stamped her feet. Tried again to separate the Niall Maguire who might have killed his wife from the man she'd kissed on the cliff. The man she wanted to kiss again. No, she couldn't think about the kiss. She would erase it from her mind and concentrate on the article. If she could win Maguire's trust, he might talk about Moruadh. Trust was a two-way street. If she trusted him, he should trust her.

Too cold to sit still, she paced the hall. The room was about the same temperature as her freezer in Santa Monica. The air even *smelled* cold. An earthy, moldering whiff from the stone floors and walls that made her think of graveyards. Outside, the wind had picked up, producing a cacophony of ghostly whistles and sighs. A floorboard creaked behind her. Heart hammering, she turned, half expecting to find a bony skull leering at her.

Okay, enough with the Gothic. She took some deep breaths and started on a little self-guided tour of the great hall. Niall Maguire obviously owned a huge chunk of real estate. This room alone could have comfortably accommodated a couple of marauding armies. With space left over to squeeze in her entire apartment. A little short on charm, though. She squinted up at the tattered banners emblazoned with faded coats of arms that fluttered from the ceiling. Tried to avoid eye contact with the assorted fox and stag heads along the walls. Irish feudal. With strong accents of Early Taxidermy.

Still pacing, she found herself at the far end of the hall, gazing up at a wall of portraits. Stern-eyed men and women with distant stares. One dark-haired woman with fine-boned features and pale gray eyes seemed to fix Kate with a disdainful look. Probably saw her as a fortune hunter, a hussy out for Maguire's money. Amusing, but a reminder nonetheless of what—besides geography—separated the two of them. One day Kate hoped to scrape up enough to buy a condo. Maguire's second home was a sixteenth-century castle; an ancestral home in which he could look up and see his own genes reflected in generations of painted portraits. Her family, which she couldn't trace beyond her immigrant grandparents, dwelled in anonymous apartments and subdivisions scattered across America.

She wandered back to the fireplace. An eagle hung on the chimney wall, amber glass eyes, talons curled as though ready to pounce. The sight of it depressed her, and she looked away. Oscar Wilde had summed up her sentiments about hunters. *The unspeakable in full pursuit of the uneatable.* Was Niall Maguire a hunter? She didn't want him to be. Any more than she wanted to believe he'd murdered Moruadh.

"Kate." He was suddenly behind her, the dog at his heels. "Sorry it took so long. Rufus went off down the hill in search of his lady friend. Little tart of a Pekingese. I had to go and break things up." He sighed. "Ah well, the course of true love never runs smooth, eh?"

"So they say." She pointed to the eagle. "Your trophy?"

"God, no. It's been there forever. I've wanted to take it down for a long time." He waved a hand in the direction of the animal heads. "All of these things, but my former partner and I were talking about turning this place into a small hotel. She thought they added authenticity."

"So you don't hunt?"

"I don't. Never have." He gave her a quizzical look. "Why?"

"Nothing." He'd unbuttoned his dark coat and his

face was flushed from the cold. She smiled at him. "I'm just glad to hear it, that's all."

"Right." He studied the worn carpet at his feet for a moment, then looked up at her. "Helps balance all the other things you've heard about me, does it? All the gossip and speculation."

"I don't believe gossip," she said, but his eyes had darkened and the smile that had been there moments ago had disappeared. Something told her Niall Maguire wasn't quite as detached and aloof as everyone portrayed him. For some reason, the thought reassured her.

But she took the Mace with her on the tour of the castle anyway, tucked discreetly away in her pocket. As they climbed stairs and walked endless corridors, the knowledge that Annie and Patrick knew where she was stopped Kate from panicking each time the image of Maguire's hand on Moruadh's back reappeared.

An image that warred for attention with the chemistry thing.

Once, as he helped her down a steep flight of stairs, his hand touched hers; another time she looked up to find him watching her. The moment of eye contact charged the air around them. An instant later, she stared at him and imagined the cold, calculating mind of a man who had murdered his wife. And then he smiled and the image dissolved like mist.

If the brain could have whiplash, she thought as she followed him up yet another steep spiral stairway, hers had a bad case.

"Only another couple of chambers and a few flights of stairs." Niall glanced at her over his shoulder. "Knackered, are you?"

"If that means tired, I'm getting there." Breathless,

she climbed the remaining stairs and came out into a long, narrow hall. At the end, Maguire pushed open a heavy door and they walked into a dank blackness lit only by the beam of his flashlight. Involuntarily, Kate shuddered. The temperature had dropped by a good ten degrees and the silent, claustrophobic darkness seemed to close in around them.

"We're in the west tower." His flashlight cast an arc of light on moss-covered stone. "It's the oldest part of the castle, built back in the late 1500s. If you look at the building from the outside, you can see how this section juts out over the ocean."

Kate nodded, recalling the precarious tilt of the wing. It had to be safer than it looked, or he wouldn't have brought her here. Still, she wouldn't be sorry when this part of the tour was finished.

"It's also the haunted wing," he added in a matter-of-fact tone. "Well, the whole place is haunted, but most of the sightings occur here." He pulled open another wooden door, and the flicker of a smile crossed his face. "Not scared of ghosts, are you?"

"I don't believe in them." She zipped the parka up to her chin and followed him into a long, low-ceilinged room. After the darkness of the corridor, the gray morning light coming through the tall narrow windows was almost blinding. When her eyes adjusted, she saw that the room was empty, except for a small desk, some tripods and lighting equipment and several rows of black-and-white photographs tacked along the length of one wall.

"I'm a commercial photographer," Niall said. "These days, I use this room as a studio." He walked over to a small desk by the window. "Moruadh used to write up here. If you ignore my stuff, the place looks pretty much as it did then.''

"Why here?'' Kate glanced around the ordinary-looking room. "Out of all the rooms in the castle, I mean. Why this one?''

"Actually, she had another one, but when a storm made it almost inaccessible, she moved her things to this room. It intrigued her.'' He stood by the window, in profile to her. "It has a bit of a notorious reputation. She wrote a song about one of its former occupants. The White Lady. Have you heard it?''

"I'm not sure.'' Frowning, she sifted through the titles of Moruadh songs. "Something about a ghost?''

"That's it. This was the bedchamber of a young bride who met an unfortunate end on her wedding night. Her ghost is supposed to walk the halls. Crying and wailing.''

Kate tried to imagine Moruadh writing at her desk. In daylight, with Maguire's photography equipment scattered around, the room didn't seem particularly intimidating, but she was starting to feel sensitized by the castle. Maybe Kate didn't believe in ghosts, but she wouldn't choose this as a place to work. Then she thought of Rory McBride's bizarre story. Flowers for her coffin. A study haunted by a murdered bride. Was a theme emerging? Had Moruadh been fixated by death?

"I had a strange experience in this room a few months after Moruadh died,'' Maguire said. "I was painting it and I wanted to finish because I was leaving the next day to ski in Switzerland. Anyway, I was up the ladder and I felt…'' He paused as though searching for the words. "Well, someone breathed on the back of my neck.''

Kate stood in front of a framed photo of two old women, creaky and stooped. Their heavy clothes fell in blurred lines. In the glass, she could see Maguire's reflection. Her body felt light, almost weightless. She wasn't sure she wanted to hear any more of what he had to say.

"It was the strangest feeling, so intense that I stopped working for a while. The thing is, I knew, or sensed, who it was. A fellow I'd known in university. Big mountain-climbing enthusiast, killed in an avalanche. By the time I went skiing, I'd sort of put it out of my head." He paused again for a moment. "Well, anyway. The first day I went up, the cable on the chair snapped. Two people were killed. I broke my arm."

"And you connected the two experiences?"

"I did. I think Moruadh was trying to warn me," he said.

"I'm curious." She looked at him. "Why did you just tell me that story?"

He smiled slightly, as though he'd expected the question. "I used to scoff at her for seeing signs in everything, but sometimes I wonder. Who knows? Maybe the world we can't see is just as substantial as the one we can."

She stared at him, not sure if he was serious.

"Think of the way some poetry, or music, makes you feel," he said. "As though you've fallen under a spell."

She smiled.

"You've never felt that way?"

"Never." She shoved her hands deep in the pockets of her parka. In California, she would have scoffed outright at such talk. Here in Ireland, she couldn't dismiss it so easily, and the thought disconcerted her. Suddenly she yearned to be back in her modern Santa Monica apartment. A place where no ancient ghosts haunted the rooms and the bright sunshine burned away shadowy fears of the unknown. And then her cynical side took over.

"I suppose if you buy that sort of thing," she said. "Fairy rings wouldn't be that far-fetched, either."

"No, they wouldn't. A very short step from one to the other." He looked at her. "Ready to resume the tour?"

Kate followed him out of the room, back into the dark corridor, rattled and a little frightened. Not of Maguire, really, but of some huge, amorphous thing that she couldn't give a name to. As she walked along with him, it took every bit of effort she could muster not to start running.

"I'M SORRY YOU NEED TO LEAVE." Niall looked at Kate, green anorak zipped up to her chin as she backed away from him across the great hall. One minute he'd been telling her something—he couldn't even remember now what it was—and the next she was practically tripping over herself to be gone. "There's still quite a bit to see."

"Maybe we could schedule it for another time," she said.

"And when would you like to schedule it?" he asked, pronouncing the word as she had, in the American way. "Will you need to consult your calendar?"

She gave him a long look. "I'll give you a call," she said. "Maybe we could get together in town, or something."

"Right, then." Niall opened the front door for her.

No point in arguing. Clearly, she wasn't convinced that she was safe around him. And as much as he wanted her company, all the talking in the world wouldn't change her mind. Trusting him was her only choice.

CHAPTER SEVEN

"WELL, IT WAS WISE of you to leave," Annie told Kate as they walked down the high street later that afternoon. "I was worried the whole time you were up there, you can ask Pat. When I found that note of yours saying you were up to see Niall Maguire, I was all for having Rory go up there to bring you back."

"Yeah, well, I guess I was just playing it safe until I get a little more information," Kate said. Which was true, but she felt a tug every time she thought about the look on Niall's face when she'd cut the tour short. And, no matter how many times she reminded herself that she knew nothing about his temperament or character, she just had this feeling that when he said he hadn't murdered his wife, he'd been telling the truth.

"Pity I didn't put two and two together before you went off to meet him Wednesday morning," Annie said. "Him coming into the tourist office just the day before, asking did I have an American girl with long red hair staying with me? And then you all over the moon about that note. Just don't get taken in by him, Katie, that's all I'm saying."

"Don't worry about it," Kate said with more assurance than she actually felt. "I won't."

"Sure, you wouldn't be the first girl to fall for a good-looking man with a black heart," Annie said.

Kate grinned. Why couldn't she have had someone

like Annie around when she was making her first forays into the dating world? Even if she disagreed with Annie's assessment of Niall, it was great to have someone a little older, and definitely more grounded, to talk to.

"It was pretty romantic, though. Meeting him up on the cliffs like that." She smiled, remembering. "We kissed, Annie. And I didn't even know his name."

"Ah, Katie," Annie said softly.

"I know. That's what I mean, it's like it wasn't even me. I swear, I've never done anything like that in my life. Really."

Annie laughed. "Ah, come on, darlin', it's not such a crime, kissing a good-looking man, even if you don't know his name. The thing I can't picture is Niall Maguire coming down out of the clouds enough to do something like that."

"That's what I mean," she said, wanting to convert Annie. "I think people just don't know him and that's how all the rumors started."

"They know him well enough," Annie said darkly.

Kate said nothing. Annie and everyone else in Cragg's Head had known Niall for a lot longer than she had and weren't likely to be easily swayed. What she had to do was try to keep an open mind, at least until she'd interviewed some less biased sources. This afternoon, she was meeting a former roommate of Moruadh's in Galway and tomorrow a musician who had toured with her.

A bell pinged loudly behind her and she turned to see a woman on a bicycle approaching.

Black raincoat flapping like a sail around her portly

body, mouth set in grim determination, the woman rode stiff as a rock, looking neither right nor left.

"Brigid Riley," Annie whispered. "Poor old thing drops in at Dooley's every evening for a pint. Parks the bike outside and when she comes out, the tires are always flat. They say that after she's had a few, she doesn't notice anyway." She laughed. "Who knows, she might even ride better that way."

Kate watched as the woman came to a sudden and shaky stop, dismounted and bent down to inspect the back tire, her ample behind sticking up in the air. After a moment, she straightened up. A frizz of red hair poked out from the front of a head scarf patterned with horses, her eyes were dark currants in a suety pudding of a face. Kate recognized her as the woman she'd seen in Hugh Fitzpatrick's office.

"Look at that, will you?" The woman flapped her hand at the flattened tire. "There's not enough air left in there to blow out a candle. Them *divils,* pestering me all hours of the day and night. They have me patience worn out, sure they do."

"I'll fix it for you." Kate reached for the rusted bicycle pump strapped to the crossbar. "I think I can figure this thing out."

The woman stared at Kate with frank curiosity. "American? Didn't I meet you in Hughie Fitzpatrick's office?"

"Katie's here to write about Moruadh Maguire," Annie said before Kate could respond. "She's staying at my place."

Kate stuck out her hand, which the woman took awkwardly, as though shaking hands wasn't exactly an everyday occurrence. "Kate Neeson. Nice to meet you."

"She's the girl Mr. Maguire was asking about the other day?" Brigid addressed Annie. "Doesn't let much grass grow under his feet, that one."

Kate got busy pumping the tire. She didn't want to think about the grass not growing under Niall's feet, but Hugh Fitzpatrick's remarks about women falling all over Niall demanded consideration. Rory McBride had also called Niall a womanizer. A possible story angle popped up like a mechanical duck in a shooting range. *Moruadh Maguire's songs about love gone wrong were prophetic. Hoping that she'd finally found true love, Moruadh made the unfortunate mistake of marrying a man who, although handsome and charming, was also a heartless womanizer. In desperation, she killed herself.* Kate finished pumping the tire. Philanderer? Murderer. Both angles were almost equally unsettling.

Under the blue-striped awning of Sullivan's Butcher Shop, Annie and Brigid were talking in hushed voices, their heads close. Annie winked at Kate, then composed her expression as she listened to Brigid.

"…anyway, in she walks all damp from the weather," Brigid was saying. "Like a drowned rat, she was."

"Mary, you mean?"

Brigid sighed. "You know quite well who I mean, Annie Ryan. Bold as brass she goes right up to the bar and asks for a pint." Brigid paused, evidently to let this sink in. "And then she has another one."

Annie's eyes widened. *"Never."*

"Indeed. Mary heard it herself from Maureen Gallagher. Seamus was there. Of course, isn't he always?" Brigid lowered her voice. "Sure, could you imagine crawling into bed with a man who has the smell of whiskey on him every night?'' She unbuttoned her raincoat. ''Is it hot today, or just me?''

''I'm not hot,'' Annie said. ''Are you hot, Katie?''

Trying not to grin, Kate shook her head. She suspected Annie of deliberately drawing out the exchange to provide her with a little entertainment.

''Must be you, Brigid,'' Annie said.

''Must be me then,'' Brigid agreed. ''Anyway, where was I? Right, so there at the bar she was drinking as though she hadn't a care in the world. Talking to all the men and herself all tarted up like a dog's dinner.''

''A drowned rat.''

''What?''

''A drowned rat.'' Annie winked at Kate. ''That's what you said. She looked like a drowned rat.''

''Did I?''

''You did.''

''Ah well. Getting forgetful in my old age, aren't we all? Now, Annie, have you heard about the terrible fight up there at the tinkers' camp?''

''I know the girl she was talking about,'' Annie said after Brigid had mounted her bike and taken off down the road. ''You'd never know from hearing all that that she's a perfectly decent young woman, happily engaged to a fine lad and hardly touches a drop of the drink. But that's village life for you.''

Kate mentally rewrote the article's lead. *While village gossip branded him as a heartless womanizer who callously pushed his young wife to her death, the real Niall Maguire is a quiet, introspective man who...*

"WHAT I DON'T UNDERSTAND—" Kate told Moruadh's former roommate over lunch in Galway "—is why there's so much hostility toward Niall Maguire. No one really seems to know him very well and they all seem convinced he pushed Moruadh. Even though the Garda ruled her death was an accident, people just can't seem to accept it."

Rose Boland smiled. An actress currently starring in a Dublin play, Rose was starting to make a name for herself in New York. She wore her hair tightly pulled back and a great deal of tasteful, expensive-looking silver jewelry. It occurred to Kate that Rose would have looked quite at home in one of Santa Monica's trendier bistros.

"Maybe some of it is Niall's own fault," Rose said. "I suspect he doesn't want anyone to get too close. He's a beautiful man to be sure, but not an easy one to get to know. He keeps his thoughts to himself."

Kate thought again of the look on Niall's face when she'd left the castle so abruptly. The disappointment at her leaving clearly there. Swept by a sudden urge to see him and apologize, she imagined excusing herself right then and driving up to the castle. Instead, she wrote "Keeps his thoughts to himself" on her notepad and looked up at Rose Boland.

"Niall had nothing to do with Moruadh falling," Rose said. "I'm absolutely certain of that. He'd spent half his life protecting her from harm. Why would he suddenly turn?"

"Jealousy? A lovers' spat?" She thought of Rory McBride's strange story. "Maybe Moruadh became too much of a burden."

"That doesn't ring true, somehow. It's not...Niall

just doesn't have it in him to do something like that. No, he's just getting his comeuppance,'' Rose said. ''That's the way the village sees it. He's from an old-money family. Anglo-Irish. It's the whole bloody thing about the gentry getting rich on the backs of the peasants.''

Kate frowned, unconvinced. ''But that's history now, surely?''

''You'd think so, but that's where it all comes from. They mistrust his type. It's as if he thinks he's above the rest of us. People resent it. They'd just as soon see Niall locked up as face up to the fact that maybe one of the local lads could be responsible, which, incidentally, I don't believe, either. And, as I said, Niall's attitude doesn't help much. He can seem very cold and aloof. I've seen it myself.''

Kate nodded, although she hadn't seen those qualities herself. *Yet.* She made another note.

''My God, that man's had it rough,'' Rose said. ''While Moruadh was alive, she led him a merry dance and now she's dead, she's still causing him problems.''

Kate caught the eye of the waiter across the room and beckoned him over. After they'd ordered, Rose flipped open a gold cigarette case and held it out.

''No, thanks, but go ahead.'' She watched Rose light up. ''What did you mean just then about Moruadh leading Niall a dance?''

Rose exhaled smoke, peered at Kate through a pale blue haze. ''You'd never met Moruadh?''

''No. Just talked to her on the phone.''

''We shared a flat in Dublin for nearly five years.'' She laughed. ''A grand old time we had. Both of us just starting out. I was beginning to get small parts here and there and she was singing in clubs around town. But Moruadh's moods were…mercurial would be a way to describe it, I suppose.''

Kate made a note, looked up at Rose.

''So much so that at times she'd seem almost out of control. God, I can remember trying to sleep and she'd want to talk. And talk. And talk.''

Kate smiled, remembering their transatlantic telephone talks.

''And she'd get all these ideas. Songs, a line of lyrics. A thought about this or that. One idea giving rise to the next. It was as though the ideas came faster than the words she could use to express them. Like shooting stars, she once said. Her voice would rise and she'd be talking a mile a minute, faster and faster, until it seemed she would fizzle out like a firework.''

''Manic,'' Kate guessed. ''And then she'd crash, right?''

''Ah God, did she.'' Rose watched as the waiter set the food down, then she looked across the table at Kate. ''You knew about it, then?''

''I recognize the symptoms. I have a friend who was diagnosed with bipolar disorder.'' She picked at her salad. ''Manic-depression is another name for it. So where did Niall come into it?''

''When all the euphoria faded and hopelessness set in, it was him she wanted. No one else would do. I remember, once he was in America, an exhibition of some of his photos, I think it was, and this mood came on her.'' She looked at Kate for a moment. ''I worried that she would kill herself, she was that desperate. Anyway, he came home early to be with her.''

''So they had a good relationship?''

''Well, I think Moruadh needed him. And, clearly,

she was very fond of him. Although she was always a bit of a user. When life was going well, she'd less time for everyone." She smiled. "I'd call her a butterfly, just flitting around from flower to flower, never stopping long. I think she was like a lot of artists. Not really in reality. The world was an extension of her own world, it revolved around her."

"Did Niall love her, do you think?"

"I think Niall was enchanted by her," Rose was saying. "It's a funny thing to say, but you'd have to have known Moruadh. Sure, she was lovely looking. Beautiful even without a speck of makeup. She had this fanciful way of seeing things. Mystical, really. A red sunset. The way a seashell was curved. A dog's bark. Anything. Messages from an unseen world, she'd call them."

"And Niall bought into it all?"

"I wouldn't go that far, but I think something about it appealed to him. Sure, he wouldn't be alone. Yeats himself was a big believer in that sort of thing." She grinned at Kate. "You're not yourself, I take it?"

"Not exactly," Kate said, smiling back at her. "Maybe if I could keep the cynic in check." She looked down at her notes, then up at Rose. "So, about Moruadh's fall from the cliffs? What happened do you think?"

"An accident."

"You believe that? Despite her moods?"

"I do. She would have turned to Niall for help before she'd kill herself. I have no doubt of that."

They talked for a little longer, and then Rose glanced at her watch and remembered an appointment she had. As they were leaving the Quay House, she put her hand on Kate's arm. "Niall Maguire's a good man," she said. "You can quote me on that."

NIALL WAS DEVELOPING prints from film he'd shot in Sligo, when Kate rang. At the sound of her voice, he felt a grin spread across his face. The phone cradled between his head and shoulder, he finished rinsing the last print and hung it to dry. After she'd left so suddenly that morning, he hadn't expected to hear from her so soon.

"Anyway, I consulted my schedule," she said, "and I found I have this evening free. I felt sort of bad about rushing off the way I did and I wondered if I could buy you a beer to make up for it."

"You don't have anything to make up for, Kate. I understand, really."

"Good, because I thought I might have hurt your feelings."

He laughed. "Since you know nothing about me, I'd say if you had to choose between hurting my feelings or your own safety, you made the right decision."

"Yeah, well…listen, Niall, have you ever thought that maybe all the gossip got started because no one really knows you? I mean, talking to people, I get an image of an aloof, detached guy who lives by himself in this Gothic castle and, when he's not taking pictures of rowboats and thatched cottages, he's got women falling all over him—" she paused dramatically "—and he probably pushed his wife off the cliffs."

He laughed. "That is me, Kate. Except for the last part. Well, maybe not the bit about the women, either."

"I don't believe it."

"What part of it don't you believe?"

"I think there's a lot more to Niall Maguire than he reveals to most people."

He hung up another print. Looked at it for a minute. A view through a windowpane into a room, empty but for a wooden chair. "Do you have a pen in your hands as you're talking to me?"

"Actually, I do. Want me to put it down?"

"What I think you should do is take a walk up here."

"I could do that," she said. "We could finish the tour. Give me an hour, okay?"

"An hour it is." He hung up the phone and grinned like an idiot.

"YOU'RE NEVER GOING to see Niall Maguire at this hour." Hands on her hips, Annie regarded Kate. "It's after six, and I've a nice meat pie cooking and a bit of that jam roll you like with some custard for afters."

Kate exchanged glances with Caitlin, who sat at the kitchen table flipping through a bridal magazine, and tried not to smile. Annie made her feel like a teenager chafing against the restraints of an overprotective mother. Something she'd never personally experienced, but not altogether a bad thing. "I won't be late, Annie," she promised.

Caitlin hooted. "You're a grown woman, Kate. Stay out as late as you bloody well want to. All night, if you feel like it. I tell you, if I didn't have Rory, I wouldn't mind paying Mr. Maguire a little visit."

"Caitlin." Annie flicked a tea towel at Caitlin's head. "You should be ashamed of yourself."

"Well, it's true, Mam. He's a lovely man. Those

eyes of his. Half the girls in the class are in love with him. Elizabeth included, which is why she made plans to meet him when she knew we were to look for dresses.''

"That girl.'' Annie shook her head. "Four days and not a word from her.''

"Do you think maybe you should call the police?'' Kate asked, trying not to speculate on Niall and Elizabeth. "I know you said she's done this sort of thing before, but what if something's wrong?''

"We'd have heard,'' Annie said. "Besides, I've had calls from people who say they've seen her. I'm telling you, though, I won't put up with this again. Niall Maguire showing up on my doorstep asking after her.''

Kate tried to keep her voice casual. "So Niall and Elizabeth…''

"Sure, I've probably not said two words to the man since Moruadh died and there he was Monday night. Gave me quite a start, it did. No offense to you, Katie, but what was he doing arranging to meet a young girl late at night?''

"Ah God, you've been nattering with Brigid Riley again, haven't you?'' Caitlin didn't look up from the magazine. "Listening to the gossip. Just for your information, Katie, I think Mr. Maguire's a gentleman. It was Elizabeth chasing after him, I know that. Just like she does over anything in trousers.''

"Caitlin. She's your friend,'' Annie said.

"I know that, but it doesn't stop me from speaking the truth about her. And back to Mr. Maguire, as far as I'm concerned, Moruadh should have known better than to be up at the Leap, the wind blowing like it was that day. You wouldn't catch me up there, I'll tell you that.'' She flipped a page. ''What do you think about pink, Katie?''

''Pink?'' Kate refocused her thoughts and looked at Caitlin. ''For the bridesmaids?''

''No, for my dress. Pink wedding dresses are all the rage these days.''

''Pink.'' Annie measured flour into brown earthenware bowls. ''When your da and I were married—''

''You wore white.'' Caitlin winked at Kate and went on turning pages. ''Actually, I was thinking of red for myself. And maybe black for the bridesmaids. What d'you think? Elizabeth said it would be really sophisticated. Not that I'd trust her opinion, though. I don't know why I have anything to do with her.''

''Don't be daft,'' Annie protested. ''The two of you are like sisters.''

''We are not. She has the morals of a snake. The minute my back's turned she's all over Rory.'' With the tips of her fingernails she'd just polished pale blue, Caitlin flipped the magazine shut. ''Of course, he'll have none of it.''

Kate thought of the secret Rory had asked her to keep and got up from the table. Rory had insisted that nothing happened with Elizabeth, but she had an uneasy feeling. They were definitely due for a little chat, she decided.

''Listen, love—'' Annie came into the hallway as Kate was zipping up her parka to go to the castle ''—I know there's nothing I can do to stop you going to see Mr. Maguire, but how about if I have Patrick come and get you in an hour or so?''

''For God's sake, Mam,'' Caitlin called from the

kitchen. "Leave Katie be, will you. She's safe as houses up there."

"THIS NEXT AREA takes a bit of getting used to." Niall reached out to touch her shoulder. "When you go inside, stand still for a moment until your eyes get accustomed to the dark and stay very close to the wall. Hold on to me if you want to."

Kate took his hand, and the heavy door closed behind them. In the next instant, she was slapped in the face by a blast of cold wet air. Somewhere far beneath them, she heard rushing water. The sound echoed off the walls, filled her ears. Spray drenched her face and hair. The pressure of Maguire's hand intensified slightly.

"Are you all right?" His voice was almost lost in the roaring sound.

She gulped an affirmative. At first there was nothing but pitch-black, then he shone the flashlight and, in the wavering beam of light, she saw that they stood on a narrow ledge that ran around two sides of an enormous room. *A room with no floor.*

Hundreds of feet below them, the crashing ocean gleamed with a faint phosphorescent sheen. She swallowed, flattened herself against the wall, paralyzed with fear.

"This was once a banquet hall," he said. "As you can see, the center is gone. In 1640, I think it was, it crashed into the sea during a reception. The earl who owned the castle was carried off along with most of the servants. Apparently, the only survivor in the domestic quarters was a tinker who'd been off somewhere mending pots."

Kate mumbled something incoherent, felt her body

sway slightly and tightened her grip on Maguire's
hand, his skin warm around her waxlike fingers. Her
feet and nose were numb. The ocean seemed to be
surging up at her.

"Apparently the countess was never all that keen
on this part of the castle," he continued. "The waves
beating all around unnerved her a bit. When the floor
caved in, she went right off it altogether."

A bead of sweat rolled down Kate's forehead,
dripped into one eye. She blinked it away, too petri-
fied to move. Sweat broke out on her upper lip.
Heights had always terrified her. Nightmares had
haunted her sleep for as long as she could remember.
Nightmares exactly like this. A narrow ledge, churning ocean below and then falling, down through the
bottomless dark with no one to catch her. Then she'd
wake up screaming. It indicated her fear of losing
control, someone had told her.

"Over the years, more and more of it has fallen
away," Niall went on. "Now, all that's left is this
ledge, which goes around to Moruadh's—"

"Niall."

"What is it?"

"I'm gonna pass out."

IF SHE HAD DREAMED UP a way to put herself in a
compromising position, Kate decided, she couldn't
have done better than this. Her clothes, already damp
from the rain, then soaked by the west wing's driving
sea spray, were now drying in front of an electric
heater, tatty cotton underwear tucked modestly out of
sight beneath her jeans and sweater.

Still shivering, she pulled the blanket up around her
chin, clasped both hands around a tumbler of hot

whiskey. Discombobulated, she thought. There was no other word for the way she felt. In Santa Monica, she followed certain commonsense rules. Life was dangerous enough without taking unnecessary risks. And while she'd never been invited by a suspected murderer to disrobe in his medieval castle, she was pretty sure what her answer would be. Of course, in Santa Monica she'd never been tempted to kiss a complete stranger on a cliff top. In Cragg's Head normal rules didn't seem to apply.

"Are you all right?" Niall turned from the fireplace where he'd been coaxing the sullen flames. "You still look a bit shaky."

"I'm fine." She eyed him over the glass. "Mostly I'm embarrassed for wimping out. I have this thing about heights."

He nodded and turned to attend to the fire. She watched as he crouched in front of the grate. His hair curled slightly over his shirt collar. When he leaned forward to strike a match to the pile, she could see the bones of his spine through the blue chambray of his shirt. Long and lean as a whittled stick. The fire caught, and he turned to look at her, his face illuminated by the flames.

"We're in luck," he said with a serious expression. "There are demon cats living under the hearth rugs that come up straight from hell. They can make lighting fires awful hard sometimes, but I think Rufus has chased them off." He glanced at the dog who was stretched out like a tattered rug in front of the fire. "He is a good dog for that sort of thing."

She grinned, struck again by the disparity between the two versions of Niall Maguire. This one, warm, attentive, quick to smile—a man she instinctively liked—and the Niall Maguire she'd heard about from others. She sipped the whiskey. As he'd led her shaking and trembling from the west tower, she'd decided that the villagers were definitely wrong about him. This was the real Niall Maguire, a man who *couldn't* have killed his wife.

Still, she had to concede that it could be just the chemistry screwing up her thought process. Everything about Niall intrigued and appealed to her. Even his voice aroused her. The lilting accent that turned her name into two syllables *Keh-ayt,* with a soft sigh at the end. Beneath the blanket, she felt her body stir. Nipples against rough wool, warmth in her stomach, her thighs. Fantasies of entwined limbs and romps on Irish bed linens. She blocked the thoughts.

"Are you hungry?" he asked.

"I'm always hungry." She eyed her clothes. "But I should get back, I told Annie I wouldn't be late. She's made this meat pie for supper."

"Annie has you there for supper every night, I'd enjoy your company."

"Niall..." She bit her lip. "I realize that it's kind of ridiculous to be sitting here with no clothes on wondering whether I should trust you. My gut feeling tells me that I can, but my gut feeling also told me my boyfriend was teaching night school when he was actually screwing my best friend, so I'm not a great judge of these things and if I stay for dinner and..." She plucked at the blanket. "God, I have no idea what I'm trying to say."

He laughed. "That makes two of us. Will you stay for supper, though? I can't match Annie's meat pie, but I do have the things for that bouillabaisse I mentioned yesterday."

"Bouillabaisse?" She grinned. "What's with this bouillabaisse thing?" A comment about corned beef and cabbage being more appropriate almost slipped out, but she remembered her caustic comment to Fitzpatrick about stereotyping and kept her mouth shut while she tried to think of reasons why she shouldn't stay. None came to mind. "Bouillabaisse sounds pretty good," she said.

"Good." He stood, grabbed her clothes and tossed them at her. "It's not every day that I tell a woman to get dressed, but these are dry now and it might be a good idea."

"Mmm, forget the bouillabaisse, listen to this." Kate flipped through an old cookbook she'd taken from the kitchen dresser. "'Carrigeen moss pudding,'" she read. "'Take as much of the moss as will fit in your fist when almost clenched. Wash it in warm water for a few minutes, removing any grasses or other foreign bodies.'"

Niall laughed. He stood at the long wooden deal table, cutting up onions as he watched Kate move around the kitchen, her curiosity imparting a new and exotic quality to the familiar. She'd touch something that caught her eye, stop to comment on it. A piece of blue-and-white glazed pottery on the dresser, the woven seats of the *sugan* chairs. She looked up to see him watching her and smiled.

He was smitten. Gone. Besotted. She had on a pair of black corduroy trousers and a short wool jumper the color of marigolds. As she leaned over to pat Rufus, the top rode up to reveal a band of pale, freckled skin.

He reached for another onion from the basket under

the table. His head was full of her. Thoughts tumbled around, endless questions. Already, her return to America loomed like a dark cloud. Unable to tear his eyes from her, he watched as she peered inside the fireplace. Kate—with her freckles like grains of sand and great masses of red hair that escaped in tendrils from her ponytail and fell in wisps around her face. A long curl hung down the back of her neck. He stared at the onion in his hand and tried to remember what he was supposed to be doing.

"God, a family of four could camp in here," she said, her voice muffled from inside the fireplace.

He glanced over at the massive bricked wall, blackened from the fires burned over the years. It held a spit that was once used for roasting meat. "It's a bit too big to be practical, though. You saw how hard it was getting the fire started in the great hall. This one is a full-time job. Still, it would be handy if you ever feel like grilling an ox for dinner."

"Yeah, I bet you grill them all the time." With a grin, she flicked a finger at the iron cauldron that hung from a crane. "And what about this? You make your porridge in it?"

"I do. That and the gravy I serve up with the ox. And some days I even boil up the *taties* in it," he added in an exaggerated brogue.

Kate laughed and pushed back a strand of hair. Their eyes met and held. He heard the drip of water from the tap, the tree branches scratching against the window. A moment passed, and then with a self-conscious little shrug, she came across to the table and pulled up a chair opposite him. Elbows propped, she watched as he started on some green peppers.

"I'm trying to imagine your life," she said. "What

do you do, walk around this place saying, 'I'm the king of the castle?'"

He laughed. "Hardly. More likely, I walk around wondering where I'm going to get the money to repair it. It's not in very good shape. The west tower, for example. I'll need to do something about it one of these days, but it's prohibitively expensive."

"So you don't have a pile of money?"

He looked at her, tried not to smile.

"What?" she asked.

"I was just thinking that the Irish way of asking that question would be a lot more indirect," he said. "Sure, we might wonder the same thing, but we'd swim slowly around it, gradually circling in to the main point and even then we would be less blunt. Something like, 'Ah sure, it must be nice not to have worry about the cost of repair.'"

She laughed. "I've only got a few days in Ireland. I need to work fast, but you still didn't answer my question."

"I don't have a pile of money." He let a moment pass. "So you can cross off your list the theory that I pushed her to avoid paying her part of my fortune in alimony."

"You're quite an enigma, you know that?"

He shrugged, then returned his attention to the vegetables. A moment later, unable to resist, he looked up to find her watching him. Green eyed, in her sunshine sweater. Cinnamon-dusted face. If his life until now had been like one of those old black-and-white films, Kate had changed it to Technicolor. The kiss up on the cliffs had been as vivid, electrifying and as far removed from his real life as anything he'd ever seen in a cinema. It brought to mind the serials he'd watched as a boy. Every Saturday morning at the Odeon, mesmerized, his eyes glued to the screen, never sure until the very last minute how it was all going to turn out.

The peppers chopped, he sent a thin sliver skidding in Kate's direction.

"Starters," he said. "Or appetizers, as you Americans say."

"Do you often cook for women?"

"Hardly ever. Do you cook for men?"

"*Hah.* I don't even cook for myself."

"Rich boyfriends take you out to expensive restaurants, do they?"

"God, yes. Night after night. I know the best table at every Beverly Hills bistro." She sighed theatrically. "It gets to be such a bore."

He looked at her.

"I'm lying."

He smiled.

"So what about you? What do people in Cragg's Head do for fun?"

He laughed. "Not an awful lot. You'd probably find it very dull."

"But you're a photographer. Don't you go off on location, take pictures of beautiful models, that sort of thing?"

"I do a bit of it."

"*A bit of it,*" she said imitating his accent. "If I asked an American guy that question, he'd spend thirty minutes telling me all the places he went to and all the models he scored with."

"Maybe American men are more successful at that sort of thing."

She gave him a look that suggested she thought

otherwise. A moment passed. He poured wine into their glasses.

"Why are you so interested in Moruadh?"

"It's an assignment."

"That's all?"

"Not exactly. Moruadh intrigued me. She used to call me. After the article I wrote on her, we became sort of long-distance phone pals. Mostly we talked about men. Or problems with men. We were both pretty much failures in the relationship department." She paused. "Where were you married?"

He hesitated. It was public record, if she wanted to find it she could. "In France. Nearly four years ago."

"Which would have been just before my article came out. Around the time she started calling me from Paris. She'd tell me about these disastrous love affairs and sound so desperate. She never mentioned you."

He brought the knife down on a strip of pepper he'd already chopped. Too vigorously. The pepper skidded off the table. He bent to pick it up, tossed it into the bin by the sink, looked over at her. She'd shifted on the chair and now sat on it backward, her arms around the backrest. Her face was small, triangular. Pointed chin and wide-spaced eyes. Long ribbons of red hair. He couldn't look at her without posing her for the camera.

From the refrigerator, he took out a waxed-paper-wrapped slab of butter and brought it over to the table. "Let's talk about you," he said. "I'd find that much more interesting."

"God, I don't believe it." She drew her feet up on the chair, wrapped her arms around her knees. "A man who would rather listen than talk about himself. I should pinch you to see if you're real.''

He melted the butter in the pan, added olive oil and returned to the table. ''Talk away.''

''What would you like to know. Horror stories about failed relationships?''

''How did you become so cynical?''

''Mmm, let me see.'' She wrinkled up her face. ''Well, for years I swallowed all these rosy confections about true love and when I started gagging and throwing up, I realized something was wrong. You know how you're just allergic to some things?''

He smiled at her.

''That was what fascinated me about Moruadh,'' she said, her face serious now. ''Here was this incredibly beautiful, successful woman with everything going for her. We really had nothing in common except that both of us kept flunking Love 101, or at least I thought she did.'' She got up from the chair, paced the kitchen. ''All her songs were so tragic. When she died, I wondered at first if she'd finally acted upon a thought that had been there all along.''

He looked down at the shapes and colors of the vegetables he'd chopped. Squares of green. Slivers of white. A tomato, vivid red quarters reflected in the knife's steel blade. Outside, the dark night. Branches scratching against the window. ''Relationships go awry,'' he finally said.

''Yeah.'' She picked at her thumbnail. ''I've noticed. Personally, I've discovered that my life flows a lot more smoothly without men tramping around in it, so about a year ago, I took myself off the market.'' She reached past him, picked up a head of garlic and began separating cloves. ''Sort of like a house that doesn't sell. The hell with a bunch of jerks tramping through it every weekend, not appreciating its fine architecture and great views.''

He turned his head to look at her and she grinned. And they were both smiling.

"Not that it really matters," she said, "but I want you to know that I don't usually go around blabbing out my life story to complete strangers."

"Or kissing them," he said.

"That, too." She broke off a clove. "Must be something about Ireland."

He scooped the garlic in his hand, dropped it in the melted butter. Kate drifted over to stand beside him and they stood shoulder to shoulder, the smell of butter and garlic filling the air. A wisp of smoke curled slowly upward and then suddenly she was gone and back with a handful of chopped onions. As she dumped them in the pan, fat splattered and hissed. Bits of onions flew all over the place. Her elbow in his ribs, she shoved him aside and grabbed the spatula from his hand.

"God, we've chopped enough vegetables for an army and now you're standing there communing with the butter." She started stirring the onions. "At this rate it will be midnight before I ever even see dinner."

Niall laughed as he stood aside to watch her. Sleeves rolled up above her elbows, she stirred with a look of grim determination. After a minute or two, apparently satisfied things were back under control, she shot him a look.

"Green peppers."

"Right away." Quickly, he scooped the pieces of pepper into his palms and brought them over to her.

Leaning over her shoulder, he dropped them into the pan. "All right?" He stayed there, close enough to feel the warmth of her back against his chest. "Is this a takeover attempt, then?"

"You could call it that, I guess." Her hands on the spatula had gone very still. "Or you might think of it as a lifesaving rescue to avoid death by starvation. Do you mind?"

"Not at all," he said truthfully. "Would it make any difference if I did?"

"None at all," she said, imitating his accent. "What are we doing about the stock?"

"Stock?" He locked his arms around her waist, kissed the side of her neck.

"For the bouillabaisse," she said, leaning back into him. "And you're making it very hard for me to concentrate."

"That's my intention."

"No, your intention is to make bouillabaisse. At least I thought that was your intention."

Niall smiled at her. He'd spent just a few hours with her, but it seemed like an age. He knew nothing about her, yet it seemed he knew everything. He thought he could easily fall in love with her.

He took her face between his hands and kissed her. Minutes passed, then he kicked out a chair and pulled her down on his lap and they kissed with an urgency that blotted out everything but heat and sensation. She moved to sit astride him, her hands in his hair, her mouth open to his tongue. Finally, she drew back.

"What are we supposed to be doing?"

"Do we care?"

"Yeah, I think we do." She got up from his lap,

lifted the hair off her neck and went over to the stove. "Fish. You were getting fish."

He handed her several paper packages from the refrigerator. "Shrimp, mussels, a couple of different kind of fish. Swimming a few hours ago."

"Great." Without looking at him, she opened one of the packages. "They'll be really fresh."

He shook his head to clear the fog of sexual desire. "There's a Provençal saying," he told her. "Something about eating your fish while it's fresh and marrying off your daughter while she's young. My French isn't that good, so I can never remember whether I'm saying, marry your fish or—"

"Eat your daughter." Kate gave a little laugh. "So what's the plan here? Dinner, then we mosey up to the bedchamber?"

He took a breath. "Actually, I hadn't thought that far ahead. What do you think?"

She brushed past him to gather another handful of chopped onions, dumped them in the pan and stood back as they splattered in the hot grease. "I think that I can't believe I just said that. In fact, I should probably leave."

"Is that what you want to do?"

"No."

"Why then?"

"I think if I stay I'll end up going to bed with you."

"And that's not what you want to do?"

"Actually it is, but I think it would be a mistake." With thumb and forefinger she retrieved a large piece of onion from the pan. "This needs to be chopped some more. The problem is my body would like a fling, but my head is nixing it."

"How can we get your head to shut up?"

"It won't."

"Hmm." He buried his chin in her shoulder. "Is your head ever likely to give your body permission?"

"Eventually, I'm sure. The thing is, Niall, I don't want to sleep with you and then make a bunch of promises about staying in touch when we both know that's not going to happen." Spatula in hand, she turned around to look at him. "Besides, it would ruin my objectivity."

He struggled to keep a straight face.

"Jerk." She hit his arm with the spatula. "I'm usually very objective."

"I'm sure you are." Heat from the stove had turned her face pink. He wanted to kiss her again. "I think we should do all we can to preserve your journalistic integrity, so as much as I'd like to accommodate your body, I'm going to agree with your head. No jaunts to the bedchamber and no more kissing."

She grinned at him.

"I mean it. Kissing is verboten. Try it and I'll throw you outside." He flapped his hands at her. "Get over there, far away from me. You're a corrupting woman and I'll have none of it. Go on, move. After we've eaten, I'll show you my pictures. That should cool your ardor."

"A MAN OF MY WORD," he said, as he pulled a large cardboard box from the drawer of a heavy old dresser. "See, I really am just like all the other men you mentioned, I love to talk about myself." He dumped the pictures on the floor between them. "Or at least my work."

Kate studied the picture he had handed her. An old

man, his face heavily seamed. Behind him, a simple white cottage. A distant view of the sea.

"One of a dying breed," he said. "He has a farm on one of the western islands. A very hard life, it is. I was out there recently. Years ago, when his father started farming, the old fellow told me, the ground was so rocky, he literally had to make the earth. They'd haul seaweed and sand on donkeys and spread it out over the land. It was too hard for his sons, they went off to America."

She nodded, remembering the stories from her childhood. "My grandfather left Clare as a young boy and he used to tell me how difficult life was. He said that when a family emigrated, the neighbors kept turf fires burning for the day they would return."

"There were an awful lot of turf fires burning in these parts." He put the picture aside. "A lot of people went to America from all these western counties. Galway, Clare, Mayo. Ireland lost more people from here to emigration than to the potato famine. It's always been a difficult place to make a living."

"Is that something you've ever thought of yourself?" she asked. "Leaving Ireland?"

"I never have, no. I've been to America, but it's not for me. For a while, I lived in England and France, but I'd never leave this country. I'd never leave the west, for that matter."

As she took another picture, she stifled a pang of disappointment at his answer. What did she expect him to say? *"Now that I've spent a few hours with you, I'm ready to throw it all up. Let's buy a condo in Santa Monica and start having children."*

"Annie feels the same way about Ireland," she said after a moment. "She's horrified that I've moved around so much. According to her, the reason I'm not married is that I don't know who I am or where I belong."

He laughed. "What do you think?"

"I don't really think that has anything to do with my single state. But it might be nice to live in a little village like Cragg's Head, where a person really feels as if he belongs. To have the kind of rootedness you and Annie have."

"But I know what it's like not to have that," he said. "I went to boarding school in England for quite a few years and I was always this Irish boy. The accent, attitudes, everything. I never quite belonged. I'd pine away for home, go back to Ireland and feel just as out of place. I still do, really. It's the land more than the people that keeps me."

"I have that disconnected feeling about California," she said. "I have this idea that life is probably more real somewhere else."

"But that's the image of California, isn't it?" he said. "Movies and Disneyland, that sort of thing. Nothing quite real. I was there some time ago. Around Christmas and it was very hot. Eighty-five degrees, and people had on shorts. The Christmas trees were wilting in the shopping centers."

"Yeah, I know. We all have our illusions, right?" She glanced at the picture he'd handed her. A young girl at the edge of a cliff looking out to sea. A strand of long pale hair had blown across her face, and she'd raised her hand as though to brush it away.

"She's beautiful." Jealousy tugged at her. "Someone you know?"

"Beautiful and very young and naive." Niall took the picture from her, looked down at it. "Actually, she's a student in a class I teach at Galway College. Or at least she was. She hasn't been to classes for a few days.'' He put the picture on top of the one of the old man. ''You've not met her then? Elizabeth Jenkins? She's the daughter of Annie Ryan's friend.''

Kate reached for it again. ''This is Elizabeth?''

''It is. I was to meet her on the cliffs, the night I saw you,'' he said. ''But she didn't turn up.''

''She still hadn't when I left tonight,'' Kate said. ''Annie didn't seem too worried, though. Apparently, Elizabeth has done this kind of thing before.''

''I'm not surprised. She's a bit of a wild girl,'' he said.

Kate watched him for a moment—his expression preoccupied now—and wondered whether Elizabeth was more to him than a student. The question lingered in her brain as they went through the rest of the pictures. And then she looked up to see him watching her, a quizzical look on her face.

''I promised these would drive lascivious thoughts from your mind,'' he said. ''I didn't realize they'd send you to sleep.''

''They didn't.'' She smiled, formal and polite. ''They're good. You're very talented.''

''Something cold just came into the room,'' he said.

Kate looked at him. He sat on the floor facing her. His eyes steady on her face. She turned away first.

''Five minutes ago,'' he said, ''it wasn't here.''

''Maybe it was the White Lady.''

''Or maybe it was fear.''

''I don't know what you're talking about.''

''I think you do,'' he said. ''Just now, you suddenly went very quiet. Were you telling yourself to run for your life?''

"You're losing me.'' She focused on a spot beyond his shoulder. "Run from what?''

"From what you're feeling. Or, rather, what you'd feel if you let yourself.''

"I always hate it when guys tell me what I'm feeling. It's so damn arrogant.''

"You're right, it is. Tell me yourself then.''

She shrugged. "I'm attracted to you. Other than that, I don't really know much about you, so what else could there be?''

"But something's happening, isn't it? I know I feel it and I think you do, too. And what's more,'' he added, "I don't think it was just a random thing that you first interviewed Moruadh and that you came to Ireland and we met the way we did,'' he said. "I have a sense that somehow it was meant to happen.''

She said nothing, but the idea sent a small thrill of excitement through her. And then the cynic spoke up. *Get real. He wants to get you into bed.*

"Some things can't easily be explained,'' he said. "You try and reason them out and sometimes you're right and sometimes you're wrong. Sometimes you just have to trust, even though you don't understand.''

"Want to hear my theory?'' she asked.

"Sure.''

"I come to Ireland to write an article about your wife. I'm on the way up to the castle to see you and we run into each other. Cragg's Head is a small village, it was inevitable that we meet. There's this really strong mutual attraction, and I'm thousands of miles from home so it suddenly it seems okay to be a little more impulsive than I would normally be. We kiss." She shrugged. "It's a vacation fling."

"A vacation fling," he repeated. "I thought you told me you don't do this kind of thing?"

"I lied." She grinned at him. "Happens all the time."

"Is that so?"

"No. It's never happened before." She stared into the fire. "The bottom line is that I live in the States and you live here. So whatever we tell ourselves now, nothing can change that fact."

"But you'd fight it anyway, wouldn't you? Even if we'd met in America."

"Probably."

"Because, like all men, I'm a self-serving bastard who wouldn't recognize a genuine emotion if it bit me in the arse."

She laughed. "Something along those lines. I haven't been wrong so far."

"You could single-handedly reduce your country's divorce rate," he said. "Hire yourself out. Anytime you meet someone in love, you give them your philosophy. No one would ever get married again."

"You can laugh, but it's true."

"Well..." His eyes didn't leave her face. "Here's a theory. Maybe every man you've met so far hasn't been the one for you. After all, you're a bit young to have built a whole body of evidence against love. Maybe it just hasn't happened yet."

Self-conscious suddenly under the intensity of his gaze, she looked away. "Maybe," she conceded.

He laughed. "Ah, Kate. What's to become of you?"

"I'm wondering about that myself."

"What about the next few days? Are they completely filled?'

"Oh, I can probably fit you in."

He reached across and pulled at a strand of hair that had fallen over her shoulder. His fingers brushed her face and she felt an electric edge of desire so strong, her breath caught. A moment passed. He sat up and swung her legs under him so that they lay face-to-face on the floor.

"Hi." With her finger, she lightly traced his eyebrows and lashes, drew a line down the bridge of his nose to his mouth and chin. "You probably hear this all the time, but you have unbelievable eyes. Pale as fog. It was the first thing I noticed about you."

"You have one freckle on the very tip of your nose. It's very sexy."

"Yeah, right." She grinned at him. "Cover Girl's begging me to be in their ads."

He smiled.

"I've been thinking..." she said.

"Always a dangerous practice."

"...that perhaps kissing wouldn't be a bad idea."

"But I made you a solemn promise."

"Break it. I won't tell."

He kissed her forehead.

"Nice, but not quite what I had in mind." She kissed him on the mouth, felt his lips open under hers. His body pressed hard against her own, and the kiss became harder, more insistent. After a while, he pulled her on top of him, and they kissed until she thought she would swoon. Her mouth wet from his, she pulled away for a moment. Niall's face was buried in her neck, his head covered by her hair.

"Was that more like that?" he asked, his voice muffled against her skin.

"I'm not sure. Do it again and I'll tell you."

He did.

"Yeah, definitely." She lay above him, raised her head slightly to smile into his eyes. "But it's like potato chips. Once you start…"

He slid out from under her, flipped her onto her back and pressed his mouth to the band of exposed skin between her sweater and pants. "I want to carry you up to my bedchamber and ravish you. What do you say?"

"A bedchamber would definitely be a new experience." She lifted her hand to stroke his back, felt his lips move on her body.

"What about ravishing? Would that be new, too?"

"I'm not sure. That word is kind of open to interpretation." His tongue circled her navel and the sensation sent a spasm through her. Breathing ragged, she pulled him on top, wound her legs around his. His erection pressing into the crotch of her jeans, she writhed beneath him. His hands, under her sweater now, fingers beneath her bra.

Niall was the first to hear the front door open.

CHAPTER EIGHT

IN A FLASH, Niall was up on his feet, eyes heavy lidded as though he'd just woken. Kate sat up, tugged at her sweater, raked back her hair with her fingers. A tall blond woman in a long dark coat stood in the doorway, a little uncertainly, like an actor who'd missed a cue and arrived on stage at the wrong time.

"Today at three?" She looked ostentatiously at her watch. "The bank? The second time we've missed our appointment? Women distract Niall so easily," she said with a glance across the room at Kate. "Last time it was an art student, this time it's..." A taut smile briefly appeared on her face. "Sorry, I don't know your name. I'm Sharon Garroty, Niall's business partner. Or ex, I should say."

"Obviously you didn't get the message I left in the studio," Niall said, his face dark. "I said I was canceling the appointment with the bank."

"Did you?" The smile flashed again. "Well, obviously I missed it. Oh well, there are some things I need to talk to you about, anyway." She pulled off her coat, revealing a formfitting black dress beneath it, then she started for the fireplace.

"Sharon." Niall caught her arm. "Now isn't a good time. Why don't you ring me tomorrow?"

Kate stood, her heart banging against her chest. Her legs shaky, she mustered all the poise she could and walked across what seemed like miles of flagstone floor. From a row of hooks on the wall by the door, she retrieved her parka. In her peripheral vision she could see Niall and the woman standing together. The tension between them seemed to suck the air from the room.

"I need to go," Kate told him. "Maybe we could schedule some time to talk again in the next few days." With a smile that felt as patently false as the other woman's, she pulled open the door. Niall followed her out, closed the door behind him.

For a moment neither of them spoke. Kate shoved her hands in her pockets, hunched her shoulders. After the warmth of the fireplace and the exertions on the couch, the night air felt cold and sharp on her face. Wind billowed his shirt, tossed his hair. His expression was unreadable.

"All right. You've no need to tell me what you're thinking, it's clear on your face. My relationship with Sharon is over. I want you to know that. Over."

"Maybe for you." Her teeth were chattering. "Clearly not for her. Look, it was fun. You're a great kisser. I'm sure everything else would have been great, too, but maybe I'm not cut out for a fling." She flicked her finger against his arm. "Go inside before you freeze to death."

"I'll get my jacket and walk you back to Annie's."

"No. I'm fine, really. It's not that far."

He watched her for a moment. "You're so bloody convinced that you're right, you're not even willing to give it a try, are you?"

"Oh, come on, Niall." Beyond his shoulders, the narrow road leading away from the castle disappeared into a clump of trees. She hunched her shoulders against the cold. "Give what a try?"

ANNIE AND PATRICK WERE in the sitting room with their evening tea when Kate walked in. The scent of baking lingered in the air, and the fireplace and amber lamps glowed invitingly. The Ryans both smiled at her like storybook concerned parents. Swept by a wave of emotion she couldn't name, she rubbed her sleeve across her eyes.

"I was just after sending Patrick up to get you," Annie said.

"God, Annie, I'm sorry. I just…" She shook her head.

"No, it's only a little after ten. But you being up there and all." Annie jumped up from the armchair. "We were going to give it another five minutes. Have you eaten?" She touched her hand to Kate's cheek. "God, you're half-frozen. Come on out in the kitchen and talk to me, I'll put on the kettle."

She followed, half listening as Annie went on about Caitlin's cold, Brigid Riley's tumble from her bicycle, plans for the music festival and the latest sighting of Elizabeth at a coffee bar in Galway.

An image of Elizabeth's face in the picture Niall had taken flashed across Kate's brain, followed by one of his glamorous blond business partner. As Annie bustled about, Kate picked at the edge of the tablecloth. The business partner had long red nails. Kate's nails were chewed to the quick. She dug her knuckles into her eyes. God, her head felt like the kitchen junk drawer. Cluttered images. Bits and pieces of things Niall had said. Odds and ends of thoughts, impressions.

"All right are you, Katie?" Annie peered at her, her face anxious. "You look all in."

"Yeah." She shook her head to clear it, forced a smile. "I'm fine."

"A sweet biscuit?" Annie put a cup of tea in front of her and sat down at the table. "I've some treacle bread still."

"No, thanks, I'm not hungry." God, she was going to cry. Tears were massing in her throat, in the back of her nose. Filling up her eyes. She bit her lip, hard. Across the table, she felt Annie watching her. "I'm sorry. You're very sweet."

"Ah sure, I'm Mother Teresa and the Virgin Mary rolled into one. Now, are you going to tell me what is wrong? You were on top of the world when you left, and now here you are looking as though the world's collapsed about you. You might as well tell me what it is because I'll not leave until you do."

Kate looked at her, convinced she meant it. "No one wants to hear your problems," her mother had once told her. She'd been about five at the time and grieving over a kitten. It had darted under the wheels of a neighbor's car. The message had stuck. Tonight she was breaking all her rules.

"I think I've made a big fool of myself, Annie." She traced the rose pattern on her tea cup. "I don't know what happened, what I was thinking. It's like I just took leave of my senses."

"We're talking about Niall Maguire, are we?" Annie asked.

"Yeah." She took a deep breath. "I know you warned me, but...well, he made me dinner and we talked and it was great and we—" She broke off. She'd been about to say that she might well have gone to bed with Niall. Annie didn't need to hear that. "And then," she continued, "this woman came in, and I made my exit."

"Sharon Garroty, that's the woman," Annie said. "But word is, she's more than his business partner."

"I know, he told me. He said it was over, but from the way she looked at me, I'm not sure she believes that." Suddenly weary, Kate put her elbows on the table and stared at Annie. "God, I really, really want to trust a man. I want to look at him and just know he's telling the truth."

Annie sipped her tea but said nothing.

"I can't even believe I'm saying this, but it's as though there's a connection with Niall." She shook her head. "My friends would think I'd lost it if they could hear me. I just have a feeling deep down inside." Embarrassed, she paused. "On the other hand it could be jet lag."

Annie smiled.

Kate got up, pulled a sheet off the roll of paper towels, blew her nose and sat down again. She met Annie's eyes across the table.

"You probably think I'm nuts, don't you?"

"Not at all. You want someone of your own. It's a natural thing, Katie."

Kate stared hard at the embroidered daisies on the tablecloth. The tears were threatening to swamp her again, but this time she didn't even try to stop them. She looked at Annie. "Want to hear a sad story?"

Annie nodded. "I'm all ears."

"After my father walked out on my mother to shack up with one of his students, I watched my mom drink herself into a stupor every day. Finally, when the booze couldn't blot out the pain, she shot her-

How To Play:

1. With a coin, carefully scratch off the 3 gold areas on your Lucky Carnival Wheel. By doing so you have qualified to receive everything revealed—2 FREE books and a surprise gift—ABSOLUTELY FREE!

2. Send back this card and you'll receive 2 brand-new Harlequin Superromance® novels. These books have a cover price of $5.25 each in the U.S. and $6.25 each in Canada, but they are yours ABSOLUTELY FREE.

3. There's no catch! You're under no obligation to buy anything. We charge nothing—ZERO—for your first shipment. And you don't have to make any minimum number of purchases—not even one!

4. The fact is thousands of readers enjoy receiving books by mail from the Harlequin Reader Service®. They enjoy the convenience of home delivery…they like getting the best new novels at discount prices, BEFORE they're available in stores… and they love their *Heart to Heart* subscriber newsletter featuring author news, horoscopes, recipes, book reviews and much more!

5. We hope that after receiving your free books you'll want to remain a subscriber. But the choice is yours—to continue or cancel, any time at all! So why not take us up on our invitation, with no risk of any kind. You'll be glad you did!

A surprise gift

FREE

We can't tell you what it is…but we're sure you'll like it! A

FREE GIFT!

just for playing LUCKY CARNIVAL WHEEL!

Visit us online at
www.eHarlequin.com

LUCKY Carnival Wheel

Find Out Instantly The Gifts You Get **Absolutely FREE!**

Scratch-off Game

Scratch off **ALL 3** Gold areas

YES! I have scratched off the 3 Gold Areas above. Please send me the 2 FREE books and gift for which I qualify! I understand I am under no obligation to purchase any books, as explained on the back and on the opposite page.

336 HDL DNWU   135 HDL DNWK

FIRST NAME

LAST NAME

ADDRESS

APT.#

CITY

STATE/PROV.

ZIP/POSTAL CODE

The Harlequin Reader Service®—Here's how it works:

Accepting your 2 free books and gift places you under no obligation to buy anything. You may keep the books and gift and return the shipping statement marked "cancel." If you do not cancel, about a month later we'll send you 6 additional novels and bill you just $4.47 each in the U.S., or $4.99 each in Canada, plus 25¢ shipping & handling per book and applicable taxes if any.* That's the complete price and — compared to cover prices of $5.25 each in the U.S. and $6.25 each in Canada—it's quite a bargain! You may cancel at any time, but if you choose to continue, every month we'll send you 6 more books, which you may either purchase at the discount price or return to us and cancel your subscription.

*Terms and prices subject to change without notice. Sales tax applicable in N.Y. Canadian residents will be charged applicable provincial taxes and GST.

If offer card is missing write to: Harlequin Reader Service, 3010 Walden Ave., P.O. Box 1867, Buffalo, NY 14240-1867

BUSINESS REPLY MAIL
FIRST-CLASS MAIL   PERMIT NO. 717-003   BUFFALO, NY

POSTAGE WILL BE PAID BY ADDRESSEE

HARLEQUIN READER SERVICE
3010 WALDEN AVE
PO BOX 1867
BUFFALO NY 14240-9952

NO POSTAGE
NECESSARY
IF MAILED
IN THE
UNITED STATES

self.'' She laughed, a short harsh sound. ''I came home from school to quite a mess that day.''

''Ah God, Katie, that's a terrible thing.'' Annie stared at her, clearly appalled.

She met Annie's eyes for a moment, then looked away before she started bawling at the sympathy she saw there. ''The thing is, I was always hearing my father tell this story of how he met my mother at a faculty party. She'd walked into the room and he'd looked up, stunned by her beauty. 'Who is that black-haired woman?' he asked another professor. Then he predicted that he would marry her. It was love at first sight, he said.''

Annie clicked her tongue.

''I mean, it's pretty ironic, considering he spent most of their married life cheating on her. He said he couldn't make my fifth birthday because he had to teach a seminar. And then, just before she died, my mom told me, she'd found a motel receipt for that date. He'd apparently managed to score with his teaching assistant. By the time he actually walked out on my mom, I'd learned not to believe a word he told me.''

''Well, you wouldn't, would you?'' Annie reached over and patted her hand. ''But not all men are that way. You'll see. You just haven't met the right one.''

Kate looked at her. ''That's what Niall said.''

Annie's mouth tightened. ''Sure, Niall Maguire would know all about not being the right one,'' she said darkly. She poured more tea into Kate's cup. ''Have you never been in love at all then, Katie?''

''Not really. I don't know, I think I'm so scared of the same thing happening to me, that I put up road-blocks when guys get close...'' The tears started up again with a vengeance, dripping off her nose and chin. She swiped at them with the back of her hand. "Sometimes, though, I feel so lonely and empty. I *want* to let someone in, I just can't seem to do it."

"I think it's like jumping into the water, Katie. You know it's going to be cold and, God forbid, you might even drown, but you probably won't. You just have to take the risk. And if it was anyone but Niall Maguire, I'd tell you to go and talk things over, clear the air and just have a bit of fun. Life is so short. Every day you don't do your best to enjoy is like a present you haven't opened."

"But you don't think Niall's the one for me?"

"I don't. I'd say you're courting trouble with that man."

Kate sighed. "You're probably right. I need to focus on the article, and Niall would definitely complicate things." She shook her head. "You want to know the really irritating part about all this? I was so distracted by the chemistry stuff, I didn't even take my notebook."

Annie grinned knowingly. "Sure, he was counting on that, Katie. He knew quite well what he was doing when he asked you up there." She got up from the table, gave Kate's shoulder a squeeze. "I'll tell you what," she said. "Tomorrow night, I'll have Hughie over for supper. It'll be nice for the two of you to get to know one another. Hughie's a bit of a lonely soul."

Annie hadn't added the word *too,* Kate reflected, but she might as well have done.

"ALL I CAN SAY is the two of you got friendly very quickly." Sharon followed Niall out of the kitchen.

"What was she doing? A little research into your mouth?"

"Look, Sharon, if there's nothing else, I've got some work to do." He picked up the photos he'd shown to Kate. "By the way, the frames and canvases are all yours. Take whatever else you want from the gallery. I'll talk to the solicitor tomorrow and have everything written up."

"So." She watched his face. "We've moved on already, have we?"

He said nothing.

"I remember how it was with us at first. You could hardly wait until we were alone, could you?" She grabbed his arm. "But she'll learn, this new girl. Just as I did. She'll start poking around, asking questions, and that's when you'll move on to someone else until *she* starts poking around in your head.

"You know what you are?" She grabbed the pictures from his hand and threw them onto the table. "You're like one of these. Take this one—or this one of Elizabeth. Sure, it's a lovely image, isn't it? Lots of character on that face, look at it. Aren't you just intrigued? Don't you just wonder what's going on in her head. Sure you do. Just as this girl tonight probably did when she looked at you. Well, I could save her the trouble. She might as well ask the bloody picture."

He stood at the window, looking out at the dark night. In the windowpane, he could see his own reflection. Behind him, Sharon, prowling the room. He turned to look at her. "Look, it's late and I've got a long day tomorrow."

"I have a confession to make. Those letters I gave

you the other night, the ones you wrote to Moruadh. I did read one of them.''

''Sharon.'' He covered his eyes with both hands, dragged them down over his face. ''Please.''

''All those calls from her in Paris last year, all your trips over there. A bit more than simple visits, weren't they? You were cleaning up after her.'' Sharon's face flushed. ''Sure, a spoiled, selfish girl who wanted only to have her own way and to hell with your life. It was always Moruadh first, wasn't it?''

''That's enough, Sharon.''

''It was Moruadh who really came between us.'' She laughed. ''You never stopped feeling responsible for her, did you? Even after she'd slept with every—''

''I said that's enough.'' He caught her arm. ''Look, if you have any feelings for me at all, I'm asking you to forget whatever you read in that letter. We've all our reasons for behaving the way we do. Sometimes they turn out not to be the best ones, but then it's too late.'' He stopped. ''I'm making a mess of saying this, but leave it alone, please. There's a lot of pain you're tromping around in.''

''I'm sorry.'' She touched his arm. ''I should know better than to ask whether I can help, but I'll ask anyway.''

''You can't, but I'll tell you this. Your words didn't fall entirely on deaf ears. Maybe it's time to unlock the gates. I just have to find the key.''

She smiled. ''They say there are three keys that unlock thoughts. Drunkenness, trust and love. And if that little redhead is the one to do it, I'll scratch her eyes out.''

''Don't.'' He smiled back at her. ''She's a fine person. It's the issues of trust we both have to work out.''

KATE STOOD in the shower the following morning, arguing with herself. She'd hardly slept and she definitely had no appetite for one of Annie's huge breakfasts, nor did she want to face her. Last night, Annie's advice about forgetting Niall had made sense. But this morning, all Kate wanted to do was head out across the cliffs, look down the footpath and see him walking toward her.

She wanted to see his face again. To feel his arms around her again. To hear him say her name. She tried to conjure up the cynic, but for once the voice was silent.

Water sluiced over her body, and she pictured Niall. Long dark overcoat flapping in the wind, relaxed, loose-limbed, as though he'd spent most of his life striding across fields, a dog at his side. Not that she couldn't lead a rewarding, productive life without a man, she could, but, God, the thought of coming home every day to someone she loved, to someone who loved her.

She soaped her breasts. Bubbles encircled her nipples, trickled down her stomach and thighs. To love with no holds barred and to be loved in return. To fall asleep with his arms around her. To wake next to his face on the pillow. To do all those mundane, couple things. Buy groceries together, rent a movie, plan a vacation. The hand with the sponge paused on her breast. Have children.

But where would they live? He'd said he could never leave Ireland. Could she really be happy in Cragg's Head? She imagined herself, married to Niall, living in Ireland. Rattling around a medieval castle with animal heads on the wall and ghosts in the bedroom? Would she feel a little homesick after a while?

Start missing people? She grabbed a bottle of shampoo from the bathtub, lathered her hair and tried to think of who she would miss.

Ned and his family, of course, but she was kind of peripheral to their lives and she hadn't spoken to her father for more than a year. And there would be the children, of course. Gray-eyed children with red hair. Or maybe green-eyed children with dark hair. Maybe one of each.

Oh, stop. The cynic finally spoke up. *Let's not even consider the fact that you know nothing about this guy and you're already moving in. Let's not even imagine how you'd hoot if you met him in Santa Monica and he started yammering on about destiny. Let's look at the real issue here.*

You're daydreaming about a guy who may have murdered his wife.

"ABSOLUTELY NO DOUBT in my mind," the musician said. "Niall Maguire pushed Moruadh down the cliffs."

Kate blinked. After Rose Boland's reassurances about Niall's innocence, she'd started hoping that maybe all the speculation would turn out to be village gossip that no one outside of Cragg's Head really gave any credence to. But this was a guy from Dublin, who used to play in clubs with Moruadh, pretty much echoing what everyone in Cragg's Head, from Annie to Hugh Fitzpatrick, believed.

"Between the two of us, Moruadh played around a bit." The fiddle player drank some beer. "I never could understand why she married Maguire anyway. Far too lively for him, she was. Money, no doubt. It'd have to be."

Kate made a note. Behind them, half a dozen men, seated on wooden chairs, played fiddles, bottles of Guinness at their feet. "But Moruadh must have been doing okay financially," she reasoned. "Surely there was more to it than just money."

"Ah well…" The man she'd come to interview winked. "As I said, she was a lively girl. Took her out a time or two myself. Before she married him and…" He grinned. "A time or two after as well."

"Was she ever in love with Maguire, do you think?"

He laughed. "Ach, I doubt that Moruadh knew the meaning of love. She was like a child. Whatever was set before her eyes was what she wanted at that moment."

Kate glanced across the road at a throng of school-girl dancers in green tartan dresses. Flags of green, white and orange strung from wall to wall fluttered in a gentle breeze. Ballincross, the neighboring village where she'd come to do the interview, was holding its music festival. She'd caught the fiddle player between sets.

"It was a bit of a one-sided affair if you ask me," he said.

"How d'you mean?"

"I remember years ago, when Moruadh first started out, we were playing at a pub in Galway." He laughed. "Mostly doing 'Danny Boy' and 'Mountains of Mourne' for the tourists. He would come in almost every night. Just sit quietly at the back of the room, eyes only for her."

She thought of what Hugh Fitzpatrick had told her about Moruadh resenting Niall's intrusion into her life. Yet that seemed to contradict the roommate's assertion that it was Moruadh who had sought Niall out.

"I think she got tired of him." Chin resting lightly on the top of the fiddle, he looked across the street at a man who had broken into an impromptu performance on a flute. The notes lingered in the air. "I'm sure it was fine enough at first, when she was playing the clubs around Galway, but when things started picking up…" He shrugged. "She was after more, it seemed."

Kate looked down at the notebook, opened on her lap. She hesitated, mentally framing a question.

"So, all the talk about how she died? What do you think about that?"

"They say it was an accident."

"Is that what you believe?"

"Ah God, that's a hard one." He looked out at the crowd for a moment. "Moruadh was a very high-spirited girl and…" He hesitated. "Well, she'd definitely an eye for a good-looking fellow and I've no doubt it didn't set well with him."

"You mean he was jealous of her?"

"Sure, Niall Maguire's not a man who gives away his feelings, so you wouldn't know by looking at him, but that's the feeling I had. He'd had enough of her running around, making a fool of him."

"And what?" Kate felt a sad inevitability. "You think he pushed her in a fit of jealousy?"

"That's my take on it."

ON THE WAY BACK to Cragg's Head to meet Niall, Kate got lost. Through the windshield, she peered at the row of small cottages. Had she seen them earlier? According to her directions, she should be back in the village, but something didn't look right. Either she'd taken a wrong turn, or had fallen victim to the infamous signpost twisting. A man standing outside one of the houses waved as she passed and she slowed the car and backed up next to him.

"Hi." She smiled. "Can you tell me how I get to Cragg's Head?"

He leaned into her car window, his eyes on the map at her side and appeared to give the question great thought.

"Cragg's Head, is it?"

"Right."

"It's not around here."

"You're kidding." She showed him the map. "I didn't think I was that off. How far is it from here?"

Pulling at his earlobe, he thought for a minute, appearing perplexed by the dilemma her question presented.

"Well, I wouldn't start from here," he began, then interrupted himself. "See there's a wee wudden brudge... Ah, no, the road is closed up, you see. With all the rain. It's all bog holes." Another pause. "Of course, you could go on up a bit and go left where the road turns. There's a bit of a sign, you'll see just down from there. Not much, mind, but if you go left there, you can't miss it."

Kate thanked him and drove on, shaking her head. Exactly two miles down the road, no wee wudden brudge in evidence, she found herself on the road leading into Cragg's Head. He could have just pointed directly. But then, this was Ireland. Nothing was straightforward.

CHAPTER NINE

NIALL SAT in the car looking out at the harbor. Or what he could see of the harbor through the fog. An hour ago, he'd driven past the Pot o' Gold and he'd been driving around ever since. Up and down the high street and Market Street, down by St. Joseph's, along the seafront, past the Pot o' Gold again.

He had to see Kate. It was like a fever burning in his brain.

He listened to a tin can clatter past the car. This wasn't like him. He could block anything out when he needed to. Banish those thoughts he didn't want to dwell upon. Kate would not be banished. She stayed in his brain. Talking, laughing, demanding his attention.

Another tin rolled by. Probably from the Travelers' camp up the hill. The village regularly got into an uproar over one transgression or another committed by the Travelers. Gypsies or tinkers, as they were still called by a lot of old-timers. Lawless vagabonds, the grumbling went. Niall had been out at a camp a couple of weeks ago on a photo shoot. A small girl with a mop of curly red hair had tried to convince him to have his fortune read. He'd declined.

Out on the water, the fog muted the painted hulls of the fishing boats. Much farther out, but invisible in the fog, a cluster of small islands, some little more than rocks, strung out like the beads of a necklace. Legend had it that one of the islands in the chain had disappeared in a dense fog and was never seen again. Moruadh had written a song about it. "Gossamer Island," it was called. It involved, naturally, star-crossed lovers. The girl poisoned herself with hemlock. Grief-stricken, her lover walked into the sea and drowned.

Niall's thoughts turned to Kate. What he couldn't be sure of was her true motivation. Up there on the cliffs, of course, there'd been no doubt. But later, after he'd told her his name, he couldn't help wondering. His blathering on about destiny. Would it wind up in print? *Eccentric widower bares his soul.* Discerning a woman's real agenda had never been his strong suit. None of which lessened his desire to see her again.

And then, as though he'd summoned her, she appeared.

She stood at the sea rail, her back to him, red hair billowing around her shoulders. He blinked, for a moment not believing she wasn't just a figment of his imagination. But it was Kate. In the same green anorak she'd been wearing when they met on the cliffs. He was out of the car in an instant.

"Kate," he said over her shoulder, "I was just sitting here in my car thinking that if I tried hard enough, I could conjure you up. It worked."

Kate turned, her eyes wide. Then she smiled, a polite formal smile. A smile that suggested that today she wore the reporter's hat. "Niall. Hi. How odd, I was just thinking about you, too."

"May I ask *what* you were thinking?"

"You may," she said. "Actually, I just drove back from Ballincross where this musician who used to tour with Moruadh seems to think you pushed her down the cliffs.''

He stared at her, stunned into silence. ''I have to keep telling myself,'' he said a few seconds later, ''that you're in Ireland for a reason.''

''I'm sorry but that's true.'' She frowned. ''And even if I were just here on vacation, I'd still be a little disconcerted to know there are people who think you murdered your wife. I want to believe you, but you're not exactly forthcoming.''

''If I said let's find somewhere quiet, and get to know each other over a pint or two and you said yes, would it mean that you wanted to be with me, or that you wanted material for your story?''

A strand of hair blew across her face and she brushed it away before she answered. ''The truth?''

''I'll be brave.''

She hunched her shoulders against the cold. ''Months from now, when you probably won't even remember my name, I'll still have bills to pay, so it is kind of important that I turn in a decent article. You're pretty pivotal to getting the information I need.''

''Months from now, I don't think I'll have any difficulty at all remembering your name,'' he said. ''But I understand your position.''

''Good.'' A moment passed. ''But on the other hand…''

''A beer sounds like a good idea?''

''That and the getting-to-know-each-other part.'' She grinned. ''Purely for personal reasons, of course.''

''YOU KNOW SOMETHING?'' Kate asked a little later as they nursed their beers. ''I've changed my opinion about you so many times in the last few days, I'm getting dizzy. All the talk about you being a womanizer, for instance.'' She pointed in the direction of a well-endowed waitress with a low-cut Lycra top. ''Every guy in the place has been eyeing her boobs and you haven't looked once.''

He laughed. ''I'm a bit shortsighted. Where is she? Point her out.''

''No way. I love having a man's undivided attention.''

''Well, you've got mine.'' He glanced around the bar which, ten minutes earlier, had been empty, but was now filling up. ''Although this lot is giving you some competition.''

Kate grinned and leaned into him slightly, enjoying the contact even through layers of clothes. They'd found a spot in one corner and they stood, backs against the wall, holding pints of Guinness, watching the action.

He'd told her about growing up on the family estate. An only child who spent much of his time with the children of the housekeeper and gardener, Hugh Fitzpatrick and Moruadh. Was tutored with them until he was sent away to boarding school. She heard no animosity when he mentioned Fitzpatrick, which, perhaps, wasn't surprising since Niall hadn't been the one forced to wear castoffs. They hadn't talked about his adult relationship with Moruadh, and Kate didn't push it. In fact, she kept forgetting her reporter's hat. She liked this guy. *A lot.*

''About this womanizing reputation I seem to have acquired,'' he said.

She turned her head to look at him. ''Yes?''

"It's absolutely true. Every word of it. A different woman every night. Sometimes two, or even three in one night. I can't help it, it's a terrible sickness I have."

"Yeah." Smiling, she drank some beer. "I kind of figured that."

"As you might imagine, my work often involves taking shots of models. I've dated a few of them, but nothing serious. And then there was Sharon who you met the other night and that's about it."

"Listen, Niall. You don't have to do this. I mean you don't owe me any explanation."

He nodded, his face suddenly serious. "It's important to me that you don't get the wrong impression."

"It's funny you should say that. You don't want me to get the wrong impression and yet you can live with everyone seeming to believe you murdered your wife?"

A few moments passed, and she thought he wasn't going to answer.

"I've been accused of living in my head," he said finally. "Often to the exclusion of people around me. A woman I know once told me that I only ask questions to get people talking so that I can escape to my own thoughts." He swirled the beer in his glass. "It's a protective thing, I suppose."

"So you can just shut out all the talk, is that what you're saying?"

"Right. I'm aware of the gossip, of course, but in a distant, unfocused sort of way that doesn't really touch me."

"Have you always been this way?"

"I think it started with my father. He had a knack

for cruelty." He set his beer down on the bar. "Have you had enough of this place yet?"

She nodded. Outside in the cool dark night, Niall took her hand and they walked through the narrow streets to the harbor where she'd met him. Whatever doubts remained were like tiny shoots, withered by the warmth of his hand in hers and, she had to admit it, by the fact that she just plain liked him and *wanted* to believe whatever he told her. At the door of her car, he caught the ends of her scarf.

"I felt awful when you left last night," he said. "It had been so good. Seeing you again, making supper together."

"We didn't do a very good job with the bouillabaisse, though, huh?"

"We could try again," he said, moving closer. "Want to?"

She nodded. "Yeah," she said softly. "Let's."

And then he kissed her, and it was so magical to be standing in the cool foggy Irish air, with the sound of water lapping and his arms around her and mist beading on their skin and hair, that nothing else really mattered. And they kept on kissing, trading places after a while so that she was leaning back across the car with Niall almost lying on top of her, kissing so hard she felt his teeth against her lips.

"You have far too many clothes on," he whispered. "I'm convinced there's a body under this padding and I'm determined to find it."

"You're definitely headed in the right direction." He'd found the skin beneath the layers needed to keep out the Irish weather, and worked his way up to her left breast. With his thumb and forefinger, he very gently squeezed her nipple. They both felt the spasm that shuddered through her body.

He smiled at her.

"You are very wicked." Arms locked around his neck. Jelly legs, her heart a drum gone berserk. "I like wicked."

"Good." He flattened his palm into the waistband of her jeans and down over her stomach. A tight squeeze, but easier once he'd unfastened the top button and easier still with the zipper down.

"Niall. What if someone sees?"

"It's pitch-dark and quieter than a tomb."

"I guess." Her brain wasn't thrilled with the metaphor, but her body was indisputably in charge and doing all it could do to help his fingers slide under the crotch of her panties and up inside her and... "Oh my God." She dug her chin harder into his shoulder, felt the sheepskin against her face. "Oh..." she said again.

"More?"

"Yeah."

He removed his hand, made a halfhearted attempt at zipping up her jeans and kissed her on the nose. "I've had enough of all these clothes, but I think Brigid Riley might hear about it if we disrobed right here."

"Yeah, and it's way too cold," she said.

"So I see no alternative but to take you up to the castle."

"Absolutely no alternative." Weak with anticipation, she smiled at him. "Take me to the bedchamber."

Halfway up the hill to the castle, she remembered Annie's supper.

THEY WERE ALL SEATED around the dining table when she walked in. Annie and Patrick, Rory and Caitlin. And next to the place that had been set for her, Hugh Fitzpatrick. All looked up expectantly when she walked in. Her mouth felt bruised, her bra a little skewed, and for one horrifying moment she couldn't remember whether she'd finished zipping up her jeans. *Hey, guys, look at me. I've been making out with Niall Maguire.*

"We were about to call out the Gardai." Annie disappeared into the kitchen, then returned with a covered dish. "Sit down, Katie. Where were you, love? I thought you were coming straight back here from Ballincross."

"Mam, that's her business." Caitlin shot her mother a disapproving look and winked at Kate. Her hair had been cropped even shorter and newly dyed a bright orange. "As long as she was having fun. Right, Katie?"

"Listen you guys, I am really sorry. I went down to the harbor to think things over and then…" God, she did not want to bring up Niall's name. "I just completely forgot about supper. I apologize, Annie, for keeping you waiting. It was just that—"

"Well, not to worry," Annie helped her off with the parka. "Sit down, love. Next to Hughie," she said with a smile. "The two of you can natter about writing. Now help yourself to some ham, Katie. And there's soda bread I just made. More ham for you, Hughie?"

Kate slipped into her seat next to Hugh. His hair looked newly washed and he'd tied it back in a neat ponytail. He wore black dress pants and a safari jacket with a black silk scarf tucked into the neck. She felt

a stab of guilt. Something told her he'd dressed carefully for the evening. Perfecting his wardrobe, while
she'd caroused with Niall. His chair was so close that
when she reached past him for bread, her arm brushed
his.

"Sorry." She withdrew her hand. "Boardinghouse
reach."

"Not at all." He leaned slightly in her direction.
"Work progressing well?" he asked in a low voice.

"Not bad." She glanced over at Annie who was
hovering over Rory, urging food on him. Under the
table, Hugh's leg brushed hers. *This was going to be
a long evening.*

"Have you met Maguire yet?"

"I have." She drank some water.

"And?"

Irritated, she turned to look directly at him. "And
what?"

"Is he being helpful?"

"Not particularly," she replied truthfully.

"And have you been able to resist his boyish
charms?"

Kate speared a slice of tomato. "Annie, these are
fantastic tomatoes," she said in a voice that carried
over all the others around the table. "A hundred times
better than anything we get in California." Everyone
stopped talking to look at her. She smiled. "Really
delicious."

"Well, help yourself to all you want, love." Annie
beamed. An expectant hush settled, as though the real
show was about to begin. A *loooong* evening. Kate
buttered some bread and tried to think of something
to say. Moruadh, as a topic, would set Hugh off on a
Niall hate fest. Niall was obviously off-limits. Annie

cleared her throat. Caitlin whispered in Rory's ear.
Hugh's thigh moved suspiciously close to hers.

"No word from Elizabeth yet?" Dumb question,
she realized. If they'd heard anything, she'd know
about it, but the spotlight was uncomfortable. "It's
been, what? Five days now?"

"She'll turn up," Rory said quickly.

"Of course she will," Caitlin agreed. "Doesn't she
always?"

Hugh piled lettuce and tomato on his plate. "Still,
it's a bit funny that she hasn't phoned."

"There's nothing funny about it." Rory shot Hugh
a thunderous look. "It's the kind of girl she is."

"Well, you'd know that better than I would,"
Hugh said.

Kate watched Rory's face darken. The atmosphere
was suddenly tense and she wondered if Hugh knew
more than he was letting on.

Patrick, in an obvious attempt to change the subject, mentioned the music festival in Ballincross. Kate
tuned out. Thoughts of Niall drifted in. His face, his
voice. The things he'd told her. His openness. *Openness?* the cynic inquired. *How much more do you really know about his relationship with Moruadh? And
what about Elizabeth? What about the little rendez-
vous they were supposed to have had Monday night?
What about the picture he took of her? How come
you didn't ask about all that?*

"Katie's woolgathering." Annie smiled at her
across the table. "Where are you, love?"

"Sorry." Kate shook her head. "Just drifting. No
reflection on the company."

"I was asking what you think of Irish music," Patrick said. "I'm partial to the Saw Doctors myself.

Ever heard them? They're a local group, from Tuam, not far from here. Making it big in Europe, they are.''

''I'll have to check them out,'' she said. ''Maybe I'll pick up a CD.''

''The thing with Elizabeth is she has no thoughts in her head for anything but having a good time.'' Rory stuck his finger in his collar. ''No concern for who might be worrying about her. She does it all the time.''

Beautiful and very naive, Niall had said. *A bit of a wild girl.* Kate took a sip of water and set the glass down too hard. Water splashed onto the tablecloth. She looked up to see Annie watching, an anxious smile fluttering around her mouth.

''When was the last time?'' Hugh leaned forward slightly to address Rory. ''Just wondering. Months? Weeks?''

''How would I remember that?'' Rory threw down the knife he'd been using to smear mustard on a slice of ham. The clang of metal against china hung in the air for a moment. ''What is this, a bloody inquisition?''

''Rory.'' Caitlin put her hand on his arm. ''What's the matter with you? Hughie just asked a simple question.'' She smiled at Hugh. ''He's a bit tense tonight. Problems down at the station.''

''Leave off, Caitlin.'' Rory pushed his chair away from the table and stood. ''I don't need you fighting my battles for me.''

''Something in the air, if you ask me.'' Annie started to clear the dinner dishes. ''Everyone seems a bit on edge.'' She put a restraining hand on Kate's arm. ''No, you leave those, Katie. Go have a little chat with Hugh.''

"I SUSPECT RORY KNOWS more about Elizabeth's disappearance than he's letting on," Hugh told Kate later that evening. "He has a bit of a problem with the bottle. Drinks to the point where he doesn't remember much at all the next day."

Kate said nothing. Everybody else had disappeared to different parts of the house. A calculated move by Annie, she suspected, to leave her alone with Hugh. They were sitting out on the back steps where she'd gone to escape the overheated house and sort out her thoughts. Hugh had followed. Smoke from his cigarette drifted up into the night.

Irritated, Kate flapped at the air. She didn't want to deal with Hugh's company, his cigarette smoke or, no fault of Hugh's, the niggling question about Niall and Elizabeth. Why *hadn't* she just asked him?

"The thing is, Rory was with Elizabeth on Monday, a friend of mine saw them together in Galway, and I saw her later in his car up on the cliffs. My guess is they'd had more than a few drinks together and then something happened. Of course, he has no recollection of what it was."

Kate pulled up the collar of her parka. The cold had started to seep through and her nose felt numb. "Something happened? You don't mean he did something to her?"

"No, no." Fitzpatrick waved the suggestion away. "Rory hasn't got it in him for anything like that. No, I'm speculating that she left, for some reason or another, and has either just neglected to call, or…"

"Or?"

"She met up with someone who had more sinister motives." He ground out the cigarette with his heel. "Maguire comes to mind, of course," he said after a moment. "She was apparently supposed to meet him."

Simmering irritation ignited into anger. "Excuse me for saying so, Hugh, but you're hardly an objective party here." *And you are?* the cynic inquired. Kate pushed on, "I don't know exactly what happened between the two of you, but maybe it's time to move on."

"Annie thinks we're a good couple," he said. "She told me that. She'd like to see the two of us together."

She looked at him. "What exactly does that have to do with what I just said."

"Maybe you're what I need to move on with my life," he said. "Someone to replace Moruadh." He caught her hand. "I'm very attracted to you, Kate. Give me a chance, would you?"

"Hugh." She pulled her hand away. "This is embarrassing. I'm really not—"

"You have a boyfriend in California?"

"Kind of." She wanted to spare his feelings. "Not only that, but I'll be gone in a few days, so there's not much point in—"

Suddenly his arm was around her shoulders in an awkward embrace, and his mouth was grinding into hers. She tasted smoke and beer. "For God's sake—" She broke away, pulled herself up off the steps and glared at him. "What was all that about?"

"It's Maguire, isn't it?" He remained seated on the steps, looking up at her. "I don't stand a chance, do I?"

THAT NIGHT, she dreamed Niall tried to kill her. They were making love, the sound of water all around them. His body over hers, her legs locked around him, her hips moving under him. Faster and faster they moved in a growing frenzy until she cried out. Suddenly she was staring into his eyes, and his hands were locked around her throat as he sent her tumbling down in the roaring abyss of ocean and rocks, and then Annie was there saying, "I told you not to trust him."

She woke the next morning to the sound of the phone ringing somewhere in the house. Moments later, Annie knocked on her door.

"Mr. Maguire for you." Annie handed her the phone, her face stiff with disapproval. "If you'll keep it short, I'd appreciate it. I'm expecting my brother to call with news about Elizabeth. They've got someone out looking for her."

Kate rubbed sleep from her eyes, fluffed up her pillow-flattened hair as though Niall could actually see her. "Want me to have him call back?"

"No, no, that's all right." Annie turned to leave. "I'll have your breakfast waiting when you're through," she said, and closed the door behind her.

"I had the distinct feeling Annie was not at all pleased to hear from me," Niall said.

"I know." Kate sank back into the pillows, the phone cradled between her ear and shoulder, memories of the nightmare erased by Niall's voice. And in the morning light, last night's agonizing over his possible involvement with Elizabeth seemed overwrought. Probably how rumors got started, she thought. An innocuous incident fanned into flame by a fevered imagination. All she had to do was ask him. Which she would soon.

"Annie is convinced Hugh and I are destined for

each other,'' she said. ''Hugh's thinking is along similar lines.'' She decided not to mention the attempted kiss. ''You're kind of messing things up.''

''Am I?''

''Yeah.'' She could picture his face as he spoke. That hint of a smile. *God, she had it bad.* *Ask him about Elizabeth,* the cynic urged.

''Should I back out?'' he asked.

Her stomach knotted ever so slightly. ''Would you do it that easily?''

''Not without a duel to the death.''

''I'm not interested in Hugh,'' she said. ''If you're concerned.''

''It wouldn't be the first time he and I've been in competition over a woman. While I was off at university, pining away for Moruadh, she was back here taking moonlight walks along the beach with Hugh.''

Uh-oh. Kate shifted the receiver to her other ear. *Time to don her reporter's hat.* Hadn't Hugh accused Niall of stealing Moruadh away from him? She'd have to check her notes. Right now, Moruadh's long-ago relationship with Niall didn't interest her nearly as much as her own brand-new one with him. The cynic spoke up. *New what, exactly? Not relationship, surely.*

''Hello?'' Niall said. ''Did you nod off?''

''Nope.'' She sat up in bed. ''Wide-awake.''

''I wondered if you'd like to go to Kerry with me. I have a photo shoot there this afternoon. I'll need to stay overnight. There's a very quaint B&B.'' A pause. ''Of course, we'd have separate rooms.''

''Oh, of course.'' The smile returned, stretched from ear to ear. Would she like to go to Kerry with him? Stay in a quaint hotel? *Make love all night.* Nah, didn't sound like much fun. Reality check. There were interviews she couldn't cancel. She knew that, even before she reached for her appointment book to confirm. "I don't think I can. Today I'm interviewing a professor who tutored Moruadh and tomorrow I'm having lunch in Galway."

"Trenellen," he said. "That's the professor's name. He gave Moruadh piano lessons. Actually, he tried to work with me, too, but he gave up in disgust. I'm absolutely tone-deaf. Where are you going for lunch?"

"Drummond House. Do you know it?"

"It's on Quay Street. Nice place. Built by a marquis during the potato famine. Sensitive man that one, kept himself busy trekking in chandeliers while the peasants were leaving the country in droves."

Kate smiled and sank back against the pillow again.

"I'll be back tomorrow evening," he said. "Would you be free then? Bouillabaise? Bedchamber? Anything?"

"All of it," she said.

"Right, then," he said. "See you tomorrow. Oh, and Kate, Trenellen's a little dotty. Just don't get him talking about the elf king."

"Elf king?"

"You'll see."

Still smiling, Kate hung up the phone. And remembered she hadn't asked him about Elizabeth.

CHAPTER TEN

IT DIDN'T TAKE Kate long to see that Niall's assessment of Trenellen was correct. Though charming and courtly, the old man was definitely dotty. His head, smooth, except for a fringe of white hair, sloped steeply like a hard-boiled egg, and his eyes were a pale, guileless blue. During the brief periods of lucidity that shimmered through his rambling discourse like sunshine through the clouds, there were small but revealing glimpses into the young Moruadh's life. Her gift—in the Celtic tradition of storytelling—had been apparent at an early age, he said.

"Have you heard the word *seanachai?*" he inquired. Then, without waiting for Kate's reply, went on to explain. "It was the old men mostly who would go from house to house telling the stories. And these were passed down from one generation to the next, you see. That was how Moruadh started, making up her little stories that eventually she set to music."

Kate made some notes, asked a few more questions and was ready to ask about Moruadh's childhood disposition, although she didn't have high hopes of an informative response, when the housekeeper appeared with a tea tray. The professor watched as she set the tray down on a small table by the fireplace and quietly left. Smiling, he pushed the teapot toward Kate, then delicately lifted the edge of one of the sandwiches.

"Ah sure, and I hope it's not potted prawn." His head trembled slightly. "She knows I can't stand that." He took a tentative nibble and seemed to find it to his liking.

Kate eyed the plate of tiny sandwiches and the small, neatly sliced, chocolate cake and estimated that, left to her own devices, she could polish it all off in five minutes flat. Already, she was beginning to regret turning down Annie's breakfast although it probably had been a good idea. That morning, for the first time in her life, she'd had difficulty zipping her jeans. *And tomorrow, in the bedchamber, Niall would see her naked.*

She forced her thoughts back to the professor and nibbled politely. As he ate, he discussed the complicated domestic relationship between the sun goddess and the elf king Midir who had apparently been cuckolded by the eastern horse king of Tara.

The elf king. She bit back a smile, remembering Niall's warning. God, the man kept invading her thoughts. Again, she dragged her attention back to the professor. How soon could she bring the session to a halt without offending him? Not long, as it turned out. In the middle of a riveting account of the sea god Etar's marriage to the virgin Aine, Trenellen fell asleep.

Just when the tale was getting good, too. Another minute or so and they'd have consummated the act. Kate closed her notebook and stood, not sure whether to rouse him or quietly leave. As she tried to decide, the housekeeper appeared in the doorway.

"He seems to have nodded off," Kate said. "I think I have all I need, though, so I'll just go. If you could thank him for me."

"Writing about Moruadh, are you?" The house-keeper bent to pick up the tray. "I worked as a maid for the Maguires for nearly twenty years. Old Maguire was a right terror." She shook her head. "If there's anything I can tell you…"

"Do you have a few minutes right now?"

"I do. If you don't mind my getting on with things while I talk."

With her hip, she pushed open the door, and Kate followed her down a narrow hallway into a large kitchen, cheery with yellow gingham curtains. She sat down at a small table and opened her notebook. Off in one corner, a green parakeet in a cage carried on a noisy exchange with its reflection.

"I've got to get a move on with his supper," the housekeeper said. "As soon as he wakes, he'll be wanting food." She looked over her shoulder at Kate. "When they're that age, food is the one thing in life that matters. Very finicky he can be about it, too."

Kate smiled sympathetically.

"Sure, the old man was the same way, too. Niall's father," the housekeeper added. "Nothing he wouldn't complain about. Gave young Niall a hard time of it, he did."

"How do you mean?"

"Well, of course, he never had any room for the boy to start with." She opened a pantry door and took a string bag of vegetables from the shelf. "Likes a few parsnips with his roast chicken, he does." She emptied the bag into the sink. "Would you like another cup of tea, miss?"

"Oh, no, thank you." Kate flipped through her notebook for a blank page. "You were talking about the old man, Niall's father."

"Ah right. Well, as I said he was hard on the boy. Expected far too much of him, it always seemed to me. Ferocious temper he had on him, too," she said, scraping the parsnips as she talked. "I can well remember his voice roaring out from the library, tearing into the child for one thing or another, threatening to send him off to the orphanage."

"The orphanage?"

"Aye, well, it hadn't been an orphanage for some years, it was just a spooky old place that people still spoke of as the orphanage. It's been a number of things over the years, but about ten years back, Annie and Patrick Ryan bought it and turned it into a guest house. The Pot o' Gold, it's called these days."

"No kidding?" Kate scribbled a reminder to ask Annie about it. "I'm staying there."

"Ah well, it's a lovely place today, Annie Ryan's done wonders there. Back then, though, it'd strike terror in the heart of a child to walk past. The old man knew that. He would rant and rave, and young Niall would get a look on his face—hard to describe, really—as though his head was somewhere else entirely. I think the boy was a disappointment to Maguire. His nose always stuck in a book. Very drawn into himself. It irritated the old man that he couldn't get a rise out of him."

Kate watched her chop parsnip into small pieces. Niall had described his habit of mentally disappearing. Apparently, something he'd learned to do at an early age. Probably explained how he could live in a small village like Cragg's Head and be practically oblivious to all the gossip about him. Struck by a thought, Kate chewed the end of her pen. If you constructed an invisible wall to shut out the things you didn't want to deal with, could you remove it at will when you *wanted* to feel something? Like love. Caught up in the question, she realized the housekeeper had asked something.

"Sorry?"

"I said have you met Mr. Maguire?"

She felt her face go red. "Yes, I have actually."

The housekeeper glanced over at her. "Always very protective of Moruadh, he was," she said. "Lucky for the child. too, or she'd have no doubt gone to her coffin at an earlier age than she did. Very willful and spirited. A right little mischief-maker, that one. Her and the Fitzpatrick boy. I can't tell you the things those two would get up to. Young Niall would usually end up taking the blame. Moruadh could twist him around her little finger."

Kate wrote "manipulative" in her notebook. She had the weird feeling she was snooping, rather than gathering information for an article. Moruadh had become a scheming temptress who had callously broken Niall's heart. Journalistic objectivity was a distant memory.

As she was leaving, the professor made another appearance. He held a sheaf of papers in his hand and appeared revived by his nap.

"I have here some early examples of Moruadh's work." Bright blue eyes looked directly at Kate. "Would you like to see them?"

"I'd love to." She took the sheets of yellowed paper he held out to her.

"Read it aloud," he said.

She glanced at him, then down at the sheet in her hands.

"You don't see me through your far-off lens.
I'm a pebble washed up on your shore.
Random, scattered here or there.
Directionless, but can that be?
The salmon in the vast gray sea, swims home because
It was meant to be."

After she'd finished, Kate looked up at the professor. His fringe of white hair, backlit by the lamp, floated like a halo around his head. His smile was beatific. Angelic, Kate thought, looking at him. And then, as though he'd whispered in her ear, she heard Niall's voice that night at the castle. *"I have a sense that somehow it was meant to happen."*

AN OVERDOSE OF CELTIC mystery. Kate diagnosed her condition as she trudged down the lane from the professor's house. If you want to believe this destiny stuff, she told herself, you can find signs to support it. If you wanted to, you could find meaning in a laundry list.

Cold rain swept down, puddled the sides of the road with mucky brown water. She unfurled her umbrella, cursing her decision to walk to the professor's instead of taking the car. Although the sun had been shining when she left Annie's, she should have known better. Little in Ireland—especially the weather—was entirely predictable.

As she walked past muddy fields and isolated cottages, she tried not to imagine steamy scenes with Niall tomorrow night. Tried to focus instead on what she'd learned about Moruadh so far. Bits and pieces of a puzzle, but not really a complete picture. The bizarre coffin scene Rory McBride had described, details Niall had let slip that suggested a certain preoccupation with death.

She dodged a puddle. It was impossible to speculate on Moruadh's state of mind the day she died without bringing Niall into the picture. Equally impossible to believe that he was responsible for his wife's death. Suicide remained a possibility, but even that was now questionable. What woman would want to leave Niall by taking her own life? He could have dumped her of course, and brokenhearted, she'd jumped to her death. *And tell the world, I died for love.*

Or it was an accident. The wind-driven rain battering her umbrella, Kate walked on. At the edge of a field, she passed a small gray cottage. Scabrous cars and empty beer bottles littered the threadbare grass. A handwritten wooden sign read: Pleaze Do Not Run Over Childrun or Horses.

A sheet of newspaper fluttered across her line of vision and landed near a cluster of battered mobile homes. Voices and raucous laughter floated to her from across the field. Drawing closer, she saw three men clustered around a smoky campfire, seemingly oblivious to the weather. Nearby, two donkeys were tethered outside a painted wooden caravan, their long, coarse coats ruffled by the wind. A Travelers' camp, she guessed.

"Will y'gimme fifty pence, miss?" one man called out. "T'send me three sons to Trinity College?" Another burst of laughter broke from the crowd.

She ignored the men but stopped to pat a small black-and-white terrier that came running up to her. In an instant, she was surrounded by children who seemed to appear from every direction. Small hands tugged at her parka, her fingers, her legs. Childish voices entreated her for money.

She looked into the crowd of upturned faces and met the eyes of a girl of about eight or nine, freckle-faced with a mop of thick red hair, exactly the same color as her own. The child smiled at her, and Kate dug in her pocket, retrieved a bar of chocolate and broke it into several small pieces. She held out her hand, grinning as the kids jostled each other to get a piece.

"What's your name?" the red-haired girl asked around a mouthful of chocolate.

"Kate." The chocolate dispersed, she stuck the empty wrapper in her pocket and started walking. The girl kept pace beside her, thin cotton trousers stuffed into black rubber boots. She shot Kate a sideways glance.

"You here on holiday?"

"Yeah," Kate said. "Kind of."

"My mam'll tell your fortune." She waved in the direction of the trailers. "She's right over there."

"No, thanks," Kate said. Not that she believed in that sort of thing, but if there was bad news in her future, she didn't want to know.

"Ah, come on now." The girl ran over to the nearest mobile home and pulled open the front door. "My mam's in there waiting for you."

"Sorry, maybe another time." But as she stepped around a pink plastic flamingo someone had positioned to drink over a puddle, she saw the look of disappointment on the girl's face and relented. What the hell?

She picked her way across the muddy ground and

up the trailer's front steps. Maybe the woman's forecast would tie in with Niall's destiny prediction. *I see you both a year from now, holding hands in your Santa Monica condo. He is cooking bouillabaisse. You are pregnant. It is destiny.*

Inside the smoky, dimly lit room, a stout middle-aged woman sat at a wooden table, intent on trying to insert a straw crucifix into an empty whiskey bottle. Half a dozen completed bottles were lined up on the table. Souvenirs, Kate guessed, for sale to tourists.

The woman glanced up and motioned her inside. "Cross me palm."

Fishing a pound from her pocket, Kate sat down opposite the woman. The room was warm and heavy with the smells of stale cigarette smoke and cooked cabbage. A few feet away, a kettle set over a blue gas flame began to hiss. Something brushed against her legs, and Kate looked down into the amber eyes of an orange cat.

The woman reached across the table, touched the gold hoops at Kate's ears and pointed to the similar pair in her own lobes. Deep lines wreathed her brown leathery skin, bracketed eyes as blue as periwinkles. A small clay pipe was tucked behind her ear.

"'Tis a *dudeen*." The woman had seen Kate's eyes go to the pipe. She took Kate's hand in her own. "A bit of *auld Oireland*, isn't it?" She winked. "Sure, I hate the thing, but visitors like yourself, well, that's what they expect to see, isn't it?"

Kate watched as the woman examined her palm, tracing the lifeline with a long painted fingernail. It was true, she supposed. Tourists had certain expectations, regardless of reality. Like the college friend from Nebraska who'd visited one summer in Santa

Monica and expressed disappointment that she hadn't bumped into a single movie star at the supermarket.

"You've traveled over the water."

An easy enough guess, she thought. It would apply to any visitor to Ireland.

"There's a man. You might have met him, or you might not." The woman rubbed her forehead and closed her eyes. *"Far Liath,"* she said slowly, the words almost a chant. "He covers the land and sea with his mantle."

"Far Liath?" Kate looked at the woman. "What does that mean?"

"Far Liath is the gray man who obscures. With *Far Liath,* all is not as it appears." The gypsy eyed Kate for a moment. "Now, this I don't like saying, miss. Bad news," she added with a sly smile, "is not good for business." Then her expression sobered. "But I'm telling you as a warning. There's death around you. 'Tisn't here on your hand, but I sense it."

Kate swallowed. The faint smile, meant to show she wasn't taking any of it seriously, congealed. She moved to pull her hand away, but the gypsy's fingers held it tight.

"Beware of *Far Dorocha.*" Her eyes seemed to bore into Kate's. "Several have stood at the edge with him." Her voice had taken on the chantlike quality again. "Fewer have joined him on the homeward journey." Suddenly, she released Kate's hands and folded her arms across her chest. "The cards tell more," she said, her voice brisk now. "Will I do them for you?"

"No, that's okay." Kate shook her head. All the air seemed to have gone out of the room, and she could hardly breathe. The cat sidled against her leg. A child wailed somewhere. "I've got to go."

"There's no charge." The woman held out a pack of cards.

"I don't think so." Kate rose, then backed toward the door. "Thank you, though. Maybe some other time."

The woman nodded. *"Far Dorocha,"* she said again. "Mind yourself."

Outside, the clouds had darkened, and Kate heard a distant rumble of thunder. Once again, the children surrounded her, but this time she ignored their entreaties and hurried past the camp. With the woman's voice jangling in her brain, she picked up her pace as though she could somehow outdistance any lurking danger.

By the time she reached the road that led back into Cragg's Head, she was running. Five minutes later, still breathless, she let herself into the Pot o' Gold. She stood in the hall, trying to catch her breath. Embarrassed now by the irrational fear that had gripped her. *A fortune-teller,* the cynic scoffed. *You have definitely overdosed on Celtic intrigue.*

Then something odd struck her. The house was in darkness. By now, Annie always had all the lights on and the fire burning. Puzzled, Kate pushed open the sitting-room door. In the dim light from the window, she could barely make out someone sitting in the armchair where Patrick usually sat. As her eyes adjusted, she realized it was Annie.

"Annie?" She came into the room. "Is something wrong?"

"My brother Michael was just here. They've found Elizabeth's body at the bottom of Cragg's Head Leap."

CHAPTER ELEVEN

"I JUST CAN'T GET IT through my head," Annie told Kate the next morning. "Nothing seems real. It's like something you read about in the paper, but this isn't some girl in Dublin I've never heard of." She blew her nose into a tissue and dabbed her eyes. "Elizabeth sat in this kitchen, Katie. She slept in the bed upstairs. The very one you're sleeping in."

Kate leaned over to fill Annie's cup. They'd been up most of the night, sitting at the kitchen table drinking pot after pot of tea. From where she sat, Kate could see the pink-tinged morning light through the window. Daffodils bobbed in windowsill containers, their cheeriness somehow all wrong.

The Garda had found marks on Elizabeth's neck. The locket she always wore, gone. A struggle, apparently. Foul play was suspected. Kate poured more tea. The brown teapot wore a green-and-white woolen cozy, the kind of thing her grandmother used to knit with yarn left over from sweaters and scarves. On the wall hung a cross-stitched sampler in Gaelic. Roughly translated, Annie had told her, it said: Tell A Good Story, Tell A Lie, Or Get Out. Advice Niall Maguire should take to heart, Annie had muttered darkly.

The scene on the cliffs played like an endless video in Kate's brain. The two figures she'd seen. Niall's sudden appearance. Her stomach felt as if someone had punched it. She'd intended to ask him about Elizabeth when she saw him tonight. Promised herself she'd do it before she got distracted by chemistry. Now she wondered whether she should cancel the date. But how would Niall interpret that? And what about Rory? Time for him to clear up a few things, she decided.

As soon as she walked into the Gardai station, Kate knew she'd made a mistake. If Rory did know anything about Elizabeth's death, he was hardly likely to confess it to her here, surrounded by fellow Gardai all looking grim-faced and preoccupied.

"He's in the toilet," one of them said when Kate asked for Rory. "Where he's been much of the morning. I think he might have decided to take up residence." He called Rory's name and rattled on the doorknob. A moment later, Rory emerged. Sweat beaded his forehead and, as he came over to the counter to where she stood, Kate caught the faint, but unmistakable whiff of alcohol.

"Kate." He ran a hand through his hair. "You've heard the news then?"

She nodded and then the front door opened. Annie's brother, Sergeant Michael Riordan, walked in. He wore a heavy blue overcoat and vapor streamed from his mouth.

"It's bitter out there this morning." He shot a concerned glance at Rory. "Are you feeling all right? You're white as a sheet."

"I'm fine." Rory took a peppermint from his pocket. "Just got to me a bit, seeing Elizabeth like that. I mean, knowing her and all."

"Ah sure, it would, wouldn't it?" Michael looked at him. "You'd have to be awful coldhearted if it didn't. A young girl like that. And it's always worse if it's someone you know. Well, just remember this is your first big test. Now you've got something like this under your belt, you'll never be the same again.''

Kate watched as Rory started checking the booking entries. He'd studiously avoided looking at her directly.

"Rory, I'll need you to hold down the fort here," Michael told him. "There's a bit of a panic in town. Everyone's talking about how it's just like what happened to Moruadh." He shook his head. "I'd not been here for five minutes this morning when Brigid Riley rang to say we should be looking at Niall Maguire's whereabouts last Monday night.''

Kate stared at him. She felt exactly as though she'd been punched in the stomach. Words scrambled around in her brain. Surely no one really believed that Niall…it was preposterous. Anyone who really knew him would know… Her thoughts stopped short. Who really did know Niall Maguire? Including herself.

"Will you be doing that then, Michael?" Rory looked up from the ledger. "Talking to Maguire, I mean?''

"Sure, him and a few others. We'll follow all the leads." He leafed through a stack of papers on the counter. "I'll not have this turn into a witch-hunt for Maguire, though. The talk aside, we've nothing much to go on with him but the whole thing with Moruadh's death. Although our new superintendent's been talking about opening that up again.''

"That's ridiculous," Kate said, and both men turned to look at her. "Niall Maguire is not a murderer.''

Michael gave her a look that said he didn't appreciate her input. "That's exactly what we intend to find out."

She would talk to Rory tonight, she decided as she left the station and headed to the superette on the high street to pick up some things for Annie. A cold wind whipped around her head, and she huddled into her parka. The shock of hearing Niall's name as a suspect in Elizabeth's murder was already giving way to the numbing realization that no one even considered the possibility that anyone else could have done it. Everywhere she went, people huddled in shop doorways, their heads close. And the name on everyone's lips was Niall Maguire.

In the superette—a tiny store that would have fit into one corner of the Ralph's Market she shopped at in Santa Monica—she tried to remember what it was Annie wanted. Bread? Butter? Her brain refused to focus. In the adjacent aisle, two women she couldn't see were talking about the murder.

"Sure, well, it's not surprising, is it?" A woman's words floated over to her. "My Elaine takes his class at Galway and she says the girls flit around him like flies. I'm telling you, it was only a matter of time until something like this happened."

"Mind you, though," another voice said, "he's been very good about helping out when he's asked, and every time I've ever spoken to him, he's very polite."

Before she could hear more, Kate walked away. Was it butter or jam she was supposed to pick up? She tried to think. Where had she put the shopping list? Her pocket? She felt around. Not there.

She felt as if her head had been placed in a spin drier, then tossed and tumbled until she could no longer think straight. Had Annie said something about honey? Or was it lemon curd? Playing it safe, she picked up a jar of each, added them to her basket. A pound of butter, a piece of cheese at the dairy counter.

In a daze, she found her way to the checkout. Again, she saw the shadowy silhouettes on the cliffs. Had they been fighting? Embracing? She thought of the way the short one had disappeared. She saw Niall's face emerging from the fog. But Rory had also been up on the cliffs. She'd seen him herself. The cashier said something and Kate stared at her blankly. Money, right. She produced some notes, left the shop in a daze.

Plastic bags in hand, she walked slowly along the high street. Intuition told her she could trust Niall, but intuition about men had not served her well in the past. She lined up all the evidence against him. He'd been up on the cliffs Monday night. He knew Elizabeth. He'd taken her picture. "Elizabeth is beautiful," he'd said. "And very naive." But, so what? Most teenage girls are naive.

Maybe *she* was also naive. Annie certainly thought so. "If you have to go up to the castle again," she'd said, "you'd be a fool not to ask Rory or Patrick to go along with you. Not that I'm rushing to judgment, of course."

Kate glanced at a shop window, optimistically crammed with things to catch a tourist's eye. Aran sweaters, Waterford crystal, Connemara pottery. Racks of postcards that showed a verdant Ireland under improbably blue skies. Next door, she saw a display of Claddagh rings. Two hands holding a heart. Tidily cradled in a crown, the rings symbolized hope, promise or eternal love. Take your pick, she thought, moving on. Maybe she *was* naive.

Hadn't everything with Niall happened a little too rapidly? What if he was some sort of clever, attractive sociopath? A Ted Bundy type? How many college girls had succumbed to Bundy's charm and good looks? None of them suspected his real character.

In the window of the bakery shop, she stopped to look at the shelves of breads and sticky-topped buns. Behind them she saw her own reflection. Hollow-eyed, shoulders hunched in her green parka, hair shoved up under the black knit hat.

What did he see in her anyway? She recalled Caitlin's simpering remarks about his eyelashes and the girls flocking around him. What would he want with a thirty-four-year-old writer with freckles and invisible lashes when he could, apparently, have any nubile young coed he wanted? Unless he really was just a womanizer. Impressionable young girls, lonely American writers. Makes no difference. Fill them with blarney and get them into bed. *And murder them?*

With a shiver, she thought of the narrow ledge in the west tower. A slight push would have done it. Why had he taken her over there anyway? Planned to push her, maybe, then changed his mind? Seduce her first, then kill her. God, her imagination was running away with her again. She didn't know what she believed anymore.

By THE TIME Niall drove back into Cragg's Head from his overnight trip to Kerry, the sun had already gone down. The tide was out as he drove past the harbor. Lights from a boat on the horizon appeared as pinpoints in the darkness. He drove slowly, then decided on the spur of the moment to take the Cliff Road toward the Pot o' Gold instead of the road up to the castle.

Tired, he turned his head from side to side to ease the tension. It had not been a good day. Most of the shoot had been done around Killarney, a town that had let its natural beauty become eclipsed by tourism. All day his mood had swung between anger and depression at the sight of the pony carts and tawdry souvenir stands, and a dreamy yearning to be out on the narrow roads. Meandering across the heather-dotted moors with Kate at his side.

She'd never left his mind. He thought of the things they would talk about, the places he'd show her. He'd take her up to Sligo. "Connemara has this stark beauty about it," he'd tell her. "The gorse and rocks and trees all stunted and gnarled by the winds off the Atlantic." He wanted her to see it all.

The thought of being with her again had fueled him for most of the day. But he was exhausted now, and the gloomy fear that maybe all his mystical mumbo jumbo and talk of destiny had scared her off began to overwhelm him. After all, wasn't she an American? Pragmatic and cynical—as she herself had put it.

Maybe he'd gone too far. Sure, it was one thing to think such thoughts himself, but he should never have said anything to her. No doubt, she'd thought him completely daft. In fact, it was a miracle that she'd even wanted to see him again. They might be destined for each other, but at times even destiny needed a bit of a push.

Flowers sometimes helped, too. He glanced at the bunch of daffodils on the seat beside him. He'd bought them from a stand in Killarney intending to give them to her tonight. What he'd wanted were marigolds, the color of the jumper she'd had on the night they'd cooked dinner, but it was too early in the year for marigolds, the shop girl had said. The daffodils had wilted a bit on the drive back, and the things he'd been rehearsing in his head to say to her now seemed all wrong. Naive and overly romantic.

God, a woman like Kate was probably used to long-stemmed red roses. And himself with a bunch of wilted daffodils, he thought as he pulled up outside the Pot o' Gold. He looked up at the boardinghouse and felt an edge of panic. It wasn't good to feel this desperate over a woman. It had happened once before, and he should have learned his lesson. He stared through the windscreen, thinking of how he'd sat here like this just a few days ago. He'd known nothing about Kate then, not even her name. Tonight there were no lights on in the sitting room, and he wondered if she was even in.

Only one way to find out. He got out of the car, closed the door behind him, then remembered the flowers. A moment later, daffodils in hand, he opened the latch on the garden gate. Up the path, his footsteps loud on the gravel, up the two steps to the front door.

Annie usually had all the lights on, but through the panels of amber glass he could make out only a dim lamp at the back of the house. He lifted the polished brass door knocker, let it fall back. Not sure it would be heard, he lifted it again. No one came, and he rang the bell. A light went on in the hallway, and after a moment he saw Annie. She wore a black skirt and cardigan. There was no smile on her face as she pulled open the door.

"Mr. Maguire."

"Evening, Mrs. Ryan." Her face was pale, her eyes red as though she'd been crying, and Niall thought for a moment of asking what was wrong. Then he saw her eyes go to the bunch of flowers in his hand. He shifted his feet, awkward suddenly as an unwanted suitor. "I've come to see Kate," he said. "Is she in?"

"She is not." Annie dabbed her nose with a handkerchief. "But if she were, she'd not want to see you."

He looked at her, at a loss for words. Had Kate told her to say that?

"And you'd be doing everyone a great service if you'd stay away from that girl." One hand on the door, as though to close it, she apparently saw something on his face, and her forehead creased in a frown. "Have you not heard then? They've found Elizabeth."

"Found her." He shook his head, confused. "She's home, is she?"

"They've found her dead, Mr. Maguire." Annie spat the words at him. "Dead at the bottom of Cragg's Head Leap where you said you were to have met her last Monday. She'd been pushed by someone, Mr. Maguire. Pushed to her death."

Niall stared at her, too stunned to speak. Shocked as much by Annie's anger as he was at the news. He took a step back as though from a fire. Her eyes blazed at him, and her hands were clenched at her sides. It seemed all she could do not to claw at his face.

"And you'll excuse me for saying so, but it seems a bit of a coincidence that you yourself should have asked about her just that very night."

"Mrs. Ryan, you're not saying you think I—"

"What I'm saying is neither here nor there. I'm sure the Garda will have plenty to say to you and if you'll take a bit of advice, you'll not come calling here anymore. You've more than enough on your plate as it is. So, good night to you, Mr. Maguire."

The door slammed, and Niall felt a rush of air across his face. For a moment he just stood there feeling as though the whole thing had been a vivid dream and if he rang the bell again, Kate—not Annie—would answer the door with a smile on her face. Across the road, he could hear the sea crashing against the rocks. He smelled smoke from the chimney, the tang of salt in the wind. From inside the Pot o' Gold, he heard a clock chime the quarter hour. He glanced again through the door's glass panels to the dim light at the end of the hall, then, daffodils in hand, he walked back down the path to his car.

CHAPTER TWELVE

KATE LOOKED UP from buttering bread for sandwiches to see Rory watching her from the doorway, still in his uniform, tie off, shirt collar unbuttoned.

"I thought I heard Annie's voice down here," he said as he sat down at the kitchen table.

"You did." The kettle whistled, and Kate got up, scooped tea into the pot then poured in the boiling water. "She's upstairs now with Elizabeth's mom. Annie was talking about calling the doctor for some tranquilizers; maybe you could see if she needs someone to pick them up."

Rory nodded, but stayed put. "I wanted to say something to you," he said after a moment, "While there's no one around."

Kate glanced at him. Elizabeth's mother, Maeve, had arrived earlier in the day, and the house had been full of people; an endless stream of friends and neighbors bearing plates of food, the doorbell and the phone constantly ringing. She'd left a message on Niall's machine, cancelling their plans to get together that night. She'd also postponed her interview in Galway, and she and Rory had pitched in to help Annie. Shirtsleeves rolled up, he had brewed endless pots of tea and stood alongside her as she cut and buttered bread for countless platters of sandwiches.

Kate had used the time to rehearse what she wanted to say to him.

"I need to talk to you, too," she said. "Who else knows that you were with Elizabeth on Monday?"

"No one." He frowned down at his hands. "Look, I know what you must be thinking. I mean, I can see it looks suspicious, but all we did was kiss a bit."

"Hold on." Kate had started to place a slice of ham on the buttered bread. Meat in her hand, she looked up at him. "You told me there was nothing between the two of you."

"I know I did." He sighed and scratched the back of his neck. "I was worried you'd get the wrong idea about me if I told you. Look, I've never run around on Caitlin, you can ask her. Honest, Kate. I don't know what it was with Elizabeth, it was like I had a drug in me, I swear. D'you know what I mean?"

"Not really." She pushed away images of Niall. "The problem now is that Elizabeth is dead, and you were up on the cliffs around the time it happened."

"So were a lot of people. So was Niall Maguire. I saw him."

"Rory, you were with Elizabeth. You'd both been drinking. Maybe—"

"Who told you that? Fitzpatrick?"

"Yeah." She sighed, mad at herself for mentioning Fitzpatrick's name. "Look Rory, maybe you had nothing to do with this, but I'm not comfortable with keeping your secret anymore. I want you to tell your supervisor that you were with Elizabeth Monday night."

"Ah, Katie…" He dug his knuckles into his eyes. "Look, I swear to God I'm telling you the truth. Ask

Caitlin if I've ever laid a hand on her. She'll tell you I haven't.''

She nodded. "I'm sure that's true, but—"

"Come on, Katie. You don't understand. We'd had a few drinks and sure she was all over me, but that's all it was."

"So if your conscience is clear, you have nothing to worry about, right?"

"It won't be like that, though. Right now they all think I was on the Galway Road. If it gets out that I was up on the cliffs, the whole thing with Elizabeth will come out. And then I might as well kiss my life goodbye."

"Rory…" Kate hesitated. "You're a Garda, for God's sake. You're supposed to be investigating Elizabeth's death and you're sitting here figuring out how to cover your tracks. Shouldn't you at least try to get off the case or something?"

"It'll be fine. The only people who know I was there are you and Hughie, and he's not going to say anything."

"How do you know that?"

"Because he wants to see Maguire get what he deserves for Moruadh. He wants this pinned on Maguire, and so does everyone else in Cragg's Head."

Kate shook her head, speechless. Any minute someone was going to wake her from this nightmare.

"I know what you're thinking right now," Rory said. "You're thinking that if I won't make a report, you'll do it yourself. Well, you might as well save yourself the effort. There's no one who doesn't know you've a thing for Maguire, and if you think the Gardai are going to take your word over mine, you're soft in the head."

Kate watched as he got up from the table and went over to the fridge. With the door open, he perused the contents, removed a beer and sat down. As he popped the top on the can, the door opened, and Annie came in.

"Katie." Annie patted her on the shoulder. "I wasn't going to mention this, but then I thought about the article you're writing and decided it was something you should know. Mr. Maguire was by to see you a little while ago. Maybe I shouldn't have, but I told him you were out." She paused. "Holding a bunch of daffodils in his hand, he was."

Daffodils. Kate felt the burn of tears in her throat. She could picture Niall's face as Annie turned him away. She watched Annie pick up a knife and start hacking away at a loaf of bread as if she had a personal grudge against it. After a moment, she put the knife down and came over to sit beside Rory. Hands on her knees, she leaned forward, looked directly into his eyes.

"Rory, love, I've got to ask you something," she said, her voice barely above a whisper. "Maeve upstairs, would like to have the locket Elizabeth always wore, but she was told it wasn't on the body. Would you or any of the Gardai know what might have happened to it?"

Her mind still on the daffodils and the exchange with Rory, Kate had gone to the sink to rinse out dishes. Her hands, immersed in soap bubbles, froze. She barely heard Rory's reply. All she could see was the glint of the locket Niall had dropped that night on the cliffs.

A BAG OF DOG FOOD under his arm, Niall stood outside the superette, looking at Brigid Riley's pudding of a face. If Rufus hadn't been completely out of food, Niall would never have driven back to the village. Listening to Brigid, though, he was sorry that he hadn't simply sacrificed the roast beef.

"I used to clean up at your family's house," she said.

Niall nodded slightly.

"Terrible thing about the murder of that young girl, isn't it? Terrible thing indeed. It put me in mind of poor Moruadh and the way she died. Sure, what a tragedy that was, don't you think, Mr. Maguire? And what a strange coincidence that this poor young girl was discovered in almost the same spot as Moruadh."

"What exactly is your point, Mrs. Riley?"

"Oh, nothing at all, Mr. Maguire," she replied, her eyes wide. "Nothing at all. Sure, 'twas just a tragic coincidence is all I meant."

Later, in his darkroom, Niall poured developer into a tray and watched the image slowly come into focus. Moss-covered gates—no sign now of the castle they'd once guarded. Barren hills behind the gates. A Celtic cross. Usually, he could lose himself in the process; tonight he was simply going through the motions. Brigid Riley's voice still rang in his ears.

Distracted, he paced the room. It was happening all over again, as it had after Moruadh. The gossip, the whispers. Tomorrow, there would be a visit from the Gardai. No doubt there was already a message on the machine downstairs. With no direction in mind, he left the room, wandered down the ancient corridors of the west tower. The haunted part, he'd told Kate. That day seemed long ago now.

Down on the first floor again, he opened the door

to the library. Switched on the light. The room was
much as it had always been. In one corner, the massive mahogany desk the old man had used. Around
it, shelves of books. On the desk, a Maguire family
photo. He picked it up.

The old man standing, hands on his wife's shoulders. Smiles on their faces. And himself. A schoolboy
in short trousers and a blazer, standing off to one side
as though he'd tried to slip into the picture unnoticed.

The mind plays tricks, he thought. Changing and
shading memories so that they become unreliable.
With a photograph, though, the truth—for that second, anyway—is captured. He replaced the picture
and sat down at the desk. From a drawer he took out
a large tan envelope. He'd pulled together a collection
of pictures after his father died. Childhood pictures,
himself and Moruadh. Hugh Fitzpatrick. The three of
them together, apart, paired up, alone. Now he emptied the envelope onto the desk, studied a picture
taken just a few months after the family photo.

Two children, playing together at a table set for
Christmas dinner. Moruadh, laughing as she reached
for the paper hat Hugh wore. Niall stared at it for a
moment, remembering. He had ducked his head to
stop her taking his hat, too, held the flimsy paper in
place with one hand. Happy children, frozen in time.
Happy only in the moment the picture was taken. Just
after it was snapped, Niall had been summoned to the
library, where his father had told him he was an in-
grate, a worthless disappointment. Unless he mended
his ways, he would be sent away with just the clothes
on his back.

Niall riffled through the pictures, his thoughts drifting back through the years. Summer days and russet

autumns. Winters of thickened clouds and low gray skies. Scenes captured by the camera.

A picture with Moruadh, the summer he'd returned from university. He had put the camera on a tripod and set the timer, but as he'd dashed around to be in the picture with Moruadh, he'd tripped and barely made it to where she stood. They were both laughing, and his arm was around her waist. Standing under a chestnut tree, its branches dripping rain. Patches of damp on Moruadh's blue cotton dress. And, through the trees, barely visible, a watchful Hugh.

A month after the picture was taken, Niall had left Ireland. Lived in London and then Paris. A dark time, full of loneliness and yearning. And then Moruadh had come to him in Paris.

He put the photos back into the envelope and returned it to the drawer. Glanced at his watch. It was nearly one in the morning. Tired, he walked downstairs. There were three messages on the answering machine. He pressed the button to hear them. One informed him that his gallery show had been canceled, the other that his college class had been closed due to low enrollment. The third was from Kate. He listened to it once, then rewound the tape and replayed it.

"Hi, it's Kate. I'm sorry, I don't think it would be a good idea to…well, I can't see you tonight after all. Could you meet me tomorrow, at the harbor at noon?" A pause. "Some questions I need to ask you." Another pause. "If that doesn't work, please leave a message at Annie's and let me know what would be more convenient."

He ground the heel of his palms into his eyes. In his head, he heard the American accent, the flat im-

personal tone. He went into the kitchen, took down a
bottle of Jameson's from the cupboard. Poured an
inch into a glass, ran water from the tap. As he raised
the whiskey to his mouth, he heard tires on the gravel
outside. Moments later, glass in hand, he opened the
front door to find Kate standing there.

"This is probably the most stupid, impulsive thing
I've ever done in my life," she said. "But I just had
to see you."

Stunned, he shook his head. Her shoulders hunched
against the cold night air, she stood in the small circle
of light cast by the lamp above the door. He couldn't
read her expression or the tone of her voice.

"You're shivering." Beyond her shoulder, he
could see her car. The driver's door was wide open.
"Come inside."

"No." She looked down at the keys in her hand.
"I told you I just wanted to see you."

"Kate, I…" he started, then realized that he had
no idea what he wanted to say. No idea what this visit
meant, or what she wanted from him. Bemused, he
watched her for a moment. "Annie told me about
Elizabeth," he finally said. "I stopped by earlier. She
told me in no uncertain terms to stay away from
you."

"She's worried. Any moment now, you'll probably
hear the Garda coming up the hill."

"What can I say to you?"

"Right now?" Eyes on his face. "Nothing."

"Profess my innocence?"

She shook her head.

"Tell you a load of lies?"

"Stop."

A moment passed. He felt the wind on his face, the

chill of it through his clothes. Kate's nose was pink
from the cold, her face pinched. He felt a rush of
impatience—not with her—with himself. With whatever it was about him that had led to this moment.
To a woman fighting with herself to trust him. He
thought of Brigid Riley's face, of the suspicious eyes
in the village. Of Kate's voice on the machine. He
felt weary, exhausted. Tired of dragging around the
past.

"Kate." He touched her arm. "Come inside."

"I can't." She took a step back. "I have to go."

"That's it? You drive up here in the middle of the
night to stand on my doorstep for two minutes?"

"I told you, I wanted to see you."

"And now you have."

"Right."

"And?"

Her expression softened, a flicker of a smile.

"What did you learn?"

"Enough."

He shook his head at her.

"Ireland has addled my brain," she said. "Or
something has."

He smiled.

"I'm serious. I don't even know myself anymore."

"Will I still see you tomorrow at the harbor?"

She nodded.

He caught the ends of her scarf.

"Niall..."

He watched her face.

"I really have to go."

"Tomorrow then?"

"Tomorrow." She turned and walked to the car.

As she climbed in, she looked up at him. "Hey, Niall. Do you know what *Far Liath* means?"

"*Far Liath.* It's Gaelic, I think."

"What about *Far Dorocha?*"

"*Far* I think is 'man.' *Darocha* is 'dark.' The dark man." He looked at her for a moment. "What's all this about?"

"I had my fortune told yesterday." She gave an embarrassed laugh. "Who knows why? She said something about watching out for *Far Dorocha.*"

He tried to remember the mythology he'd learned as a boy. "*Far Dorocha* was the sinister one." It was coming back to him now. "He never looks around him, just rides until he finds who he's looking for. No one ever turns him down."

Kate nodded slowly.

"She warned you, you say?"

"Yeah." With a grin, she fluttered her fingers at him and got into the car.

He stayed at the door, watching until the car's tail-lights had disappeared down the hill and out of sight.

KATE LAY BACK IN BED, hands locked behind her head. Annie had been waiting up for her when she got back from Niall's. "You've taken leave of your senses," Annie had said. And maybe Annie was right. Maybe her brain really was addled. Maybe it had contracted some sort of Celtic malaise that rendered it unable to engage in anything but dreams and fantasies.

She'd planned to ask Niall about the necklace, but any doubts she'd had about him had disappeared the moment he'd opened the door. She had tried to look at him dispassionately—a tall man, pale and a little weary, with a shadow of beard on his jaw—but it had taken every bit of self-control she could muster not to fling her arms around his neck and tell him she knew he was innocent.

Wide-awake now, she got out of bed and wandered over to the window, stared out at the dark night. The turrets of the castle had disappeared in the blackness. Why did no one else share her belief? Even Patrick, who had previously dismissed the gossip about Moruadh, now saw Niall as the most likely suspect in Elizabeth's death.

Back on the bed, she sat cross-legged, gnawing at her thumbnail as she tried to think. Why *hadn't* she asked him about the locket? Should she report it to the Gardai anyway? Regardless of her feelings. As if they needed more ammunition against him. Tomorrow, she thought. She would definitely ask him about it tomorrow. The cynic scoffed. *Sure, he's bound to have a great explanation. Lots of men carry lockets around in their pockets. Just a coincidence that a murdered girl happened to be missing hers. But you'll buy whatever he says, of course. One question, though. Would you be such a staunch believer in his innocence if he weighed three hundred pounds and had a glass eye?*

THE QUESTION KEPT KATE awake for much of the night. And by the time watery gray light filtered through her bedroom window, she still couldn't answer it. Bleary-eyed, she pulled on her navy UCLA sweatshirt and jeans and went downstairs. As usual, the smell of bacon frying greeted her, but in the kitchen, she found Annie weeping at the stove.

"Annie." Kate came to stand beside her, put her arm around Annie's shoulders. "What can I do?"

"There's nothing anyone can do short of bringing Elizabeth back," Annie said. "All we can hope is that they bring him in before he does it again."

Kate went still. *Bring him in.* Annie hadn't needed to say Niall's name. Kate knew exactly who she meant. Annie obviously had no doubt about who had murdered Elizabeth. Kate watched the steam rising from the blue-and-white kettle on the stove, saw Niall's face as he'd stood at the door to the castle last night. She took two cups from the cupboard, reached into the refrigerator for milk. It struck her that this bright kitchen with its blooming daffodils and baking aromas felt more like home than her own kitchen in Santa Monica. "We were worried about you," Annie had said last night. Just before she'd accused Kate of taking leave of her senses.

The image of Annie and Patrick, both in their dressing gowns, drinking mugs of cocoa as they stood at the window watching for her car, clogged her throat with tears. In just over a week, Kate reflected, Annie had managed to fill the spot in Kate's heart that had been vacant since her mother's death.

Annie. Niall. Two people who had suddenly become the center of her world. Did loving one mean betraying the other? The phone rang, and Annie went off to answer it.

"That was Michael," Annie said a few moments later. "I shouldn't be telling you this, but they've found another piece of evidence that links Mr. Maguire to Elizabeth. A film box up there on the cliff, right where the detectives say Elizabeth was pushed. It's only a matter of time, Katie, before they bring him in."

CHAPTER THIRTEEN

NIALL MAGUIRE IS JUST another interview subject, Kate told herself as she pulled into the harbor to meet him. *Ultimately, his guilt or innocence isn't your problem. Either way, you've still got a story to write. A paycheck to earn, bills to pay. Objective, detached, that's the attitude du jour. Objective, detached.* She kept saying the words in her head like a mantra. *Objective, detached. Objective, detached.* They rang as hollow as the feeling in her stomach.

Engine idling, she waited for a truck, loaded with bales of hay, to pull out then drove into the empty spot and turned off the ignition. Spots of rain splashed on the windshield. Huge purple clouds, bruised and sodden, massed over the ocean. On the car's hood, a couple of gulls fought over an orange peel. According to the dashboard clock, it wasn't quite twelve.

She pulled down the driver's mirror and peered at her reflection. Frizzed-out hair and freckles in bas-relief. With a sigh, she dug in her purse for lipstick and a compact, did a quick repair job. Okay, maybe he wasn't *exactly* just another interview subject, but there would be no long, lingering looks and she absolutely would not kiss him. And, somewhere in the far recesses of her mind, she would *try* to accept the idea that his innocence had not been entirely established.

Rain spattered down on the roof of the car. The windows began to steam. Where was her brush? She dug it out, dragged it through her hair. The green numerals on the dashboard clock clicked over to 12:05. He was late. She folded her arms across her chest, unfolded them, opened the sack of raisin buns she'd bought at the bakery in Cragg's Head. Picked three raisins out of one of them. Checked the time by her watch. Seven minutes past.

One of the gulls on the hood flew off. *Objective, detached. Objective, detached.* Even if he explained everything. Even if he removed every single doubt about his innocence. She pulled down the mirror again. Checked her teeth. Two schoolboys in green uniforms raced by the car, laughing as they swatted each other with their schoolbags. *Objective, detached.* A tap on the window made her start.

Niall. Looking through the glass at her. Eyes exactly the same color as the ocean. Gray eyes from now on would always remind her of Ireland.

She rolled down the window. A burst of cool, damp air hit her face. He wore the same sheepskin jacket he'd had on the first night she'd seen him. In the damp air, his hair curled slightly. *Objective, detached.*

"You're late," she said. "Do you know what time it is?"

"The time? I do." He didn't look at his watch. "Between noon and one exactly."

"It's twelve-ten." *A womanizer,* she told herself. *As soon as you're gone, there'll be someone else.* "Twelve-ten," she repeated. "Which means you're ten minutes late. Fifteen minutes is my limit. For anyone."

"D'you know the Irish philosophy on time?"

"No, I don't." He had nicked himself shaving. Just above his lip. *Objective, detached.*

"God made plenty of it, so it doesn't hurt to waste a little."

"Time is money," she retorted. "That's the American philosophy. I make sixty bucks an hour, which means you owe me about seven dollars."

"Will Irish currency do?"

"I'll send you a bill."

"Right." A drop of water trickled down the side of his face. He wiped it away with the back of his hand. "Am I to stand out here in the rain then?"

She unlocked the door, pushed it open and scooted back against the driver's door as he climbed inside. All arms and blue-jeaned legs, he grinned and shook off water, filling the small space with the sort of barely restrained exuberance that made her think of a schoolboy in a stuffy parlor.

"Uh-oh." He reached beneath him, pulled out the bakery bag and peered inside. "I think I've squashed your buns a bit. Sorry."

"It won't affect the taste, I'm sure." She offered him the bag. "Lunch is on me."

"Thanks." He took one, held it in his hand. "Hello, Kate."

"Hi." As she met his eyes, the charge that zipped through her body told her that the front seat of a small car with fogged-up windows was not the best place for an interview. *Objective, detached.* She brushed a crumb from her lap, sifted among the ashes of her resolve. Tried to fan them into flame. *Thinks he's going to charm you into bed. Bad news. Don't look at him again.*

"Did I warn you I'd come armed with questions?

If I didn't, I should have.'' To demonstrate that she meant business, she reached into the back seat for her notebook. As she did, her arm brushed his shoulder. She took a quick breath. ''There's a lot of talk in Cragg's Head. About Elizabeth's murder. Actually, that's an understatement. The village is consumed by it.''

''I'm sure that's true.''

''Almost everyone seems convinced you did it.''

''I can well imagine.''

''Tell me about Elizabeth.''

''What specifically about Elizabeth?''

''Was she more to you than a student?''

He broke the bun in half, studied the two pieces for a moment. ''If you're asking whether I slept with her, I didn't.''

Her head lowered, Kate stared at the notebook on her knees. Words blurred into meaningless scribble. In her peripheral vision, she could see the knees of his jeans, the sleeve of his jacket. The air in the car seemed to have congealed. She moved in the seat to screen the notebook from his view. Drew a square and then an interlocking square.

''So she was just a beautiful young girl that you were supposed to meet Monday night? A date, you might say?''

''Elizabeth was a student in my class who showed some promise,'' he said quietly. ''I offered to help her with a new camera she'd bought. Looking back, I can see that it probably wasn't a wise thing to do, but I'm not always a very good judge of things like that.''

''Meaning.''

''Meaning that I should have recognized that her

motives for meeting me might not have been the same as my own."

"She had a crush on you, you mean?"

"She might have. If she did, I didn't recognize it."

"The locket she always wore was missing when they recovered her body." She drew another square. "I happened to see a necklace drop from your pocket Monday night." She looked at him. "Just a coincidence?"

"No, Kate. It wasn't a coincidence. It was probably Elizabeth's necklace. I turned it in to the Gardai when I went to the station yesterday. As I told them, I found it on the cliffs."

"And did they buy it?"

"If you're asking whether they believed me, I don't know. They've got a new superintendent who seems eager to prove his worth. I'm their star suspect. Small wonder."

She met his eyes for a moment.

"Sure, it's the constant stream of women I have up to the castle day and night, not to mention the suspicious similarity to Moruadh's death. It's a miracle I'm out walking the streets."

Kate stared very hard at the frayed patch on the knee of her jeans. When she was ten, she'd been falsely accused of taking a school friend's lunch money. Later, the girl discovered that she'd mislaid the money and apologized. Even now, Kate realized, she could feel the stinging sense of shame. She looked up at him. In the car's shadowy interior, he looked pale and a little weary.

"What are you going to do?" she asked.

"Do?"

"Have you spoken to an attorney?"

"It will all blow over," he said. "There'll be a bit of a witch-hunt for a few days, as there was after Moruadh, but it will blow over."

"Speaking of Moruadh…"

"What about her?"

"Why won't you discuss her?"

"Because I've no interest in reading anything more about her in print."

"Even if it helps to clear your name?"

He shrugged. "My conscience is clear," he said, an edge to his voice now. "It's enough."

"Someone described you as overprotective of Moruadh." She flipped through the pages of her notebook for Fitzpatrick's quote. "'An intrusive presence in her life.' Any thoughts on that?"

He said nothing, sat facing the windshield, his expression unreadable.

"Why did you feel she needed protection?" She thought of Rory McBride's bizarre tale of Moruadh stretched out, naked, in the flowers. "Was she mentally unstable?"

He rolled down the window and flung out the crumbled remains of the bun. Immediately, a flock of gulls swooped down. Their raucous cries filled the air. After a moment, he closed it. Shut out the damp chill, the bird sounds.

"One of Moruadh's friends called her 'mercurial.'" Again Kate consulted her notes. "'Had her ups and downs,' was the way she put it."

His face remained completely blank.

"Did you love her, Niall? Did she love you?"

He said nothing. He remained completely still.

"I came to Ireland because I wanted to know for sure how she died. I thought you'd killed her. I absolutely can't buy that now. I don't care what people say. So that takes me back to another possibility. Suicide. Did she kill herself because of a man? Was it you?''

"Who's asking, Kate?" He looked directly at her. "You or the journalist wanting to fill in the blanks of her article?"

"Maybe both. What difference does it make?"

"All the difference in the world. I'll tell you anything you want to know, but it's between the two of us, because I want *you* to know. It's not for your article.''

"What if I use it?"

"You won't."

"How do you know?"

"I'll trust you."

She looked at him, and neither of them spoke. His eyes, pale as the sky, fixed on her face. His words— I'll trust you, he'd said—lingered in the air. Her nose prickled with tears, and she stared at her notebook, not trusting herself to speak. A moment later she looked up and met his eyes again.

"God, Niall..." She swallowed, tried to speak and then all pretense at objectivity fled. Her arms went around him, and they sat holding each other, her face buried in his collar. Through his open coat, she felt the warmth of his body, his heart beating against her chest. She closed her eyes, pressed her mouth and nose into the sheepskin, breathed in the smells of wool and rain and ocean. *She wanted not to think.* The hell with reason and logic and everything else. All she wanted was the feeling she had when she was with him. He pulled away, looked at her for a moment.

"Moruadh killed herself. I hid her suicide note from the Gardai." He sighed. "It's a long story…"

THEY WERE MARRIED in Paris. He was on assignment; Moruadh, touring throughout Europe. He'd found an ancient flat near the Pompidou Center. Three flights up over a Chinese restaurant. The whole flat reeked of chop suey. It was April and, as he walked home along the Rue de Bouberg, he found himself humming. Life felt good, full of promise. Plans to go down to Provence for a week, an upcoming exhibit. The one cloud was Moruadh. He'd not seen or heard from her since she'd left almost a month earlier. Typical, but hardly the relationship he'd once envisioned. Still, he'd long ago resigned himself to the fact that the weather around Moruadh would never be calm.

As he turned the corner to his street, he saw a line of dustbins along the curb and, alongside them, what he first thought was a bundle of old clothes. It wasn't until he brushed past to press the security code on the front door that he saw something move. Then he looked down and did a double take.

"My God. Moruadh." He hardly recognized her. Strands of matted, unwashed hair poked out from under the dirty blue scarf she'd tied around her head. Her face was pale, her eyes red-rimmed. He pulled her to her feet. "What happened? I've been trying to reach you—"

"No. Don't speak." Weeping, she clutched his arm, fell against him. "Just hold me. Please."

They stood in the middle of the narrow street, his arms around her as she sobbed on his shoulder. Through her clothes, her body felt boneless, limp with grief. Eventually, he grabbed her small bag and managed to get her up the flights of stairs. Inside the flat, whatever reserves she had briefly drawn upon disappeared. She collapsed facedown onto the bed.

"I'm pregnant." Her voice was muffled by the pillow. "He went back to his wife." Her body shook. "I thought he loved me, but he lied." In a sudden movement, she was up from the bed, pacing the room, her eyes wild and darting. "He said he loved me, but he lied to me. God, I can't stand this. Why? Why?"

He said nothing. He had no answers. The only thing to do, he knew from past experience, was to let it play out. So he sat in the filtered late-afternoon light as the woman he loved hurled herself about the room. A wild bird who had accidentally flown in through an open window and was trapped. The light faded and the room grew dark and, in the way it had happened so many times before, Moruadh finally exhausted herself and fell asleep.

He woke the next morning to find her sitting on the edge of the bed watching him. Her hair still damp from the shower, her eyes the clear blue of the sky after a storm. They left the flat and walked down to the Seine.

"Sorry." Her back against the railing, she smiled up at him. She wore a long red dress with pearl buttons down the front and flat black shoes like ballerina slippers. "Can you forgive me?"

"There's nothing to forgive, Moruadh. We've been down this same road too many times before. You're a storm that swoops into my life every so often, tears it all apart and then you're gone."

"Until the next time I show up." She turned to face the water. A moment later, she looked directly at him. "Something has changed, hasn't it?"

He felt a stab of impatience. "I don't hear from you for God knows how long and then suddenly you're back as though nothing's amiss. How could you not expect things to change?"

"It's the spells."

"You've stopped taking the medicine."

"It was making me fat."

"My God, Moruadh." Exasperated, he shook his head at her. "Couldn't you have just spoken to the doctor?"

"You don't love me anymore."

"I'll always love you."

"But not as you did."

"I want a life of my own. I'd prefer that it be with you, but I can't go on this way. I hate this sense I have of myself as some sort of self-sacrificing saint with nothing more to do than to be swept up into your vortex."

"That's not the way I see you."

"It's the way I feel. Something in me dies every time you leave."

"If I could undo it all, I would." Tears filled her eyes. "All that I've done to make you unhappy."

He said nothing.

"I love you." She wiped her eyes with the back of her hand. "When I'm feeling all right—like myself, you know—there's no one I want in my life but you. But then something comes over me. It's like a wave that sweeps all inhibitions away."

"Reason, too," he said with a wry smile.

"Reason, too," she agreed. "I feel that there's nothing I can't do. I have ideas, thousands of them, and I feel wonderful. I want to make love to the world. Then suddenly it's all gone, and I'm scared to

death. I can't think. I panic. All I can do is run. And
then I return to you.''

He turned his back to the river, the scenario she
had described all too familiar. Moruadh leaned
against the metal railings. On the other side of the
street, a group of students in blue jeans and anoraks
stood beside a newspaper kiosk arguing loudly in
German.

"What will you do now?" he asked her.

"I don't know." Her fingers tightened on the rails.
"I can't have the baby."

For a while, neither of them spoke. Then holding
hands, they walked across the street to a café. Moruadh sat outside on a green iron chair while he went
to order coffee for them both. He brought the drinks
out and set them down on the table. He watched her
spoon sugar into her coffee.

"Have you seen a doctor?"

"About the baby?"

"The other thing." A police wagon screamed
down the boulevard. He watched it for a moment,
then looked at her. "Your mental state."

"I will." She lowered her head, stirring her coffee.

"You've made the same promise before."

"This time I mean it."

"So do I, Moruadh. If we're to have another
chance together, you have no other choice. This is
it."

"BUT OF COURSE, she broke that promise, too." He
sat with his back against the car door, facing Kate.
"For a time, things were great. The medicine worked.
We were happy. And then she started complaining
again that the pills were making her fat. She promised

me she'd talk to the doctor, swore she wouldn't stop taking the medicine.''

''But she did.''

''Apparently. Around Christmastime I came home to find candles burning all over the flat. Fifty of them maybe, and they'd obviously been burning for hours. She was gone, her suitcases with her. It was months before I saw her again. She'd lost the baby. A miscarriage, she said. I'd had enough by then and I came back to Ireland.''

''So it was over for you?''

''I thought it was. I bought the lighthouse up in Sligo and I was trying to get the photography studio started. One day she just showed up at the studio.''

''You hadn't seen her since France?''

''Hadn't heard a word from her, which wasn't unusual. She seemed stable enough, although with Moruadh I could never be sure of anything. I always felt as if I was holding my breath, waiting for another calamity. This time, though, she seemed to have adjusted. She told me she thought her life was finally back on track.''

''Did you believe her?''

''I wanted to. Unfortunately, it soon became clear that she hadn't got things together.'' He shook his head, remembering. ''She was caught shoplifting in Galway a couple of times. One night I had a call from the Gardai that she'd broken into a flower shop.''

He paused, his expression distant. Kate waited for him to go on.

''She told me that she'd wanted to get my attention,'' he finally said.

She shook her head.

''It was a nightmare time. I had the sense of her

twirling faster and faster and I knew that unless she got help, something awful would happen. But she absolutely refused. Finally, she went back to Paris, but she called me almost every night. I think she may have been seeing Hugh Fitzpatrick again. I gather she was phoning him, too. At one point, she told me that if I didn't love her anymore, she was going to marry him.''

Kate nodded. ''It sounds as though that hadn't changed since childhood. Moruadh was always fueling the rivalry between you and Hugh. Pitting you against each other.''

''We both loved her,'' he said. ''In our own ways. Neither of us could really claim her.''

''Although she married you.''

''Which he's never forgiven me for. As far as he's concerned, I stole her from him. When things went bad with us, she turned to him and vented her unhappiness, which I'm sure confirmed his belief that she never really wanted to marry me in the first place.''

''And he didn't see the signs of mental illness?''

''Apparently not, although how she managed to keep it from him, I don't know. Hysterical phone calls almost daily, begging me to give her another chance. Eventually, I went to Paris again; I had to. I thought I'd try and get her some help, but I got there to find Hugh with her, and Moruadh insisting that she was fine and that I should leave her to lead her own life and stop interfering.''

''What did you do?''

''At that point, I'd had it. I felt as though I was drowning. When I got back to Ireland, I wrote her a long letter, told her that unless she got help for herself, I wanted no part of her life. She came back to

Ireland, but I didn't see her. Six weeks later, she was dead. When I went through her papers afterward, I found a letter she'd written to me, dated the day before she died.''

"The suicide note."

"Yes. She apologized for all the trouble she'd brought to my life and said she knew of only one way to rid me of the burden.''

"To take her own life?"

He nodded. "They made a preliminary ruling that it was an accident, but then all the talk started, stirred up to a great extent by Hugh's reporting. By the time the Garda searched the castle, I'd already found the note. It was with her journals in the west tower. When they opened the door and saw only the ledge, they assumed there was nothing there.''

"And you let them believe that?"

"It was better that way. No one needed to know."

"But didn't all the rumors bother you? I mean, you could have cleared your name if you'd shown them the note.''

"I suppose I thought about it a couple of times, but I knew if I did, everything would come out. Moruadh's emotional problems. The reason she took her life. And that would be the image of her that people would be left with, the one they remembered.''

"So instead you let them think you'd killed her?"

"How many people really believe that? There's the gossip, but that's part of life in a village, isn't it?"

She didn't answer. It was something she would definitely take up with him later. "So what was your relationship based on? Did you really love her, or was it just...I don't know, an overdeveloped sense of responsibility? She needed someone to take care of her and you took on the job?''

He smiled. ''You do like to get directly to the point.''

''But Niall...it sounds like a nightmare. She ran around on you, made your life hell, and you're still covering for her.'' She took a breath before she went on. ''You loved her, though? You must have. No one could be that self-sacrificing.''

''Of course I loved her, Kate. I always have. I also recognized that life was very difficult for her. Painful a lot of the time. She held up as much as she could, but with me she didn't have to keep up the pretense. She'd always been a part of my life and her ups and downs were just...'' He shrugged. ''Just Moruadh.''

''Part of the package, huh?''

''She was a lot like Irish weather—changeable from hour to hour. And I loved her, despite it all. Everyone did. You've no doubt picked that up in your interviews. Cragg's Head was proud of her. The local girl becomes a star. I'm sure most people wondered why she married me in the first place.''

''For your money,'' Kate said.

He gave a wry laugh. ''I suppose that's the perception. Little do they know. Actually, my father had the perfect candidate. The daughter of a family who really had money. He thought me selfish and ungrateful for refusing to cooperate, but I couldn't get past this one small problem. I didn't love her.''

Kate leaned her head against the back of the seat, thinking about what he'd told her. Thinking about Moruadh. About love and loss and loneliness. *And tell the world that I died for love.* God, it was so damn senseless. A woman surrounded by people who loved her, but so lonely and desperate she took her own life. She hadn't died *for* love, she'd died *despite* it.

"Hey." Niall tapped her shoulder. "Come back."

"I was just trying to fit all the pieces together."

"Moruadh was mentally ill, Kate. Her reality was distorted. There's no logic or reason to what she did. Between the bouts of illness our life together was fine. We were happy. It just didn't last. And you can't sum it all up in a tidy little sentence. It won't work that way." After a moment, he put his arm around her shoulder, pulled her toward him. "Let's go for a walk."

"It's raining."

"You won't shrink, I promise."

"A walk where?"

"The bogs."

"Bogs?"

"They're an interesting part of Irish history. A bit dangerous if you don't know them. Lots of strange characters out there. Madmen. Lunatics. Don't worry though, I'll protect you."

"*You'll* protect me?" She grinned. "Kind of ironic, isn't it?"

"Nothing wrong with irony. It's my favorite emotion."

"Irony isn't really an emotion," Kate said. "It's a literary device."

"If you're Irish," Niall said, "irony's an emotion."

CHAPTER FOURTEEN

"ALMOST EERIE, isn't it?" Niall said softly, his collar up against the cool damp air. "Twelve thousand years of Irish history beneath our feet. From the bog to glacier to lake to fen and then to bog." He leaned over the railing of a small wooden platform, peered down at the pool of dark water. "At least I think that's the way it went," he said with a grin. "When I was a boy, I was warned not to go near these things because they have no bottom."

Kate shot him a sideways glance. "And did you listen?"

"Not at all." He laughed. "I'd spend hours out here by myself, flinging stones into the water. The bogs have always fascinated me. Irish folklore is full of tales about them. Odd creatures that inhabit them, strangers being led astray by eerie lights coming off them."

She looked around, awed by the silence and isolation. Whatever way she turned, for as far as she could see, lay bogs. Light brown, like a blanket draped over the land. No sign of civilization anywhere. Not a house in sight, not a single vehicle on the narrow road that ran down the middle of the vast boglands. No sound but the faint hush of the wind.

Mist, soft as cobwebs, brushed against her face. Wraithlike drifts of it hovered over the small black pools of water, shrouded Niall's head and shoulders. They might have been the only two people in the world.

Her hair blowing around her face, she watched as he climbed down a couple of steps cut into the turf bank.

"There's a quality to the bog that preserves things. Before electricity, people put their butter in wooden boxes and buried them in the bogs to keep it fresh. They've pulled up dogs and animals, even a body or two, all perfectly preserved."

"That's a reassuring thought," she said, and then it occurred to her that he might read something she hadn't intended into the remark. "I mean, if you'd done something you wanted to hide." She felt her face color. "What I mean..."

Niall laughed.

"You think it's funny, huh?" She followed him off the platform, and they set out across the desolate landscape. "Watching me trip all over myself not to offend you."

"I do." He caught her hand, guiding her across a piece of marshy ground. "Careful, you need to watch where you walk. There are deep water holes with a little bit of plant material over them. You step on one, thinking its safe, and the next thing—"

"You're in deeper than you thought?" she suggested.

"Well above your head if you're not careful," he added, keeping her hand in his.

She grinned.

"Listen, Kate," he said a moment later. "You don't have to edit what you say. I hardly think you'd be walking out here with me if you were afraid."

Impulsively, she pressed his arm to her side, watched their legs and feet as they walked. Her jeans were several shades lighter than his. His Wellingtons, her own battered hiking boots. Ankles, knees, thighs. His arm around her shoulders now, hers around his waist. Bodies bumping. Smiles and stolen glances as they tramped across the misty boglands, fine rain in their faces, the drift of turf smoke from distant chimneys hovering in the air.

As they walked, she would think of something he'd told her about Moruadh and start to examine it in more detail. Treating Moruadh's mental illness as a shameful secret did her a disservice, Kate wanted to argue. Better to try to explore it through the article and maybe help others. But sensing Niall's reluctance to say more, she said nothing.

Besides, at least for one afternoon, she wanted nothing more than to just be with him. Something had changed between them, a door had opened. All afternoon, they'd swapped stories about themselves. Little things he'd told her whetted her appetite for more. She wanted to know everything. Nothing was too small or insignificant. Did he sleep on his back? As a child, had he had chicken pox, measles? What was he like in the morning? Did he dream? Take vitamins? Brush his teeth from right to left, or the other way around?

She'd fought the feeling, ridiculed it, denied it. Then gave up. Might as well acknowledge it. She was, as Annie would put it, over the moon about Niall Maguire. Just to be with him, to listen to his voice, to watch his face. She couldn't think ahead. Even tomorrow was too far off. If this walk could be encapsulated, years from now she would take it out and remember exactly how perfectly happy she'd been.

The mist gave way to light rain, and they kept on walking. With one hand, Niall reached for the hood of her jacket and pulled it up over her head. She turned to grin at him and he stopped abruptly, took the edges of the hood in both hands and kissed her on the mouth. Moments later, laughing, they resumed their walk.

"A day of uncertain weather," Niall said with a look at the sky.

"Uncertain?" Kate hooted. "What the hell is uncertain about it? All it's done is rain. Not only that but it's damn cold."

"Ah, a bit of a soft day is all. But then you're a California girl, accustomed to blue skies and sunlit beaches. "This—" he caught the fabric of her parka "—might be all right for California, but you need something a lot sturdier to keep out Irish weather."

"In a couple of days, I'll be back in eighty-degree sunshine." She felt a hollowness in her stomach. "Not a cloud in the sky."

"You'll be glad to get back?"

"Sure." She took a deep breath. "Although I have to admit, the bogs would be a good place to visit if you're feeling melancholy. You could walk and weep and revel in your misery. Very lugubrious. In California, you sort of feel perverse being miserable in all the sunshine."

"Do you spend a lot of time walking and weeping?"

"Nah. I'm deliriously happy."

He shot her a glance.

"What?"

"You're not, are you?"

"Not what?"

"Deliriously happy."

"Who is?"

"Maybe you need a change." His arm tightened around her as he guided her around a puddle of still, black water. "If California sunshine makes you melancholy, perhaps you need a place where the winds howl and the sky is always weeping."

"Ireland?" She felt her heart pound.

"It's a thought."

"Too unpredictable. Ever since I've been here, I don't know from one day to the next what's going to happen."

"Riding down the wrong side of the road, you mean. Falling into fairy rings?"

"That, too."

"But that's a good thing. I hate sameness. Hate it when things get too predictable."

"Women, too?"

"I've never known a predictable woman."

She grinned. Tried not to speculate about all the unpredictable women he might have known.

"By contrast," she said, "I like having order. Predictability is good. I want to know what to expect."

"Deadly dull."

"Not at all. It's the devil you know. That's one reason I want the staff job at *Modern World*. Freelance life is just too uncertain. At home, I have certain routines. I get up at six-thirty, check my e-mail. Run five miles. Eat half a bagel with nonfat cream cheese."

He laughed. "Is the rest of the day just as exciting?"

"Yep. I'd describe it, but you might fall asleep."

"And that's really the way you like it?"

"Yep." Did it really sound as desolate to him as it did to her? She tried again. "It's like being with people I know versus being with strangers. I know what to expect from my friends, I know how they're going to respond in a given situation. There's a certainty and stability, and I need that."

"Maybe you only think you need it." He looked at her. "I've lugged a load of...mental baggage around for years. Maybe we all have. Ideas and beliefs that always seemed so important. They've shaped us, made us who we are and then one day we realize that we've outgrown them. In fact, maybe they're dragging us down."

"So dump them?" Kate asked. "Is that what you're saying? Find something new to believe in?"

"Maybe that's the only way to move on."

She thought about her life in Santa Monica. Contrasted it with the past week in Ireland. Could she honestly say she was happier in Santa Monica? No. But Santa Monica was reality. She knew its warts and imperfections. Ireland was an illusion. Nothing felt quite real or dependable. The misty rain and green hills and sudden rainbows. Walking across deserted boglands with a tall gray-eyed man's arm around her shoulders. It was all beautiful and magical but almost dreamlike. As soon as she reached out her hand, it would vanish. The best she could do was enjoy the moment.

But then she looked up at Niall and felt such a wave of tenderness that she wondered if, against all odds, the impossible had finally happened. Had she ever, *ever* felt like this before? Ever felt this dreamy yearning that only one person in the whole world could satisfy? Her body literally ached for him.

They walked back the way they'd come. The sky had darkened and a drop of rain worked its way under her collar. At the edge of the bog, they started back into town. A few moments later, they came to a field where a crowd was watching a soccer game. Men in colored jerseys, one team in blue and yellow, the other in red, hurled themselves around the field, bodies clashing, cleats thudding against the turf, splattering mud on the crowd of onlookers.

Kate watched as the ball soared high and wide beyond the midfield, then sailed down into a clump of rushes. The crowd roared its disapproval.

"Go home and get your auld lady's apron."

"Me mother'd do a better job at it."

"One of Rory McBride's criticisms of you," Kate told Niall, "was that you weren't one of the lads. Not the sort to kick a ball around."

"Sure, it's true enough," Niall said with a smile. "One of those habits that should be dumped, maybe. I'll have to talk to them about giving me a try."

She smiled up at him.

"Your turn," he said.

"Huh?"

"If I throw out a worn-out idea, you have to toss one, too."

"How about if I modify that comment I made that night at the castle," she said. "The one about all men being no-good jerks?"

"Go ahead. Modify it."

"*Most* men are. There are exceptions."

He smiled again, and they walked on in silence,

arms around one another. Back at the harbor again, they stood at her car.

"Have you anything to do for the rest of the evening, Kate?"

"No."

"Do you have to rush back to Annie?"

"No."

"What about tomorrow?"

"Nothing."

"Will you come up to Sligo with me?"

"Yes."

WHEN SHE PULLED UP outside the Pot o' Gold to get an overnight bag, Kate saw with relief that the sitting-room lights were out. Annie's anxious inquiries into how she was planning to spend her day, while sweet and caring, made Kate feel more like a teenager than a thirty-four-year-old woman. Not that she didn't appreciate Annie's concern, but right now she had other things on her mind. She parked, got out of the car and sprinted to the front door.

In her room, she threw her bag on the bed, then surveyed the open suitcase. In Santa Monica she had, on a whim, splurged on a pale apricot silk bra and panties. Now she wondered whether Niall was onto something with the destiny thing. She stuffed them into the bag, added a pair of jeans, a couple of shirts and another sweater. As she started down the hall for her toiletries, she heard the front door open.

For a moment she froze, as guilty as if she'd been caught stealing the silverware. Then someone called her name.

"Hi." She peered over the banister, down into the hallway where Hugh Fitzpatrick stood looking up at her. "I, uh…" She felt her face color. "I just came back to grab a few things. What…do you need something?"

"I had some letters I wanted to show you. Annie said you might be here. I wondered if you'd like to go into Galway. I'll show you around a bit."

"I'm sorry, Hugh." She remained at the top of the stairs, for some reason a little unnerved by him. His hair, damp from the rain, was flattened against his skull. He wore a long black plastic raincoat over a dark shirt and dress pants. The dim amber light from the window cast an eerie glow on his face. "I've, uh…got plans."

"With Maguire?"

She looked at him. It was none of his business, of course. Still, she recalled his remarks about Niall getting everything he ever wanted and felt a stab of sympathy. "Maybe we could look at the letters when I get back," she said. "I could meet you in your office."

"You're taking a risk, you know." Hands in his pockets, he looked up at her. "I was talking to one of the detectives today. They're not actively looking at anyone but Maguire. It's just a matter of time before they make an arrest."

Kate said nothing. Annie had called Hugh a lonely boy. Lonely and eaten up with jealousy. Right now he struck her as a little creepy. She eyed the open door behind him, wondered how to bring this to a close.

"There's more than enough evidence," he said. "Witnesses who saw him on the cliffs that night. Footprints there that matched footprints in his house.

And then, Elizabeth had this romantic crush on him.''
He watched her face. ''It all adds up, no?''

''Look, Hugh—''

''If they charge him for Elizabeth's murder, they
may reopen the investigation into Moruadh's death.''
He moved a few feet down the hallway, closer to the
stairs. ''A man who would murder his wife, and then
take the life of a young girl. What woman in her right
mind would want anything to do with a man like
that?''

NIALL WHISTLED as he moved around the kitchen.
Into a picnic basket on the table he put a couple of
bottles of champagne, some grapes and cheese he'd
picked up that morning. He glanced down at Rufus,
who had apparently picked up a sense of excitement
in the air and was panting expectantly.

''What? You're wanting to take someone up there
yourself, is that it? Why should I have all the luck?
Sure, if you weren't such a scruff bag, the little Pekingese might have given you a second look.'' He
turned his attention back to the picnic basket. What
else? Bread. He'd bought a loaf, hadn't he? Maybe it
was still in the car, he thought, and went out to check.

The doll had been placed facedown on the doorstep. A small pink plastic doll with a mass of red hair
around its back and shoulders. Naked, but for a pair
of painted-on white shoes and a piece of paper taped
like a belt around its waist.

He reached for the doll, removed and unfolded the
paper. The scrawled message read:

Victim number three? Turn yourself in, Maguire.
If she dies, no one will believe it wasn't your
work.

CHAPTER FIFTEEN

HUGH FITZPATRICK HAD finally left, but his words lingered in Kate's mind. She stared through the windows of Niall's Land Rover and out at the dark night. Signposts appeared and disappeared in the white flash of headlights. Letterfrack. Leenane. Westport. They'd stopped somewhere to let the dog out for a moment and to buy gas. A village with a tiny harbor. From the car, she could hear the mournful low of a foghorn, the groan of boats against the moorings. Niall had hardly spoken a word since they left Cragg's Head.

What woman in her right mind... She sat with her knees clamped closely together, her hands tucked under her. Did she so desperately want to feel whatever it was that Niall made her feel, that she couldn't see what seemed clear to everyone else? Or could she, as the outsider, see what others couldn't?

Mountains appeared and disappeared in the mist, the road played hide-and-seek with the ocean. You don't know Niall Maguire, Annie had warned so many times. Kate shot him a sideways glance. Hands loose on the wheel, he seemed lost in his own thoughts. Silent, detached.

She thought of Hugh's face contorted with anger as he raged on about Niall and she made a mental note to check on *Hugh's* whereabouts Monday night. The tall figure she'd seen could have been him and the timing was right. He *could* have pushed the girl off the cliff and still kept his appointment at Dooley's. In fact, he had seemed a little rattled.

And she still had to decide what to do about Rory. The night before, she'd gone into the kitchen for a glass of water and walked into an argument between Rory and Caitlin. She'd immediately apologized and tried to leave, but Caitlin had insisted she stay.

"Rory just admitted he was with Elizabeth Monday night." Her face pink, Caitlin stared at Kate. "He said you knew about it." She whirled on Rory. "You did it with her, didn't you? Don't lie to me. I know you did."

"Listen, you guys." Kate backed toward the door. "This really has nothing to do with me."

"No, stay, Katie. I want you to hear this," Caitlin said as she confronted Rory. "Did you or didn't you?" she asked him.

"Caitlin, I already told you, I don't remember much about what happened after we got back from Galway, but I didn't do anything with her, I swear. She went off somewhere, and I just passed out in the car."

"If you don't remember what happened, how do you know?" Caitlin's voice rose. "How do you know what you did? For all I know, maybe it was you who pushed her."

But of course Caitlin hadn't really believed that. "I've known Rory almost my whole life," she'd told Kate after Rory had stormed out. "Even though I could throttle him at the moment, I know he'd never do anything like that."

Annie had walked in then. "See, Katie, we all love Rory. Sure, I've known him since he wore nappies. I know his faults as well as he does. I know he's a bit fond of the drink and he's an eye for a pretty girl, but inside he's a good lad with a heart of gold. In all the years I've known him, he's never so much as laid a hand on anyone.''

"Never," Caitlin agreed.

"Never," Annie had repeated, her voice emphatic. "But Niall Maguire now, well, there's not a soul in Cragg's Head who has a clue as to what he's thinking. Ah, he's cordial, right enough, and if the mood strikes him, you may get a smile, but he's an odd one and there's no getting around it."

They drove on. Castlebar. Ballina. And then a sharp turn onto a narrow dirt road that wound and bumped through darkened fields and out to a rocky promontory where she could see a white painted tower and a dim light in the circular window. Outside, she heard the crash of waves against the rocks.

Niall parked in the long grasses and cut the engine. Then he turned his head and smiled at her. "You're very quiet," he said. "Everything all right?"

"No..." She shook her head. "It's not."

He caught her hand, tried to pull her to him, but she resisted. "What is it?"

"I'm scared to death for you, Niall." The words came out before she had time to think about them. "Not scared *of* you, which everyone seems to think I should be. Scared *for* you. They're on the verge of arresting you—"

"They've been on the verge of arresting me before," he said. "After Moruadh."

"Well, this time they've got two deaths to pin on you."

"I'll set Rufus on them." He reached for her. "Moving on to other things."

"No." She pushed him away. "How can you just joke about this?" She told him about Hugh Fitzpatrick's comments. About the film boxes on the cliff tops. The heater blasted out warm air, but she felt chilled. She huddled into her parka. "Look, we can't just sit back and let it happen—"

"We?"

"I want to help you, Niall." She moved sideways in her seat to face him. "Maybe you're too close to the situation to see how much trouble you're in, but it's bad. First thing we need to do is find you an attorney. You should have done that already, but we'll get onto it right away. Second, you've got to show them Moruadh's suicide note. Obviously their suspicions about Elizabeth are fueled by the uncertainty about Moruadh. We need to get that letter—"

"You can forget the letter, Kate."

"But the letter will prove you're innocent."

"I'll say it again, I'm not giving them the letter. Look, this is no different than what went on after Moruadh. It'll blow over." He took the keys from the ignition. "Can we just drop it, please?"

"Niall—"

"This isn't your concern, Kate. I'll deal with it in my own way."

"Meaning stay out of your business?" She tried to read a contradiction in his expression, but there was a guardedness there now. Something seemed to go hollow inside her. "That is what you mean, isn't it?"

"Ah, come on, Kate. Look, I appreciate your concern, but—"

"That's okay, I get it." Her pulse racing, she

watched his face in the dim light from the dashboard. God, what an idiot she'd been. She'd created this little melodrama with Niall as the misunderstood and falsely accused tragic hero and herself as the wise and courageous St. Kate the Rescuer. Clearly, though, he didn't want to be rescued. Clearly, what he wanted from her was just a noninvolved little action in the bedroom. Wham, bam, then please get out of my life. *Surprised?* the cynic asked. *When was the last time you accurately figured a guy's motivations anyway?* Her arm and shoulders were squashed against the passenger window, as far from Niall as possible. If he wanted noninvolvement, she'd give him noninvolvement. That's all she wanted anyway.

"Kate." He reached for her. "Look—"

"No. No apologies necessary. Well, actually, I'm the one who should be apologizing. Sorry I stuck my nose in."

"I've hurt your feelings," he said.

She laughed. "Don't be absurd. It's much better that we each understand where the other is coming from. Makes things much easier."

He kept watching her, his expression a little quizzical. Moments passed and neither of them moved. Then he reached across the seat for her and hauled her up onto his lap and they kissed. Long slow kisses that went on and on, the culmination of what had been building all day. Sex, she reminded herself. That's all you're here for. A little romp in the bedchamber. Her hat came off and her hair fell everywhere. Strands of it around her throat, hanging down over his face. He unbuttoned his jacket, unzipped her parka, held her so tight she felt her breasts flatten against his chest. They kissed again with renewed intensity.

"My God, Kate. I've wanted to do that all afternoon." His arm rested along the back of her seat, his eyes intent on her face. "I can't tell you what it means to me that you wanted to come up here."

He reached for her again, and they kissed, his body stretched out over hers. His mouth against her skin, he whispered her name, held her to him with an intensity that shook her. She could feel herself going under, drawn into the current of his feelings. With all the willpower she could summon, she put her hands on his chest and pushed him away. Stay out of my business, he'd said. Or words to that effect. Okay, she could do that.

"Listen, Niall. I have to say something. Before we go in, we need some kind of understanding. This is…I don't know what you want to call it. A onetime thing. A fling. Total noninvolvement. All that stuff."

Niall's eyes flickered across her face. The muscle in his cheek twitched. He said nothing.

"Okay?"

"Kate…"

"Really. I mean it. Obviously, it can't be anything else, so let's not even pretend it can be."

"Right." His face grim, he took the keys from the ignition, pulled open the car door. "Let's *pretend* it's a fling."

NIALL STOOD at the doorway to the bedroom, watched as Kate flicked on the light and walked across the room. She sat down on the edge of the bed, bounced up and down. "You can tell a lot about guys by their bedrooms," she said. "Black satin sheets would be very bad news. Water beds are bad, too. And leopard-skin bedspreads." She laughed. "*Forget* it."

"What does white cotton tell you?" Niall watched her turn down the corner of the quilt.

"Safe." She looked at him. "If not particularly imaginative."

"I suppose for a fling," he said, "you'd probably want black satin. I'm sorry I can't oblige you."

Kate shrugged, and flashed a quick look as she passed him. He followed her into the living room. Something had gone wrong in the car. He'd only wanted to keep her from getting mixed up in the mess his life had become, but he hadn't expressed himself well. Then she'd made the remark about a fling and now, for the life of him, he couldn't read what was on her mind. He watched her, thought of the doll back at the castle. She'd be safer here, with him.

Arms folded across her chest, over at the window now, she turned her head to look at him. "So how long ago was this a lighthouse?"

"It hasn't been for years." He came up behind her, put his hands on her shoulders. "It was never very well thought out to begin with. They were going to use it for big ships, but only fishing and pleasure boats pass by and they know the area well enough."

They stood for a while, staring out at the dark sea. A pinpoint of a light glowed out on the horizon. He watched Kate's reflection in the window, caught her watching him.

"We don't have to do this, Kate," he said softly.

"I'm fine."

With a bright, false smile, she pulled away from him, started across the room. "What do you have to eat? I'm starving." In the kitchen, she opened the refrigerator, pulled out a bottle of Moselle. "A little sweet for my taste," she said with a glance at the label. "But it'll do. Where do you keep your glasses?"

He took two down from the cupboard, watched as she poured the wine and downed half of it in a quick gulp. She filled the glass again and raised it to her mouth, then looked up and saw him staring at her.

"What?"

"I meant what I said before. If you've changed your mind, you can have my bed," he said. "I'll sleep on the couch."

"Niall, I said I'm fine. This is what I want. Really." A moment passed. Another tight smile. "Anyway, how can we have a fling if you sleep on the couch?"

He studied her. Back against the refrigerator, arms folded across her chest. Green cardigan, a shade lighter than her eyes. Same color as the ribbon that tied back her hair. Convincing herself as she tried to convince him, even though they both knew that a fling was the last thing either of them wanted. But God, he wanted her. Wanted to make love to her.

"What are we waiting for?" Glass in hand, Kate came over to where he stood and kissed him. She drank some more wine, looped an arm around his neck. "Let's go check out your sheets."

"No." He pushed her away. "We're going to eat."

"Eat?"

"Eat." He opened the refrigerator and scouted the contents, suddenly not in the mood for the picnic he'd envisioned. "I'm famished, and you're drinking wine as if it's water." He pulled out bacon, tomatoes and eggs and took them over to the counter. "And because after the bouillabaisse fiasco, I have my reputation to maintain."

"What's that going to be?" She stood behind him, watching as he opened the package of bacon. "An omelette?"

"Nothing that complicated. A fry-up."

"Sounds very Irish." She slid her hands under his shirt, leaned her head against his back. "Is it going to take all night to make?"

"It might, if you keep doing that." He felt one small, cool hand playing with the hair on his chest, the other sliding beneath his belt, down over his belly. "Get away from me, you're a corrupting influence."

"Yeah, it's something I'm known for. Corrupting Kate, they call me, the scourge of *daycent* Irish men."

"Have you corrupted many?"

"None so far." She kissed the back of his neck, then came around to stand beside him. After a moment, she hopped up on the counter. Legs swinging, she leaned down to kiss him, her hair like a canopy over them both. "But I'm working on it."

"You're doing a fine job." He put down the knife and glanced at her faded jeans and hiking boots. With one hand, he grasped her ankle. "But these aren't exactly the stuff of the boudoir, are they?"

"What do you want?" she asked, laughing. "Marabou slippers?"

"No." He moved over to stand between her legs, unlaced the boot and slipped it off. Then he did the same with the other one. Her socks were navy, heavy and thick. He held her left foot in his hand. Beneath the thick wool, her bones felt as fragile as eggshell. Slowly, carefully, he peeled off the sock. Down over her ankle. Off her toes. When he looked up, Kate was staring straight at him with huge, unblinking green eyes.

"So what was it I was doing then?" he asked.

"Beats me." Her eyes still on his face. "Something about dinner."

"Right." He nodded at the fridge. "Mushrooms."

She jumped down from the counter, brought the mushrooms to him.

"By the way—" she stuck out her foot "—you forgot the other sock."

"So I did." He took the mushrooms to the sink.

"Typical male," she said. "Everything half-assed. Bouillabaisse. Socks. Flings."

Whistling, he separated three rashers of bacon, cut up the tomatoes and mushrooms and put everything in the frying pan to cook. Then he turned to her and undid all the buttons on her cardigan. Pulled it off her shoulders and let it fall to the floor.

A slight smile flickered on her face, but she said nothing.

Still whistling, he caught her hands, raised them above her head and pulled off her white T-shirt. Next he removed the silky camisole and dropped it on top of the rest.

Her bra was pink cotton. Ribbons of her long red hair hampered his progress as he pushed the straps off her shoulders. The bra fell to the floor beside the camisole.

Down on his knees, he unzipped her jeans and slid them over her hips. Removed them, one leg at a time, with her hands on his shoulders to steady herself. Finally he stripped off her rosebud-patterned underpants.

Beneath the harsh fluorescent light, the mass of red hair that tumbled around her shoulders was a shade or two lighter than the triangle between her thighs.

Freckles, like those he'd counted on her nose, smattered across her breasts and belly. Arms at her sides, legs slightly parted, she stood on the black-and-white tiled floor like a small and perfect chess piece.

"Half-assed, is it?" he asked.

"Half-assed," she repeated, lifting her foot. "You still haven't taken this sock off."

"I was saving that for last." He turned off the stove and took her hand. "Let's go and try out the sheets."

"Oh, no. It's my turn now," she said as she unbuttoned his shirt. "And the kitchen's just fine."

THE KITCHEN *WAS* FINE, as was the couch in the living room and, finally, the bed. Fine didn't describe it. Fantastic, incredible, mind-blowing did a better job. But now, lying in Niall's arms with the light creeping in the windows, a cloud had drifted across her horizon.

This time next week, she would be lying in her own bed in Santa Monica.

Back in Santa Monica. An empty apartment and microwaved dinners. Falling asleep alone to the sounds of the neighbor's clock radio and the traffic outside her window. Dreaming of a gray-eyed man and misty green fields on another continent.

Niall stirred, opened his eyes and smiled lazily. "You know something?" He rolled on his side to face her. "After last night, I'll never think of the kitchen floor in quite the same way again."

"Yeah, but the bed was more comfortable."

"Too conventional for a fling, though."

"Probably." She watched the play of sunlight across the rumpled bed, traced his jaw with her finger.

Tears stung her nose. She turned on her back, away from him.

"You've gone very serious all of a sudden," he said. "What were you thinking?"

She shook her head. "Nothing."

"Ah come on, Kate." He pulled her up onto his body so that she sat straddling his stomach. "Take a bold leap."

"I was thinking maybe I should move to Ireland." Her face went hot. It hadn't come out quite as nonchalant as she'd planned. "Learn to play the flute, or weave or something," she said, joking now to cover. "Entertain the tourists." *God, what an idiot she was.* She wanted to pick up her clothes and leave.

His hands on her knees, he watched her face.

"It's the sex." She forced her mouth into a smile. "It's addled my brain. Either that or the fog."

"Probably," he said, unsmiling. "Besides, I can't see you with a loom."

Embarrassed, angry with herself, she climbed off him and went to look for her clothes. He'd taken her seriously. Right now he was probably wondering how the hell he was going to get off the hook.

In the kitchen, she picked up her panties and bra. Well, he didn't have to worry about it. Her return ticket was safe in her briefcase. She stepped into her panties, glanced out of the window. Sunshine—the first she'd seen in Ireland—gleamed off the blue ocean. A long curve of sand, high rock cliffs, a grove of trees clustered darkly along the edge. It all struck her as heartbreakingly beautiful and she felt her eyes fill with tears. *Cut it out.* She moved away from the window. Bra dangling from one hand, she gathered up her jeans and sweater and then she heard Niall behind her.

Flustered, as though they hadn't spent the night making love, she hugged herself. He stood in the doorway, naked still, one hand on the doorjamb.

"Hi." She nodded at her clothes. "I was just getting dressed."

"So I see." He came over to her, put his hands on her shoulders and looked into her eyes. "All right, what is it?"

"What is what?"

"You know what I mean. Why did you suddenly bolt?"

"I didn't. It's getting late. I need to get back to Annie's."

"Kate."

"Really. I've got a bunch of things to do. In case you've forgotten, I don't have much more time here." His gaze on hers was unblinking. "Okay," she added, "I just thought maybe you thought I was serious."

"About you moving to Ireland?"

"I don't want you to think that I was going to descend on you, or something."

"God forbid."

"I mean we've had a great time, and I'm really glad I met you, but that's it."

"Hadn't we already established that it would be that way?"

"Yeah, we did, but I thought you might think I'd gone soft or something." She laughed. "You know how it is, you sleep with a woman and suddenly she's talking commitment. I just want you to know that wasn't the case. I mean, I have my life in Santa Monica, and you have yours here and that's the way it has to be.''

"Kate.''

"What?''

"Shut up and take off your knickers.''

He drew her close and kissed her. She breathed in the scent of him, felt the graze of his beard on her face, her neck, her breasts. His tongue circled her nipples, his hands moved down her back, over her buttocks and thighs. Senses aflame, she didn't even try to fight him. What was the point? Even after they'd made love half the night, she felt weak with desire for him.

With his body, he guided her down onto the floor, then stripped off her panties. She opened her mouth to his tongue, opened her legs wide as his fingers plunged inside her. Head flung back, her back arched, she writhed and moaned as his fingers kept stroking and caressing her until, in a wave of white-hot sensation, she called his name aloud.

A moment later, he slipped inside her. His mouth on her skin, his breath in her ear, she rocked with his body. Faster and faster, higher and higher. The floor creaking under them. Her hips moving under him, arms flung above her head now, her movements matching his in growing frenzy until she felt him come with a shudder that ran down the length of his body.

CHAPTER SIXTEEN

"SOME HAM, about four different kinds of cheese," Niall said later that morning. He held open the refrigerator door, peered at the packages. "An Irish cheddar, something blue, something that smells like sweaty feet. Gorgonzola. Grapes, pears. Will that do?"

"As long as it doesn't require cooking," Kate said.

He turned from the fridge to smile at her. She wore one of his old flannel shirts, black leggings and a pair of his heavy gray socks. The shirt came almost to her knees, the socks flapped beyond her toes. As he carried the cheese and bread over to the counter, he dropped a kiss on the top of her head.

"What time is your flight tomorrow?" he asked.

"Five-fifteen in the evening." She spread butter on a slice of bread. "What do you have to drink?"

"Beer, Jameson's, champagne and what's left of the Moselle you sloshed down last night. Can't you just stay a little longer?"

"I have to pack," she said from the refrigerator. "Want a beer? That wine was way too sweet."

"You seemed quite keen on it last night."

"Last night I was gearing myself up for a fling." She poured beer into two glasses. "And now the fling has flung. So to speak."

He took the food and beer into the living room, set

it down on a table by the fireplace, pulled the couch up in front of the fire. Kate sat at one end, knees curled up to her chin, arms wrapped around them. Rufus stretched out in front of the fire, opened his eyes, sighed, then went back to sleep. The room was warm, warmer than he liked it himself, but that was all right. Kate was always cold. Outside, the high bright sunlight on the water belied the chill air. Wind whipped the waves into foam-edged sheets. He sat on the floor by her feet, his back to the couch, toes tangled in the dog's rough coat. Restless, he got up and went to the stereo. From the stack of compact disks, he pulled out Moruadh's last recording and slid it into the tray. A moment later, her voice filled the air. ''Tell the World, I Died For Love.'' All things considered, not the best selection he could have made.

''I have a tape of this recording,'' Kate said as he sat down again. ''I played it the first day I was in Ireland.''

''A bit extreme, dying for love.'' He stretched his legs over the dog's back, felt the warmth of the turf logs on the soles of his feet. ''But there's almost nothing else we wouldn't do for it, is there?'' Moruadh's voice mingled with the sound of the waves breaking on the rocks beneath them, the more distant roar of the ocean. ''Sure, it's brought down plenty of very powerful people over the ages. Kings, presidents, generals. Very potent stuff, love is.''

''Kind of like booze,'' Kate said. ''You feel great while you're drinking it, but it can make you start doing stupid things that you'll probably regret.''

''Ah, but you can live without the drink,'' he said.

''You can live without illusions, too.'' She got up suddenly.

"Listen, it's getting a little warm in here, even for me. Can we go for a walk or something?"

"We can." He pulled himself up from the floor, picked up the tray with the food and glasses, took it into the kitchen and returned the cheeses and grapes to the fridge. When he turned around, Kate was watching him, tears in her eyes.

"What is it?"

She shook her head. "Nothing."

"Kate?"

"I'm fine." She bent to tug at one of the socks. "I'll go get my jacket."

He took a bag of dog food from the cupboard, poured some into Rufus's bowl. Then he wiped off the counters, grabbed his jacket from the peg behind the kitchen door and dug a scarf from the pocket. He pulled on his jacket, walked over to the window, stared outside. Watched the waves break on the shingle. He heard Kate behind him.

"My jacket was on the bureau in your bedroom," she said. "When I went to pick it up, I knocked a pile of your papers to the floor." She held out her hand. "This fell out."

From where he stood, he couldn't see what she held in her hand, but her face had gone pale. Without another word, she handed him a picture. Elizabeth. Naked, posed like a model in a girlie magazine. On the back, she had written, "To Niall. I'm all yours."

SHOULDERS HUNCHED against the cold, Kate jammed her hands in her pockets, hurrying to keep up with Niall's long stride. Seagulls wheeled and screeched overhead, and the smell of the ocean filled her nose. Her skin beneath the parka felt clammy and chilled and she bit her lip to stop her teeth chattering. He had taken the picture from her, whistled for the dog, and they'd left. Walked for nearly half an hour without speaking. The silence was beginning to get to her.

"Well?" She shot him a sideways glance.

"If you're wanting me to explain it, I'm not going to."

"Stay out of my business, right? Just like you said yesterday."

"I won't constantly explain myself and reassure you," he said. "I'm not forcing you to be here. If you feel that you're in some kind of danger, then I'll take you back."

"That's not the point, Niall. I just want to know why you would have a picture like this of a girl who was supposedly just a student. *Did* you sleep with her?"

"Sure, I slept with her then took pictures of her. Brought out my black satin sheets for the occasion. I've a whole gallery of similar shots. Is that what you want to hear?"

"What I want to hear is the truth."

"She sent it to me."

"Why would she do that?"

"Good question. Maybe I've got it wrong. Maybe I found it on the seat of my car. Ah, no—" he slapped his forehead "—now I remember. A seagull dropped it off. He was trying to frame me."

"Okay, I'm sorry I asked. Obviously you don't feel I deserve any kind of explanation. I'll try and keep that in mind from now on."

"What difference will it make, Kate, what I tell you?" He laughed. "You may believe that I'm innocent of murder, but when it comes to trusting me here—'' he stabbed at his chest ''—that's something different entirely. Trust is what it comes down to, Kate. You trusting me, trusting yourself instead of trying to turn everything into a tidy little package that you can just explain away.''

Speechless, she just watched him walk away from her, out across the soft strip of sand. He bent, picked up a stone and threw it for the dog. The tide was almost out and the wind had the tang of the sea and mudflats exposed by the low tide. It blew into her face, stung her eyes. She swiped at them with the back of her hand.

God, it was a good thing she was leaving soon. Her hand to her forehead to deflect the light off the ocean, she peered out at the water. He wore the long dark overcoat he'd been wearing the day she met him on the cliffs. Open now, as it had been then, flapping in the breeze. Niall. The man Moruadh had loved and, confused and unbalanced, died for. The answer to the question Kate, herself, had come to Ireland to find.

Hands jammed in the pockets of her parka, she walked slowly along the beach. The sand was soft and her feet sank into it, leaving little pools of water where she stepped. The long beach swept out to the ruins of something. Ireland was full of the ruins of something. Out on the horizon, a boat, like a child's toy, moved almost imperceptibly along the line of sky and water. She stood for a moment, then Niall turned and walked toward her, and they started back along the beach in silence.

When they reached a narrow ledge where the path ended and the stairs to the top of the cliff began, she stopped to catch her breath. Above her, the steep path rose, almost perpendicular to the cliff face. She glanced at Niall's back, heard the waves crashing below her and felt a wave of vertigo. Then something hit the side of her face. Startled and thrown off balance, she staggered slightly. As she tried to steady herself, she lost her footing and fell backward.

A jumble of sounds and fragmented images flashed across her brain. Niall's voice shouting out to her, his outstretched hand. A tuft of grass, the rumble of loosened rock as it tumbled down. Her fingers clawing at air, more grass, more rocks, waves breaking below. After what seemed like forever, she managed to grab a clump of weeds and the images stopped. Blood pounding in her ears, her body pressed against the rock face, she held on by her fingertips.

Above her, she saw Niall scrambling down the cliff. Showers of rock, loosened by his movements, cascaded past her head, and then he was hoisting her up onto the ledge and safety. Violent tremors shaking her body, she reached out her hand to help him up and then she was in his arms, sobbing into his shoulder.

For a while, neither of them spoke. She felt Niall's heart thudding against her chest, his hands stroking her hair. When the trembling subsided a little, he pulled away to look at her face.

"Kate. What happened?" His face was ashen. "One minute you were there and then..."

"I don't know." She felt a trickle of blood run down her cheek. "A rock or something hit my face." Her teeth started to chatter, and Niall pulled off his coat, wrapped it around her shoulders and guided her so that she stood with her back to the cliff, shielded from the wind by his body.

"Are you all right?" His arms were braced against the cliffs, his palms on either side of her head.

"I'm fine, a couple of scratches. More shaken than anything else."

As her own breathing slowly returned to normal, she realized that he was still shaking. Eyes dark with shock, he looked haunted. Unable to speak, touched by the naked emotion on his face, she buried her face in his shoulder.

"God, Niall, I'm sorry. About everything."

He looked at her for a moment, then he pulled her close and held her again. Finally, he moved away to see her face, looked into her eyes. And she wondered whether he could tell that she was in love with him.

NEITHER OF THEM said much as they walked, arms entwined, back to the lighthouse. They made love in the bedroom, woke during the night and made love again. With Niall's arms around her, she finally fell asleep. When she opened her eyes, the room was filled with morning light.

She rolled over to find Niall already awake. Hands clasped behind his head, he lay on his back, eyes wide open. Without a word, he pulled her close, and they kissed with their bodies stretched out together, soft deep kisses that seemed to meld her to him. Every cliché she'd ever heard, clamored to be said aloud. I've never felt this way before. I never thought I *could* feel this way. *I love you.*

Her eyes filled, and she buried her face in his neck.

"Kate." He pulled away to look at her. "What is it?"

She heard the choked sound from her throat at exactly the same moment they heard a loud pounding at the front door. Niall sat up beside her, then without a word, pulled on his jeans and left the room.

Heart racing, she got up and extricated her own clothes from the jumbled pile on the floor. Dressed, she ran her fingers through her hair and started to follow him out, when it occurred to her that she had no idea who the caller might be.

Minutes later, he came back into the bedroom, his face pale. Through the open door, she saw a uniformed Garda.

"I'm being arrested." Niall reached for her hand. "For the murder of Elizabeth Jenkins."

NIALL SAW THE COLOR drain from Kate's face. Her hand to her mouth, she dropped onto the edge of the bed. With a glance at the Garda standing in the open doorway, he sat down next to her, "Listen," he said softly, "it's going to be all right—"

"No." She stood, then bent to bring her face close to his, her voice low and intense. "You can't still believe that. It's *not* all right. This is what I've been trying to tell you. They're arresting you, for God's sake." She turned to address the Garda. "Look, can you give us a minute?"

"I'll be right here," the Garda said.

Kate pushed the door closed. Stayed with her back to it, arms folded across her chest. "Niall, you have to show them the damn note," she said. "If you'd cleared that up, you wouldn't be under all this suspicion now. I mean it's noble and wonderful that you want to protect Moruadh, but—"

"*Kate.*" Behind her, the Garda had reopened the door and was looking into the room with undisguised curiosity. Niall steeled himself for what he had to say.

"Go back to Santa Monica." He got up from the bed, grabbed a clean shirt from the closet and put it on. "Get married, have some children. Forget all this."

She blinked, clearly disconcerted. "What—"

"I said go home." An image of the doll with the note attached to it gave his words conviction. "This has nothing to do with you. Don't get yourself mixed up in it."

A moment passed. A range of expressions played across her face. She stood in front of him, clutching his shirt. "Quit playing the damn protector," she said. "You've done it long enough. It's time for you to help yourself."

In the hallway, the Garda cleared his throat.

Niall disengaged Kate's hands. "I will. In my own way."

"Your own way obviously isn't working."

"Kate—"

"No. I am not about to turn my back on you. I care about you, damn it."

"Well, it's not mutual." He couldn't look at her. "It was great, but now it's over. I don't need help. I don't need support. I mean it. Go. I don't need you."

CHAPTER SEVENTEEN

"WELL, HE'S WRONG, isn't he, Rufus?" As she fumbled with the unfamiliar instrument panel of Niall's Land Rover, Kate addressed the dog in the passenger seat. "He does need us. And we're going to help him whether he wants us to or not." She patted the top of the dog's head. "He's just stubborn. Like most males. No offense to you, of course."

Niall had given her the key to the castle's front door and asked her to drive Rufus back to Cragg's Head. He would call a friend to come and feed the dog, he said. He would write to her, he said. To let her know how everything turned out.

Kate peered through the windshield as the car's headlights caught the green directional sign in the distance. The dashboard clock blinked three o'clock. After Niall had left with the Garda, she'd lost thirty minutes chasing after the dog and almost an hour driving around Westport looking for an open gas station. And then, of course, the inevitable wrong turns.

She massaged the back of her neck. Her head ached and her shoulders felt stiff with tension. The Garda superintendent would need to see the suicide note to be convinced of Niall's innocence in Moruadh's death and, with Niall safely under arrest, they were hardly likely to go to the trouble of retrieving it. Which left only one alternative. She thought of the west wing's ragged ledge and Moruadh's study on the far side of it. It would be dark up there, but she couldn't afford to wait for daylight.

"Your master had better damn well appreciate this," she told Rufus. "I wouldn't do it if I didn't love him."

Her estimation had been correct. It was nearly five as she drove up the winding road to the castle; the sky was black with not a single star to punctuate the darkness. The car's headlights caught something moving in the shrubbery along the side of the road, and she stepped on the brakes thinking it might be an animal. She drove a few feet farther to the front door, parked and turned off the ignition.

Rufus jumped out of the car after her and bounded down the hill. Shivering in the cold air, Kate made her way to the front door. She turned the key in the lock, but the door wouldn't budge. Nothing about this place is easy, Niall had said as he'd fumbled with the key. He'd been right. A twig snapped somewhere, and she froze as she tried to pinpoint the location. She peered into the dark night.

"Rufus." Her voice sounded shrill in the dark night. "Here, boy."

She waited a moment, suddenly edgy and alert. The castle, in broad daylight with Niall beside her, unnerved her. At night, by herself, it had the qualities of a nightmare. Keys in hand, she thought about driving back down to the village. Maybe Patrick or Rory would be willing to help her. And then someone behind her said her name.

"Hugh! God, you scared the hell out of me." Heart pounding, Kate gaped at him. His long hair slicked back in a ponytail, he wore a battered brown-and-green tweed jacket, black cotton shirt and a Pepto-Bismol–pink knit tie. Even in her rattled state, it struck her that he either had a real sartorial flair or truly awful taste. "What are you doing here? Where's your car?"

"I walked. Needed a little fresh air." He glanced at the key in her hand. "Trouble with the lock?"

As she started to explain, he took the key from her, fitted it into the lock and shouldered open the door. "There."

"Thanks." Uneasy still, she glanced over Hugh's shoulder trying to spot the dog. "Rufus," she called again. "Come on."

Hugh smiled. "Probably has a lady friend down the hill." He blew into his hands, rubbed them together. "Bit chilly, but not a bad evening for romance. I was walking up here to see you, but I ducked into the bushes when I heard your car, otherwise you'd have run me over."

"You came to see me?" Kate frowned. "How did you even know I'd be here?"

"Since your car wasn't outside Annie's…" He smiled. "Reporters are good at putting two and two together. And you missed our appointment. Again."

"Oh God, I'm sorry." The truth was she couldn't even remember making another appointment with him. After the kiss fiasco, it had seemed better to keep her distance. "It just, um, slipped my mind."

"It's all right." He waved away her apology. "It isn't the first time I've lost a woman to Maguire. All I can hope is that it will be the last time."

Purse still in hand, she looked at him. He'd always appeared a little disheveled and pale, but now his face was almost ashen. Jingling the change in his pockets, he glanced beyond her shoulder to the dimly lit great hall visible through the open front door. From somewhere down the hill, Kate heard Rufus bark. She leaned forward to call him again, and then in a blur of movement, he took her arm and pulled her inside the room. He slammed the door closed behind them.

"Not to criticize your hospitality—" he smiled "—but it's bloody cold out there, and I don't fancy standing on the doorstep all night. I've brought Moruadh's letters for you to see."

Kate dropped her purse and car keys onto a table. A shiver ran down her spine. True, she *had* asked to see the letters and she probably had said something about seeing him again, so maybe it was reasonable for him to think he'd find her here. But in the dim light of the cavernous room, he spooked her. Eyeing the stuffed eagle over the mantelpiece and the fox and badger on the walls, Kate thought of the fortune-teller's words. Death *was* all around.

A noise behind her made her start. She turned to see a giant candelabra slowly swinging. Caught in a draft, the trembling crystals sent shadows dancing, wild and erratic, on the walls. Her teeth started to chatter. She forced herself to smile at Fitzpatrick.

"So." Arms folded across her chest. "You've got Moruadh's letters?"

"You Americans are a very direct lot, aren't you?" He shook his head. "You forget our appointment, leave me standing on the doorstep and now it's down to business. No niceties, no chat. No offer of a drink. Just a demand and not a very friendly one, either."

"I'm sorry, Hugh." He was right, but she wasn't in the mood for social calls. She took a deep breath. "What would you like? Tea, coffee?"

"A little of what you gave Maguire would be nice."

"Excuse me?"

"Sorry." He smiled. "A failed attempt at humor."

Involuntarily, Kate looked again at the door behind him. In her peripheral vision, she could see the black phone on the table beside her. Outside, the wind shrieked, branches tapped against the window. Feigning nonchalance, hands tucked under her arms for warmth, she strolled over to the table where she'd left her keys and purse.

"I'm just a bit disappointed." Fitzpatrick jingled the change in his pockets more violently. "I was so encouraged after we spoke. Finally, I thought to myself, someone who sees Moruadh's death for what it was. Murder."

"I think I told you I wanted to keep an open mind until I'd heard all the facts," she said. At the table now, she started to reach for her car keys when she noticed the open drawer. Her hand froze. A small plastic doll lay on top of some papers, beside it a note scrawled in heavy black ink. *Turn yourself in, Maguire. If she dies…* She looked at Hugh, saw his eyes register the doll. With a faint smile, he returned his glance to her.

"The thing is, I'd taken you for a levelheaded woman. A woman who wouldn't be seduced by Maguire's boyish charm. After all, wasn't it you who'd gone on about judging someone on surface appearance?"

"I'm sure I did."

"But that was before you met him, wasn't it?"

"Listen, Hugh…" She picked up the keys. In a flash, he grabbed them from her, shoved them in his pants pocket. For a moment, their eyes locked. Slowly—his eyes never leaving her face—he withdrew a pack of cigarettes from his jacket pocket. As he lit up, his hand shook slightly, then he exhaled and peered at her through a drift of smoke.

"I have to say, even for Maguire, this must be a record of sorts. What was it, three days and he'd got you into his bed? Or did he slip it to you that first day up at the castle?"

He leaned against the doorjamb, smoking, a faint smile as though he'd asked a polite social question. Kate fixed her eyes on his shoulder. Slow breaths. Think. What is it you're supposed to do in these situations? Don't antagonize. Don't show fear. Did Ireland use 911?

"Maguire did murder Moruadh, you know."

"So you've said."

"He murdered her because he was jealous. For once in his life, Moruadh's life didn't revolve around him. He couldn't stand that. He also knew that Moruadh wanted to marry me. Did I tell you that?"

"You mentioned it."

"Moruadh had accepted my proposal. She was going to divorce Maguire and marry me. When he found out, he killed her."

Kate nodded. She clenched her jaw to stop her teeth chattering. Her eyes burned from the cigarette smoke. Should she make a break for the side door?

"Something tells me you're still not convinced." Cigarette between his teeth, he withdrew some letters from his inside pocket. "Moruadh sent these. May I read part of one?"

"Go ahead."

"'Niall is a plague upon me, Hugh,'" he read.

"'He will not leave me alone. He is obsessed with me. I have no life of my own while he is around.'" He watched her face as though for reaction. "'A plague on me. Obsessed by me.'"

"You showed them to the Gardai?"

"Of course I did. Fat lot of good with the old superintendent. As good as on Maguire's payroll, that one. This new fellow, though, paid a little more attention." He smiled. "Between the two of us, these letters are part of the reason they finally stopped dragging their feet and picked him up."

"You mean you just showed them these letters and it was enough?"

"Ah, finally we get a little reaction," he said. "Lover boy's in jail. And you don't like that, do you?"

She looked at him, her brain racing. If Niall had been arrested for Elizabeth's murder on the basis of Moruadh's letters, now she *had* to retrieve the suicide note. First she had to get rid of Hugh.

"So, Hugh. Why don't you just tell me why you're here?"

He laughed. "Haven't I already told you?"

"Seriously." There were five, maybe six steps to the side door off the kitchen. With luck, it wouldn't be bolted. Her eyes fixed on his, she took two steps backward. "Maguire's in jail now, Hugh. You obviously believe that's where he belongs." She took another step. "And you may be right." Another. "I'll have to give you my address in the States and you can write and let me know how it all turns out."

She turned to run, but in an instant he was behind her. As he reached to grab her arm, she ducked and ran across the room, throwing obstacles in his way.

A chair missed him, but the lamp she hurled with both hands hit his forehead. It only slowed him for a few seconds. He grabbed a handful of her hair, jerked her head back, arching her neck and throat. With one hand around her throat, he began to press lightly against her jugular vein.

"What do I want? you ask." His voice was soft as a lover's. "What do I want? I want to have you like Maguire had you. That's what I want. Mind you, I have to say I've grown a little tired of his castoffs. It's been that way my whole life, you know." The pressure of his fingers intensified. "It's not fair, is it? But then life's not fair."

Her vision began to blur.

"No doubt you think it's unfair that lover boy's behind bars, but I'm here to take his place. When I'm through with you, you'll never think about Maguire again."

As he spoke, he half dragged her over to the couch, pushed her down and fell on top of her. One hand on her chest, he tugged at the zipper of her jeans.

"Maguire's castoff." He shoved his knee between her legs. "Sure, I'd like to have been there first, but this'll do."

With massive effort, she brought her knee up and jabbed him in the groin. As she jumped up from the couch, he caught her and hit her across the face. While she was still reeling, he slammed her back down, pinning her with his hand. Barely conscious of his face anymore, she stared wordlessly. Blackness threatened, the room seemed to tilt.

"Bitch." He grabbed the front of her shirt. Buttons flew. "Just like all women, aren't you? You'll put out when it suits you, won't you? Just like Moruadh after

Maguire had enough of her. Just like that little tramp up on the cliffs. Sure, all over me until Rory shows his face. Well, I showed her and I'll show you.''

He reached for his fly.

Kate screamed. A loud, bloodcurdling sound that filled the space between them. Kept on screaming until he shoved a hand, the one he'd been using to pin her down, across her mouth. She bit him, hard, and struggled into a sitting position.

''Listen to me, damn it,'' she said. He pushed her, but she shook herself free. ''Just listen to me. Look, we're both writers, okay?'' White spots blinked before her eyes. She struggled to rally her thoughts. ''You know what it's like, right? Gotta get the story, right?'' *Keep talking.* ''Sure, I screwed Niall. Only way I could get any information from him, okay? He's a wuss, though. Couldn't get it up.'' *Sorry, Niall.* His grip on her arm lessened slightly. ''What a joke, huh?''

''Oh, for God's sake.'' He hit her again. ''Shut up, if you can't do any better than that.''

''Okay, listen to this.'' Something warm trickled from her mouth. Her lip was starting to swell. ''I know where Moruadh's journals are.'' Something flickered in his eyes, and she pressed on. ''Remember you said the Gardai couldn't find them? You were right, Maguire hid them. He knew they'd be incriminating.''

''Where are they?''

''Right here in the castle. Want me to go and get them?''

He laughed.

''Okay.'' She swallowed, brain scrambling madly.

"I'll show you. They're on the other side of the castle. West wing. Do you know where that is?"

He made an impatient gesture, then tugged at her hair again, pulling her head back at a horizontal angle. "If this is a bloody trick..."

"It's no trick." A sudden image of the narrow ledge and the churning ocean made her feel faint. She took a breath. Her shirt hung open, her jeans unzipped. Fitzpatrick's hand clutched her hair. "Listen, Hugh. There's no electricity over there and it's about the temperature of Antarctica. Could I at least get my jacket?"

"You'll live." He yanked her to her feet. "Let's go."

His hand still holding her hair, she led him up the main staircase, along a narrow hallway and out onto a wide gallery that looked down over the main hall. Not sure she even remembered how to get to the west tower, she started down one corridor, up another. Her body shook so hard, it ached. Down more stairs and then into the dank corridors leading to the west tower.

Her pulse quickened. With a deep breath, she pushed open the heavy door leading into the tower. Instantly they were plunged into blackness. A blast of damp air struck her face. Behind her, Fitzpatrick stumbled on something, fell and let go of her hair.

Instantly, she broke loose, bolted down the corridor. Faster, faster, her breath pumping. Muscles screaming. Blind in the darkness. Another corridor, around the corner. A wall at the end. Fitzpatrick's footsteps behind her. She felt along the wall for the heavy wooden door. Steel bolts on it, she remembered. Where was it? Fitzpatrick's footsteps coming closer. Then her fingers touched the metal bolts.

As she pulled open the wooden door, she felt his fingers brush her hair and then the door slammed behind her. Salt air hit her face like a slap. Far below the narrow ledge on which she stood, she heard the roar of the ocean against the rocks. Panting, she flattened herself against the wall. In the pitch darkness, she could see nothing but the faint phosphorescence of the water. And then the door burst open and Fitzpatrick's scream echoed in the darkness. Relief washed over her.

And then a hand gripped her ankle.

FEELING LIKE A CARICATURE of every prisoner he'd seen in the westerns he'd once watched, Niall peered through the bars on the holding cell. They'd taken his watch when they brought him in, but he guessed four or five hours had passed—filled mostly with telephone discussions with the solicitor. Now he tried to make out the time on the clock at the far end of the corridor. Nearly seven, as close as he could tell.

God, it was so damn ironic. Just that morning in bed with Kate, he'd wondered how he could keep her in his life forever. Now she was probably somewhere over the Atlantic.

He peered up and down the corridor. He didn't even have her number back in the States. Annie would have it, he would ring her as soon as they let him out. They *would* let him out. His solicitor had assured him of that.

Deep in thought, he didn't hear Michael Riordan approach the cell.

"You're free to leave at any time." Riordan unlocked the cell door and pulled it open. "But first I'd like to offer my apologies and fill you in on what's happened.''

Niall followed Riordan to a small office at one end of the station.

"Sit down, will you." Riordan moved to the chair behind his desk. "It appears likely that Hugh Fitz-patrick murdered Elizabeth.''

"Fitzpatrick?'' Niall rubbed his eyes with the heel of his hand and stared at the sergeant. "Hugh Fitz-patrick?''

"It appears so. We've been watching him all week. Talked to all those young lads who congregate in Dooley's. A few things Fitzpatrick told us about his whereabouts Monday night didn't quite add up, and we had it from a couple of sources that he'd bragged about…'' Riordan cleared his throat. "Apparently Elizabeth had been quite generous with her favors.''

Niall nodded, thinking over what Riordan had told him. Hugh had openly accused him of Moruadh's murder. Framing him for Elizabeth's was probably an act of revenge.

"Hugh's been very keen to have you arrested,'' Riordan said. "And after we picked you up this morning, he was down here at the station going on about how he'd known it all along and, well, a few things he said made us suspect we'd got the wrong man behind bars.''

"Where is Hugh now?'' Niall asked.

Riordan shrugged. "When we went to the news-paper office to bring him in for questioning, he was nowhere to be found. His car's parked outside, but no sign of him. No doubt realized we were onto him and he's hiding somewhere. We've got men out looking for him though.''

Niall thought of the doll, which was almost certainly Hugh's work. Thought again of Kate. As much as he'd wanted her to stay in Ireland, he hoped to God that she'd caught her flight. He used the phone on Riordan's desk to call Annie.

"I thought she'd decided to stay in Sligo," Annie said. "Her flight would have left hours ago, but her suitcases and most of her clothes are still here."

RIORDAN DROVE HIM to the castle. Rufus was out in front, barking. Kate's Peugeot was there, parked next to the Land Rover. In an instant, Niall was out of the car, his feet crunching on the gravel. As he pulled open the unlocked front door, he felt his face freeze. The great hall looked as though a child with a tantrum had been through it. Broken lamps on the floor, upended chairs. A small table on its side.

As if in a dream, Niall bent to pick up a yellow ribbon. He'd seen it that morning in Kate's hair. He walked with it in his hand over to the couch. Something glittered on the rug. A tiny glass button. Blindly, no direction in mind, he ran up the stairs to the first floor, calling Kate's name.

His brain mapping the castle, he tore through the maze of rooms and corridors. From the state of the great hall, she must have been trying to get away from Fitzpatrick. Was she hiding? He yelled her name again. Did Fitzpatrick have her locked away? He tried to remember the areas he'd shown her. The studio. Convinced for a moment that he would find her there, he flung open the door. As he called out her name, he almost smiled in anticipation. But the room was empty, no sign that she'd been there.

He started down the corridor to the west tower. At

the heavy door to the ruined banquet hall, he paused. Kate knew that Moruadh's papers were in the room on the other side, but she'd nearly fainted in broad daylight. Alone, in the dark of night, she wouldn't try to cross that narrow ledge. He started back down the corridor, retracing the steps he'd taken, then stopped. Would she? Nothing Kate did would surprise him.

A few moments later, he pushed open the door and felt the gust of wind and sea on his face. He peered into the darkness. Even in bright daylight, it was difficult to see much. When he called out her name, his voice was lost in the roar of the water. Torn with indecision, he edged a few feet along the ledge. An image of the upturned furniture downstairs flashed across his brain. He was wasting his time. She wasn't here. Meanwhile, Fitzpatrick could be doing God knows what to her.

"Kate." He held his hands to his mouth. "Kate." Nothing. He waited for a moment, then turned back.

CHAPTER EIGHTEEN

AFTER A WHILE, Kate lost all track of time. She had no idea how many hours had passed. Reality was the stone wall behind her, the narrow ledge on which she stood. Reality was the ocean crashing hundreds of feet below. The sound of it filling her ears. Reality was blackness. Blackness above, below, all around. Blackness punctuated every so often by forked lightning.

Reality was numbing, paralyzing terror. She'd managed to shake her ankle free from Fitzpatrick's grasp, but she had no idea whether he'd fallen or managed to scramble up the rocks. She braced her back against the wall, terrified that the slightest movement would either draw his attention or send her tumbling to the rocks below.

All she had to do, she told herself over and over, was hold on. Hold on and stay alert. Eventually, it would be morning and, in the light, she could back out. *Deep breaths, don't look down. Stay back against the wall.*

More lightning. A moment of crackling silence and then a roar of thunder exploded in her ears. People made it through incredible ordeals. She tried to think of some. After the San Francisco earthquake, they'd found a man in his car under the collapsed Oakland

Bay Bridge. Alive three days later. Avalanches, too. People lost in the desert. A raft on the ocean.

If Fitzpatrick was dead, she could make it. All she had to do was hold on. Wait for the light. If she survived this, nothing would ever frighten her again. And she would tell Niall—again—that she loved him.

"No, sir, still no sign of her," the Garda said. "No sign of Fitzpatrick, either. We've had men all over the castle and we have the dogs out on the grounds at this moment."

Niall nodded. In a daze, it occurred to him that the great hall was full of people. Gardai all over the place. Detectives. Annie. Caitlin. People kept saying things to him. Asking questions. He walked to the window. Gardai cars, two of them in the rainy morning light. Another coming up the hill. Someone said his name.

"Drink this." Annie held out a cup of tea. "There are a dozen men looking for her, Mr. Maguire. All you can do at the moment is wait."

He stared at her.

"Come on, sit down."

He shook his head. Unable to stand the inactivity, he decided to try the west tower again. Five minutes later, the echo of his feet on the stone floors of the west tower rang in his ears. Then he stopped. At the end of the corridor, outside the door to the banquet hall, he saw her slumped against the wall.

FITZPATRICK WAS ATTACKING HER AGAIN. She felt him catch her arm. Breathing hard, she tried to fight the blackness. She couldn't lose it now. Screaming and flailing out with her arms and legs, she pulled free.

Teeth clenched, she kicked him with all the strength she could muster.

"God, Kate. Take it easy, will you? It's me, Niall."

"Niall?" It *was* Niall's voice. She peered at him, saw him as if in a dream. Niall's face. Niall doubled in pain. "Niall, are you...I thought you were in jail."

"I was." He straightened with obvious effort. "It might have been wiser to stay there."

"God, I'm sorry. Are you okay—"

"I am." He gave a wry smile. "Just don't expect a dazzling performance anytime soon." Then he caught her shoulders, stared into her eyes. "God, Kate. I was beside myself. Are you okay? Did Fitzpatrick...where is he?"

She shook her head. "I brought Rufus back and I thought I'd get Moruadh's note. Hugh chased me into the west wing and then..." Suddenly the horror of it washed over her and she started to shake. "*He pushed Elizabeth.* He admitted it. I played this trick on him, it was the only way I could get away." Her teeth started chattering. "I wanted to get the note from Moruadh's office, but I couldn't do it..."

He took off his leather jacket, wrapped it around her shoulders and kissed her on the forehead.

"Let's get out of here," he said.

HE TOOK HER BACK to Annie's where she slept for ten hours. When she finally opened her eyes, she saw a ring of anxious faces around her. Niall on the edge of the bed, Annie and Caitlin in the doorway. Michael Riordan.

"Break it to me gently, guys," she said. "Did I die?"

Niall grinned, but his face was pale, unshaven. "No, but Hollywood called. They're remaking *The Perils of Pauline* and you've got the starring role."

"You'll be fine," Annie said. "You've just had an awful scare, but you'll be up and around in no time. Now, I can't say the same for this lad." She nodded in Niall's direction. "He's been going around like death warmed up. Gave us all a bit of a fright, you did."

Niall stroked her hair. "Do you need to sleep some more? We can leave you alone."

"She needs to eat something," Annie said. "A soft-boiled egg, Katie? And some buttered toast?"

"Or bouillabaisse," Niall said. "Have I told you about the fine bouillabaisse I make?

"Yeah, I think you might have mentioned it. I'd probably die of starvation before you ever got it ready." She smiled into his eyes, swept by a huge rush of emotion. For a moment they were the only people in the room.

"You're an incredible girl. You know that?" His eyes lingered on her face. "I still can't believe what you did." He looked at the group in the doorway. "Kate doesn't have much of a head for heights."

"That's an understatement," Kate said, then winced in pain. "I just about passed out the first time I went up there."

"And you trying to run from Hugh, too." Annie's face was somber. "Holy Mother of God." She shook her head. "I still can't take it all in. That someone I've known since he was a boy would be capable of such a thing. All the rejection just affected his brain and that's all there is to it. Not that I'm excusing him, mind you." She came over to the bed, peered again into the water jug on the table, smoothed the bed-spread. "A good thing it was that you didn't listen to me, Katie. Lucky for you, too," she said, with a smile at Niall.

Kate looked at him. "When did they release you?"

"Yesterday morning."

"Tell me what happened."

"Are you sure?" Niall looked worried. "You've been through an awful ordeal. Maybe you should rest a bit more."

"I'm fine, Niall. Really." She looked at Michael. "Fill me in."

"Well, the long and short of it appears to have been revenge." He scratched the back of his neck. "We've not been able to talk to Fitzpatrick, of course, but—"

"He's…" Kate swallowed. "Dead?"

"Kate, you don't have to hear this now," Niall said.

"No." She shook her head. "Tell me."

"Well, we've got divers out in the water," Michael said, "but that would appear to be the case."

Kate lay back against the pillow, listening to Michael explain the events of the last couple of days.

The phone rang downstairs, and Annie went to answer it. A moment later, she was back, trailing a long extension cord.

"It's for you." She handed Kate the phone. "Your editor."

NIALL LEANED against the doorjamb of the kitchen, watching Annie move around the room. In unspoken agreement, they had all come downstairs, leaving Kate to her phone call. Michael had gone back to the station, and Caitlin sat at the table before a little round magnifying mirror plucking her eyebrows.

"Don't make them too thin, Caitlin, love," Annie said. "It makes you look awful hard." She smiled at Niall. "The things women do to be beautiful. You men have it easy."

Caitlin smiled at him. "If you don't mind my saying so, Mr. Maguire, you've got lovely eyelashes. Really long they are."

"They're false," he said. "I buy them at the chemist's. The glue's a nuisance, though."

Caitlin and Annie both laughed politely. He'd been invited to stay for supper. Annie had apologized so profusely for her past suspicions that, embarrassed, he'd asked her to stop. Clearly, though, she didn't feel entirely comfortable around him. Every so often she'd cast an uncertain smile in his direction. He felt a bit like a dog, known in the past to bite but now generally considered safe.

"It's been a difficult time for everyone," Annie was saying. "I still have a hard time believing that Hughie..." She shook her head. "I'd rather not even think about it.

"The thing is, no one really knew what to think," Caitlin said. "When I found out that Rory had been with Elizabeth—"

"She kissed me a few times," Rory said from the doorway. He removed his hat and coat and came into the kitchen. "I've told you over and over that's all there was to it." He dropped a kiss on Caitlin's cheek, then saw Niall. "Maguire," he said. "How're you?"

"Fine. Yourself?" he asked, but avoided McBride's eye. He suspected that McBride had been one of the ringleaders clamoring for his arrest and he wasn't keen to deal with him now.

"Niall's staying for supper." Annie took a bowl of peaches from the fridge, put it on the counter. "Hungry, are you?" She smiled up at him. "I thought a leg of lamb would be nice. You like lamb, do you?"

"It's great, Annie."

"And roast potatoes."

"I love roast potatoes," he said. "I can't remember the last time I had them."

"Ah well, you'll have to find a wife who'll cook them for you." She brought a saucepan over to the table, sat down and started peeling the potatoes. "I try to tell Caitlin that. 'When you and Rory are married, Caitlin,' I say, 'he'll want a hot supper on the table.'"

"Ah God, Mam, don't start that again." Caitlin rolled her eyes.

"I owe you an apology, Maguire." Rory took a couple of beers from the fridge and handed one to Niall, then sat down at the table. "Annie and Caitlin might as well hear this, too. I haven't exactly been proud of myself these past few weeks."

"Rory's having a bit of a problem with the drinking." Caitlin nodded at his beer. "Not that I'm nagging or anything, Rory, but—"

"Ah, leave off, will you, Caitlin. And I'll tell this myself if you don't mind." He looked at Niall. "Not to make a long story of it, but when I met up with Elizabeth in Galway the day it all happened—"

"They'd been drinking," Caitlin said. "The two of them together—"

"Caitlin, let Rory tell it himself," Annie said.

Rory studied the beer in his hand for a moment.

"To tell you the truth of it, I don't remember a lot about the evening except that we were in the car and we had a bit of a fight because Elizabeth wanted me to break off things with Caitlin, and I told her I wouldn't."

"Can you believe that?" Caitlin addressed Niall. "Trying to steal him right out from under my nose, she was."

"Anyway…" Rory said. "Elizabeth gets out of the car and goes off walking along the cliffs and meets up with Hughie."

"You saw this?" Niall asked.

"Hardly." His face colored slightly. "I'd drank enough whiskey. The next thing I know there's Kate banging on the window of the car."

"And, like a fool, I'm thinking he's up on the Galway road looking into a traffic accident." Caitlin reached for Rory's beer and took a swig. "I'm telling you, Rory McBride, if you ever lie to me again."

"He's apologized, Caitlin," Annie said. "Over and over." She looked at Niall. "Another beer?"

"No, thanks." He shook his head, already imagining the rest of the story.

"The first night she was gone, I didn't think much of it," Rory said. "But then the days passed and I got worried thinking about what might have happened to her."

"Not that he really thought he'd hurt her or anything," Caitlin said.

Rory got another beer from the fridge and gave it to Caitlin. "I started thinking maybe we'd had another fight and she'd fallen. An accident, like. And then when they found her, and everyone started talking about how it was like Moruadh… Well, when it came down to the choice of you behind bars or me, it wasn't a difficult decision to make."

Niall met his eyes for a moment. "You thought I was getting what I deserved, is that it?"

"I did." Rory smiled a bit, his expression relieved. "That's the truth of it. I'd always suspected you had a part in Moruadh's death. I even told Kate that, didn't I? And of course, Hughie encouraged me along those lines. Not that it takes anything away from what I did."

"The thing of it is, Niall," Annie said, "it's as though you've always set yourself apart from everyone else. It wasn't really until Katie came along, so dead set on you being a good man, that we all started thinking maybe we'd judged you a bit harshly."

Niall finished his beer. Even if he'd produced Moruadh's suicide note after her death, he doubted that he'd be sitting in Annie Ryan's kitchen today if it weren't for Kate.

"Well..." He stood, not really knowing what to say to any of them. "I have a few things to do before supper."

"You'll miss Kate when she goes back to America, won't you?" Annie asked.

"I will."

"When is it she leaves?"

"I'm not sure. We haven't discussed it yet."

"I can't help hoping that she might just decide to stay." She sighed. "No doubt you were probably hoping the same thing yourself."

"Ah well." He made a great show of nonchalance. "What can you do?"

"Did you not try and talk her into staying then?"

"Kate's a headstrong girl," he said.

"A California girl, too," Annie said. "Used to the city. Sunshine. That sort of thing."

"Right." Niall nodded. "And there's not much of that here, is there? Sunshine, I mean?"

"There isn't," Annie agreed. She looked up at him. "Would California be a place you might consider, yourself?"

"California?" He tried hard not to smile. Any moment now, Annie might just burst from curiosity. "I don't know, Annie. I've my work here."

"Could you not find employment as a photographer in California?"

"I could, Annie, but I'd find it very hard to leave Ireland."

"I know what you mean there. I could never leave, myself. Mind you, people do. I've a sister in Boston who would never come back. But you being a young man with your whole life in front of you…"

"Right." He took his jacket off the chair, put it on. "Listen, Annie. I've got a couple of things to do. Would you tell Kate I'll be back soon."

"I will."

"And Annie?" He smiled at her. "Do plenty of potatoes, will you?"

AFTER SHE'D HUNG UP the phone, Kate lay back against the pillow. Tears streamed down her face and trickled off her chin, soaking the edge of the sheet. She reached for a tissue, blew her nose and drank some water. The tears wouldn't stop.

"Katie." Annie stuck her head around the door. "Cup of tea?" Tray in hand, she came into the room, set down the tray and dropped into the chair next to the bed. "I thought I'd join you," she said, and then noticed Kate's face. "What is it, love? Bad news?"

"They offered me a job." Kate blew her nose again. "A staff job on the magazine. They like my freelance work and they want to put me on staff."

"Well, that's what you wanted, isn't it?" Annie pulled a tissue from the box, handed it to Kate. "That's what you were hoping for?"

"Yeah. It's exactly what I wanted. Benefits, stability. I could buy a condo instead of renting."

"And that's why you're crying your eyes out, is it?"

She shook her head, lay back against the pillow again. The tears kept coming, she could feel them in her throat, in her nose. Her head felt liquid with tears. "It's okay…" She tried to take a breath and it came out in a shuddering gasp. "Post-traumatic stress, or something. I'll be fine, really. Just give me a minute."

Annie stirred sugar into her cup of tea. "Mr. Maguire just left," she said. "He'll be back in a bit. I asked him to supper. The poor man's heartbroken about you going back to America."

Kate wiped her face with the back of her hand. "He said that?"

"Not in so many words, but it's there in his face. Very fond of you, he is."

"Yeah." She sniffed. "I kind of like him a little bit, too."

"Seems a bit sad when you think about it. Him rattling around in that castle, not to mention the place he has up in Sligo, and the two of you so happy together. An awful shame to have all of that go to waste. But then you've your new job back in California, all your friends. Some things are just not meant to be, I suppose.''

''Annie, I know what you're trying to do.'' Her shoulders shaking, Kate held her hands up to her eyes. ''God, I don't know what's wrong with me. Yes, I do. I don't want to go back, Annie. I don't want to leave you, I don't want to leave Niall…''

''Ah, Katie.'' Annie caught her in an embrace, rocked her for a moment. ''Stay then, love. Don't go back. Sure, we'd all love to have you here, Niall especially—''

''I don't think so.'' She pulled back from Annie, blew her nose again. ''Niall's never asked me, Annie. I've even hinted about staying here, but he made a joke of it. He's told me twice to stay out of his life.''

Annie looked skeptical. ''All I can say is, you should have heard his voice when he called from the jail. If that man isn't in love…''

''He was frightened for me. I'm not saying he doesn't care, I just think that after what happened with Moruadh, he isn't ready to share his life with someone.''

''And you've talked about this together, have you?''

''No.'' She shook her head. ''Not really. I mean, it's not just Niall. It's me, too. I'm afraid. The whole thing with my mom. She didn't want to go on living, Annie, because my dad walked out on her. It terrifies me, the thought of losing myself like that.''

''But that was her, Katie. You're not the same person. Sure, I never knew your mother, but maybe she didn't have the strength that you have. I'd bet on it, in fact. You believed in Niall, went up to that castle to be with him while we were all telling you not to. That takes a lot more strength than I have.''

"Or stupidity."

"No, you trusted your instincts. The rest of us were feeding off each other's fears.''

Kate sighed and drank some tea.

"Love is such a big part of life, Katie. It's not good to be afraid of it. If you love Niall, what you have to do is find that strength again, and tell him how you feel.''

CHAPTER NINETEEN

"YOU'RE VERY QUIET," Niall said as he walked with Kate down the high street to Dooley's. It had only been two days since her ordeal at the castle, and he worried that she hadn't fully recovered. "Are you sure you're up for fiddle playing?"

"Annie would never forgive me if I missed the Cragg's Head *fleadh*," Kate said. "It's a hundred times better than the one in Ballincross, she says. Anyway, I want to get my fill of Irish music before I go back."

Niall put his arm around her shoulder. She'd extended her stay a week, but her departure loomed like a gathering storm they were both trying to ignore. Or he was, and he sensed she was, too. He had something to tell her, but he needed the right moment, and if the noise level coming from every bar in town was anything to go by, that moment wasn't likely to occur within the next few hours.

Cragg's Head was humming with activity. People carrying drinks, talking in groups on the pavement. Music flowing from doors and windows. By the time they reached Dooley's, the dancing had started.

He stood at the edge of the room for a moment, his hand in Kate's, watching the couples whirling around the room, their shadows flickering on the whitewashed walls. Caitlin, in skintight black vinyl pants, leading Rory around the dance floor; Brigid Riley, resplendent in a green pleated skirt and newly permed hair, twirling around in the meaty arms of the local butcher.

Rory spotted Niall and nodded, and then Brigid Riley glanced over in his direction. If it wasn't exactly a smile that crossed her lips, it wasn't the look of hostility she usually reserved for him.

He brought his mouth to Kate's ear. "I'm going back with you," he whispered.

She turned to look at him. "Back to California?"

"Right. I was going to wait to tell you, but…" He grinned. "I've bought the tickets already. Three weeks."

"Three weeks?"

"If you can put up with me that long."

"God, Niall…I don't know what to say."

"Are you happy?"

"Of course." She bit her lip. "Sure, I mean that's fantastic. Great." Across the room, she spotted Annie and Patrick and she waved to them. "Listen, we can talk about it later. Annie has a table for us."

Niall followed her through the crowd, a little let down by her reaction. Or maybe she still wasn't feeling quite herself. He sat down next to her, put his arm around her shoulder. Across the table, Annie smiled at them.

"I was just saying to Pat—" Annie looked at Niall "—that I've never seen a couple as much in love as you and Katie."

"Annie." Kate frowned at her. "Please."

"Seems a shame," Annie went on, "her going back to America leaving you here to pine alone. Sure, you've been a different man since she arrived, it's a terrible shame, so it is.''

"Actually, Niall's going back with me.'' Kate gave him a quick glance. "For three weeks. Cool, huh?''

Annie folded her arms across her chest. "You're going to America for a visit?''

"Right.'' Niall saw Kate and Annie exchange looks. He was getting the very definite impression that he'd gone wrong somehow. "I'd like to see Santa Monica, where Kate lives.''

"And what then?'' Annie asked. "You'll just come back here and rattle around in the castle by yourself? And Katie in Santa Monica by herself. That makes no sense at all.''

"Annie.'' Kate drew her fingers across her throat. "Stop, okay?''

"Leave them be, Annie,'' Patrick said. "If it's meant to be, it'll happen. If it isn't, all your interfering won't do a bit of good.''

"Interfering, indeed.'' Annie shook her head. "You've lost your romantic streak, Patrick Ryan, no two ways about it.'' She sipped her beer, her eyes distant. A moment later, she set the tankard down. "Are the two of you not going over to Gossamer Island tomorrow?'' she asked.

"We are.'' Niall thought of the boat he'd borrowed from one of the fishermen he'd photographed. The *Macushla*. He had the day all planned out. Bicycles, a picnic by the water. He glanced again at Kate. She'd shredded her napkin into little pieces. When she caught him watching her, she gathered them up into the ashtray and smiled. Something was definitely wrong.

"What I'll do,'' Annie said, "is bake you a nice

loaf of barm brack to take with you. You remember what I told you about barm brack, do you, Katie? You never know what you'll find in a slice of it.''

"I WANT YOU TO KNOW that I had to pay another visit to the fairy ring,'' Niall said the following day as he maneuvered the *Macushla* into Gossamer Island's tiny harbor. "It's hard to find sunshine in February, but I thought for your last day in Ireland you should have it. At considerable cost to myself, I might add.''

"Sunshine?'' Kate peered into the misty air. "I hate to break it to you, but I think you were taken. So far we've had wind, clouds, rain and fog, but I don't see sun—''

"Come over here.'' He held his hand out to her, watched as she picked her way past the picnic basket, camping gear and bicycles stacked in the middle of the boat. "All right, California girl. What do you call that?''

Kate smiled. They were sailing out of the misty shroud that had enveloped them for the past hour and into shimmering sunlight. She blinked her eyes against the brightness. Breezes gently shook the tall green grasses on the shore, lace-curtain clouds hung in a pale blue sky and, off on the horizon, like the entry to a magical land, was a double rainbow. Wind, rain, clouds and now sunlight.

Beguiled, she turned to look up at Niall. As she did, a lock of hair blew across her eyes. He brushed it away and they stood in the soft light, smiling at each other. Sun shone down like a benediction, seabirds serenaded them. The breeze caressed her face.

And then, from out of nowhere, a powerboat roared by, rocking the *Macushla* in its wake. Knocked off

her feet by the sudden motion, Kate sprawled across
the deck, landing on a canvas bag of sails.

Laughing, she looked up at Niall.

"That's what you get for doubting the power of
the fairy ring." He docked the boat, hauled a couple
of ancient bicycles onto the little wooden pier and
held out his hand to her. "Ready to ride?"

THEY RODE for most of the morning. Across fields,
along winding roads, past small farms and cottages,
finally completing a full circle back at the harbor. Her
mind on what she wanted to tell him, Kate followed
Niall through a small grove of trees and onto the
rocky beach. After she'd thrown down her bike, she
removed her boots and socks and walked down to the
water's edge. The tide was out, the sand soft. She
stood for a while, watched the water lap over her feet,
then made her way back up to the grass where Niall
was unloading the basket that held their picnic.

"Ham sandwiches," he said, setting a waxed-
paper-wrapped package down on a red-checkered tablecloth. "Two different kinds of cheese, tomatoes,
crisps—or potato chips, I suppose you'd say, and a
bottle of plonk. Actually, it's quite a nice Bordeaux."

"Great." She dropped down onto the blanket opposite him, plucked a blade of grass and ran her
thumbnail down the middle of it.

"Are you hungry?" He glanced up at her, then
grinned. "Ah, a stupid question, I'd forgotten. You're
always hungry, aren't you?"

"Usually."

"But not today?" He sat with his back against a
tree, legs stretched out in front of him. "What is it?"

"I want to talk to you." She examined her green-stained thumbnail for a moment. "I've thought this out very carefully. It's not an impulsive decision. I'm absolutely sure it's what I want to do."

Niall unwrapped the sandwiches, then glanced up at her.

"I don't know what it is. Something's happened to me, I can't explain it. Maybe I've fallen under your stupid fairy spell."

"Remember the last time you maligned fairy spells?"

"Okay, it's not stupid. All I know is that you're incredibly important to me." She cut a tomato into sections, sprinkled salt on them and glanced down at the front of her sweater. Her heart was doing its sped-up-drumbeat thing, thumping so hard she thought it would show. "Anyway, I know things will change, but you were right about what you said about love adding a dimension. Not that it solves every problem, I know that." She sprinkled salt on the tomato, remembered she'd already done it, and tried to brush it off with her fingers.

Niall reached over and took the saltshaker from her.

"I mean, even though right now everything is all magical and shimmering and it doesn't seem as though anything could ever come between us—"

"Kate."

"What?"

"You've been talking for the past five minutes, you've emptied half a saltcellar and I haven't the foggiest idea what you're saying."

"I'm saying that I've decided to stay in Ireland."

As though it demanded meticulous attention, Niall carefully opened a bag of potato chips. "And?"

"And, well, I'll have to go and take care of things

back in Santa Monica. Tell *Modern World* I'm not taking the job, but I can still do freelance work for them. And I'd like to help Annie do some public relations for the tourist bureau. The Pot o' Gold used to be an orphanage. Did you know that?''

He nodded. ''Very well. I'll tell you about it sometime.''

''Well, Annie showed me all these old photos stored up in the attic. They would make a great visual display. I could write some promotional material. I'd be working, so I'd have my own money. I mean, I wouldn't be sponging off you or anything.'' Unable to meet his eyes, she watched an ant make its way across the checkered tablecloth. ''So anyway, that's what I wanted to say. I want to stay here.'' She made herself look at him. ''With you. Which is why I was less than thrilled when you told me you'd bought a ticket to California.''

He touched her foot with his shoe. Sunlight dappled his dark hair, cast shadows on his face. The blue ocean reflected in his eyes.

''What?''

''Look me in the eye and repeat what you just said.''

''I want to stay in Ireland. Live here. With you.''

''Why?''

''Because I hate my apartment in Santa Monica. I'd rather live in a castle and a lighthouse.''

''And?''

''Because I'm sick of California sunshine. I love cold rainy weather.''

''And?''

''Okay, damn it. Because I love you.'' She ran her

thumb along the blade of grass, felt her face color. "There. I said it."

"Say it again."

"I love you."

"One more time."

"I love you, damn it. I love you, I love you, I love you. Satisfied?"

"I am." Sandwich in one hand, he looked out at the ocean. "I love you, too. In case I haven't told you."

She looked at him. "I don't think you have."

"Well, I do. I realized it when I decided I'd rather leave Ireland and live in California than be apart from you."

"And when did you decide that?"

He laughed. "I think it was probably up on the cliffs when we kissed. But I was certain about it that night after Elizabeth's body was found, and you came up to the castle and wouldn't come in. The way you just stood there, not really saying much…"

She smiled. "For a change."

"I can't tell you what it meant to me, Kate. I thought I wasn't affected by all that was going on in the village. I thought I could shut it all out. But you made me realize how much I'd been missing."

"God…" Swept by a sudden wash of emotion, she bit her lip. "I can't believe this is really happening. I think I'm going to cry." Niall handed her a napkin and she blew her nose. "No, I'm not. I'm going to laugh." She did. "I think I may be a little hysterical." She hit his arm. "Don't look at me like that, I know what you're thinking. It's just so amazing. I figured I was this…love dropout. I thought it would never happen. It was like I lacked some basic ingredient."

"You did."

She looked at him.

"Trust."

"Yeah," she said slowly. "I think you're right. I had all these defenses—"

"No." He feigned surprise. "You mean cynicism and world-weary jaded remarks? Funny, I never noticed that in you."

"Because you were too busy breaking down my defenses."

He came to sit beside her, put his arm around her shoulder. "Maybe it's just something about Ireland."

"Maybe." She leaned back against him and they sat facing the ocean. Waning light played pearly against the water. The air started to grow cool, the ground cold under her feet. Dusk fell slowly, like a veil.

"Oh, damn, I forgot something." Kate reached into her purse and pulled out a package wrapped in aluminum foil. "Annie wanted us to have this. She said it was very important. No matter how full we were, she said, we both had to have a piece."

"Barm brack," Niall said after she'd unwrapped the loaf of dark brown fruit-studded bread. He took a piece, bit into it. "Do you know all about it?"

"Annie did tell me, but she says I'm too cynical for the magic to work."

"That's a pity." Niall held out his hand. In his palm, a small silver ring glinted in the sunlight. "A less cynical woman would be thrilled to pieces to find this."

"Yeah?" She fought to keep a straight face. "Why?"

"Because to find a ring in a piece of barm brack

means she'll be married within the year." He closed his hand around the ring. "But of course I'm talking about a less cynical woman."

"So you're saying she can't be cynical and married?"

"Well, I suppose it would depend a lot upon the woman in question."

"Good." She looked at him. "Because I kind of like the married-within-the-year part and I kind of think I might even be able to work on the cynical stuff."

"Should I consider this a proposal?"

"Might as well. I mean it's kind of like making the bouillabaisse. We either sit around all night yakking about it, or we move things along. I warned you I have this tendency to take over."

"I remember."

"So what's the answer?"

He kissed her. And slipped the ring onto her left hand.

She smiled, looked down at her finger. Up at Niall. "Perfect answer," she said.

If you enjoyed what you just read,
then we've got an offer you can't resist!

Take 2 bestselling
love stories FREE!
Plus get a FREE surprise gift!

Clip this page and mail it to Harlequin Reader Service®

IN U.S.A.	IN CANADA
3010 Walden Ave.	P.O. Box 609
P.O. Box 1867	Fort Erie, Ontario
Buffalo, N.Y. 14240-1867	L2A 5X3

YES! Please send me 2 free Harlequin Superromance® novels and my free surprise gift. After receiving them, if I don't wish to receive anymore, I can return the shipping statement marked cancel. If I don't cancel, I will receive 6 brand-new novels every month, before they're available in stores. In the U.S.A., bill me at the bargain price of $4.47 plus 25¢ shipping and handling per book and applicable sales tax, if any*. In Canada, bill me at the bargain price of $4.99 plus 25¢ shipping and handling per book and applicable taxes**. That's the complete price, and a savings of at least 10% off the cover prices—what a great deal! I understand that accepting the 2 free books and gift places me under no obligation ever to buy any books. I can always return a shipment and cancel at any time. Even if I never buy another book from Harlequin, the 2 free books and gift are mine to keep forever.

135 HDN DNT3
336 HDN DNT4

Name _____ (PLEASE PRINT)

Address _____ Apt.# _____

City _____ State/Prov. _____ Zip/Postal Code _____

* Terms and prices subject to change without notice. Sales tax applicable in N.Y.
** Canadian residents will be charged applicable provincial taxes and GST.
  All orders subject to approval. Offer limited to one per household and not valid to current Harlequin Superromance® subscribers.
  ® is a registered trademark of Harlequin Enterprises Limited.

SUP02   ©1998 Harlequin Enterprises Limited

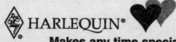

HARLEQUIN® *Super*ROMANCE®

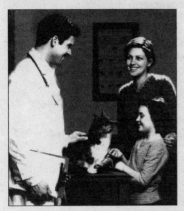

CREATURE COMFORT

Creature Comfort, the largest veterinary clinic in Tennessee, treats animals of all sizes— horses and cattle as well as family pets. Meet the patients— and their owners. And share the laughter and the tears with the men and women who love and care for all creatures great and small.

Listen to the Child
by Carolyn McSparren

Dr. Mac Thorn—renowned for his devotion to his four-legged patients and his quick temper—is used to having people listen to *him*. But ex-cop Kit Lockhart can't hear him—she was injured on the job. Now Mac is learning to listen, and Kit and her young daughter have a lot to teach him.

Coming in September to your favorite retail outlet.

Previous titles in the Creature Comfort series

#996 THE MONEY MAN (July 2001)

#1011 THE PAYBACK MAN (September 2001)

HARLEQUIN®

Makes any time special®

Visit us at www.eHarlequin.com

HSRCREAT

Princes...Princesses...
London Castles...New York Mansions...
To live the life of a royal!

In 2002, Harlequin Books lets you escape to a world of royalty with these royally themed titles:

Temptation:
January 2002—*A Prince of a Guy* (#861)
February 2002—*A Noble Pursuit* (#865)

American Romance:
The Carradignes: American Royalty (Editorially linked series)
March 2002—*The Improperly Pregnant Princess* (#913)
April 2002—*The Unlawfully Wedded Princess* (#917)
May 2002—*The Simply Scandalous Princess* (#921)
November 2002—*The Inconveniently Engaged Prince* (#945)

Intrigue:
The Carradignes: A Royal Mystery (Editorially linked series)
June 2002—*The Duke's Covert Mission* (#666)

Chicago Confidential
September 2002—*Prince Under Cover* (#678)

The Crown Affair
October 2002—*Royal Target* (#682)
November 2002—*Royal Ransom* (#686)
December 2002—*Royal Pursuit* (#690)

Harlequin Romance:
June 2002—*His Majesty's Marriage* (#3703)
July 2002—*The Prince's Proposal* (#3709)

Harlequin Presents:
August 2002—*Society Weddings* (#2268)
September 2002—*The Prince's Pleasure* (#2274)

Duets:
September 2002—*Once Upon a Tiara/Henry Ever After* (#83)
October 2002—*Natalia's Story/Andrea's Story* (#85)

 Celebrate a year of royalty with Harlequin Books!

Available at your favorite retail outlet.

HARLEQUIN®
Makes any time special ®

Visit us at www.eHarlequin.com

HSROY02